When Someday Finally Comes

A SWEET, SMALL TOWN ROMANCE

CHARLOTTE EVERHART

NEVINLY PUBLISHING

Content Warning

This is a closed-door novel containing minimal, mild language.

To My Darling Niece,

Your boundless imagination lights up every room, just like the sparkle family
you inspired in these pages. Lexi's adventures with her sparkle mommy, purple
heels, and the one-and-only Sharklove come straight from the magical stories
you dream up. Your joyful heart, brimming with love for the families you
cherish (real and imagined), is a gift to us all. This book is dedicated to you,
my sweet five-year-old muse, who reminds me that the best stories are woven
from love and a touch of sparkle.

With all my love,

Charlotte

FIRST EDITION

Cover design by Tugboat Design.

ISBN: 979-8-9996219-1-7 (print)

ISBN: 979-8-9996219-0-0 (ebook)

1. Women's Fiction 2. Family Fiction 3. Small Town/Rural Fiction 4. Contemporary Romance

Contents

Prologue

November 21, 2017

E lena Torres wasn't sure who was more relieved to hear the final bell: herself or her students. As she trudged through the snow and slush to the high school's nearly deserted parking lot, she thought about the events of the past weeks. Life had been a little *loca*. She and her cousin Leila had moved from their rented house to the Victorian home Leila had grown up in, and they'd also helped Leila's mother move out of the Victorian and into a condo. Neither move was fully complete yet, but Thanksgiving was Thursday, and that meant a shortened week at Nicolet High School, where Elena taught Spanish. She could really use the time off to get caught up with life and regain her balance.

The engine of her rusty Buick turned over—never a sure thing. "*Gracias a Dios*, she murmured before reaching into the glove compartment for a brush. Letting her car warm up as she worked through the tangles, she considered the disaster that was her fourth hour Spanish class. The moment she got home, the first thing she was going to do was draw up a nice, warm bath. She'd earned it.

She sat a few minutes longer to ensure her engine didn't stall before shifting into reverse, stepping on the gas without taking one final look behind her. Immediately, the crunch of metal drowned out the radio's static, and the car lurched to a stop.

And here she'd thought her day couldn't get any worse. A glance in the rearview mirror confirmed it: she'd backed into the bumper of the black

Suburban parked behind her. Elena groaned. Of course she would end the day by backing into the only other vehicle in the lot.

She eased forward into her parking space and climbed out. While she waited for the Suburban to re-park back in its spot, she walked around to the rear of her car and winced at the damage. Her bumper sagged like a deflated balloon. She muttered a curse and immediately crossed herself. No way could she afford a fix. She stared at the back end of her car, willing it to mend itself by magic.

The Suburban's driver door swung open, and out stepped Gabriel Wright, superintendent of Nicolet Public Schools. Her boss.

"Oh, no" she whispered.

"You alright?" Gabe's voice was low and steady—cutting through the chill of the late afternoon.

A small face peeked out from the opened back door, and a dark-haired child with wide, solemn eyes stared out at them. "Daddy?"

"It's okay, Lex. Close the door so you don't get cold. I'll be right there."

The girl obeyed, the door clicking shut.

"I'm so sorry, Gabe—uh, Mr. Wright." Elena felt her cheeks flame. "I didn't see you."

"Are you okay?" he asked again, ignoring her fumble. His eyes, a deep hazel she hadn't noticed before, flicked over her with a quiet intensity that made her stomach flip.

She gestured helplessly at the bumper. "I'm fine, but my car ..."

He knelt to inspect it, one knee sinking into the slushy snow. Fascinated, Elena watched him pull a roll of duct tape from his coat pocket, as if taping on bumpers was a daily ritual for him. "This'll hold it until you can get it in," he said, taping it with calm precision. He glanced up, catching her staring, and the corner of his mouth twitched—barely a smile, but enough to send a strange warmth through her. "What?"

"You carry duct tape?"

"In my glove box." He tore off another strip and handed her the roll. "Hold this."

Her pulse spiked as his warm fingers brushed against hers, and she mumbled a thanks, eyes darting away—only to have them land on his Suburban. A fresh scrape glared back at her. "Oh, no, your car. I'll pay for it, I swear."

"I can touch it up," he said, not looking up from his taping, his tone easy but firm, like he was used to fixing things—cars, problems, maybe even people.

"No, I insist—"

He paused, leveling her with a look that wasn't angry, just steady. "Elena, it's fine. Just don't ram me again, alright?" Her name on his lips caught her off guard. She bit her lip, torn between arguing her case and shutting up. Silently, she handed him more tape when he gestured for it, their odd little repair job wrapping up in minutes, a quiet rhythm settling between them.

After thanking her boss more times than he seemed to appreciate, Elena slid back into her car, her bumper now a silver-streaked mess, and felt a little giddy. Now, why would that be? She'd just complicated her life even further, something she definitely didn't need. Five minutes into her drive home, she was still smiling. Gabriel Wright had remembered her name. And the way he'd said it—low and sure—echoed in her head longer than it should have.

Chapter 1

April 28, 2018

Elena adjusted the placement of the framed photo that, until today, had rested on her nightstand, watching over her as she slept every night for the last few years. Now it would grace the mantel of her new home. Correction: Jackson's home. It would no longer be the last thing Elena saw before bed and the first thing she'd see upon waking. Tonight would be a trial run. She was pretty sure she was ready.

Elena pressed a finger to her lips, kissed it, and held it over the picture. "I miss you, *mamacita*. *Te quiero*." She turned as her cousin came into the living room.

"I'm finished in the kitchen," Leila announced before glancing around. "Hey, it looks really nice in here."

Elena took in the dark leather couch and matching Barcalounger that no amount of trinkets or throw pillows could feminize. The room had a very masculine energy, but she had to admit, it was a good energy. It would be, of course. Up until very recently, a good man had lived here. But it wasn't home. Not yet, anyway. Only one place had ever felt like home to her, but instead of leaving it kicking and screaming, she'd left voluntarily. Everyone knew three was a crowd, and so here she was, unpacking moving boxes yet again. The story of her life.

Leila pulled Elena in for a one-armed hug before letting her arm rest across Elena's shoulders. "I already miss being roommates."

Elena ignored the stinging in her eyes and snorted instead. "Only a few hours have passed, *prima*."

"Are you sure this is what you want?"

Ducking out from under Leila's arm, she dodged the question as best she could. "I'm ready to have my own space."

"Your own space? The Victorian is huge! You had the whole second floor to yourself."

Elena didn't answer. She loved the Victorian, and leaving it made her feel more than a little heartsick. She didn't say that, though. Instead, she stepped closer to the mantel and the picture of her mother.

"She'd be proud of you, you know," Leila said, following her. "I know you don't think so, but she loved how independent you've always been."

"*Si, claro.*" Elena's lips quirked as she caressed the edge of the frame with one small finger. She turned to Leila. "She never wanted me to go anywhere. Every time I went to work or school or to hang out with my friends, she was convinced something terrible would happen to me."

Leila flashed her a sympathetic smile before she, too, touched the ornate frame of the picture. "I remember this day. She was happy."

Elena swallowed. "Yeah." She turned from the picture and spotted her favorite wool blanket on the floor in a heap. It must have slid off the armrest of the leather couch. Grateful for the distraction, she bent to retrieve it.

"She was like her old self," Leila went on. "The way she was before *Tío—*" Leila cleared her throat uncomfortably. "You know ... before he left."

Elena kept her voice light as she smoothed out a wrinkle in the freshly folded blanket. She didn't want to talk about her father now, or ever. "There were some good days," she agreed, taking one final look at the picture on the mantel. She turned to her cousin, smiling brightly and switching to Spanish, as they often did together—telling Leila it was time to call it a day. She'd unpack the rest of the boxes tomorrow. "*Gracias*," she added. "*Aprecio la ayuda.*"

"*De nada.*" Tucking her hair behind her ear, Leila flipped back to English. "So, what's with the job applications I saw when I went out to your car? You applying for another job?"

"*Si*, for the summer, but hopefully I could start in May." Picking up the empty moving box, she carried it into the kitchen, where she could break it down properly with a pair of scissors.

Leila followed close at her heels. "May is next week."

Elena shrugged, turning away from her cousin. Keeping her voice casual, she answered, "I was thinking I might do some waitressing or bartending or something on the side." She lifted the scissors off the counter and sliced open the bottom of the box along the taped seam.

"I thought maybe that kid in your fourth hour had finally driven you away from teaching."

Elena laughed. "I can handle a few spitballs. This is just for extra money."

The room was silent with a pregnant pause. "Listen," Leila began, "if you need any—"

Dropping the scissors on the table with a clang, Elena spun on her cousin. "Do *not* offer me money again. *Nada más.*"

Leila winced slightly, but she plowed ahead anyway, spinning the engagement ring on her finger as she spoke. "I'm sorry. It's just that your bumper is about to fall off your car, and it's been that way for at least five months, and you've stopped coming out with us for girls' night—"

"I went two weeks ago!"

"And ordered water and a side salad. And I know for a fact that you're even doing your own nails now. Elena, I'm worried."

Elena studied her nails. They must not have looked as professional as she'd thought if even her cousin, a woman who'd never been to a nail salon in her entire life, could tell they were from a do-it-yourself kit she'd ordered off Amazon. "*Estoy bien,*" she insisted.

"You're always fine. You're the eternal optimist. I'm just trying to—"

Elena raised a hand, a firm signal for Leila to stop. "I know what you're trying to do, and it's sweet, okay? But I'm almost twenty-six years old, and I can stand on my own feet. Jackson's already cutting me a deal on this place—don't act like he's not. And my car, I'll fix when I'm ready. The tape is holding it fine."

"But Elena, *two* jobs?"

"There's nothing wrong with looking for ways to make some extra money and fill my time. What else am I supposed to do this summer?"

Leila brightened. "Hey, you could ask *Mamá* for work at the bookstore."

Elena returned to the task at hand, pulling at the flaps of the box and flattening it. "I don't want to work at the bookstore."

"What's wrong with the bookstore?"

Elena didn't look up, but she knew her *prima* would be standing with both hands on her hips. "Two words. Minimum wage."

"But ... I'm sure if you asked *Mamá*, she'd—"

Elena laughed and turned to hug her cousin. "Leila, *por favor*, let me be in charge of my own life. I know what I'm doing."

Leila started to say something and stopped.

"What?"

"Nothing, you'll just get mad."

Elena lifted one eyebrow.

"Okay, fine. I can't help it; I'm asking anyway. What about Marc?"

Elena felt herself go stiff, but she forced a teasing quality to her voice when she said, "You know you should never say his name to me."

"Fine, *He Who Cannot Be Named* has been commenting on your Instagram lately."

Elena pulled away and treated her to a dramatic eye roll. "I liked it better when you were too good for social media."

"I'm thinking of getting off of it already. It's such a waste. My screen time is up to four hours a week now."

Elena tried not to laugh. Leila would faint dead away if she saw Elena's last screen time report. She'd scrolled Instagram for two hours straight last Saturday night alone. That didn't include the number of times she'd gone back to re-read Marc Ghetty's comments on her photos, looking for hidden meaning.

A furrow appeared between Leila's eyes. "Seriously, Elena. You're not thinking of going back to him, are you?"

Elena didn't answer right away. She'd fallen for Marc Ghetty. Hard. And as angry as she was at him, she hated the part of herself that still felt a little something when his name was mentioned or when she saw a comment from him. But he'd hurt her and nearly ruined her career. Those two reasons were enough for her to know, without a doubt, that under no circumstances would she ever go back to that man. So what if he was a multimillionaire? And hot? And a millionaire?

Elena liked to say that she loved love, and she really did. She loved everything about it—the sparks, the feeling of being two parts of a whole, the giddy happiness that painted the world and everything in it a beautiful rose color, waking up with a smile on her face before her brain could even communicate why it was that she was so deliciously happy.

She loved relationships, and she longed for one that would last more than one or two moon cycles. But that was never going to happen for her if she didn't make some big adjustments. She'd been doing some soul searching since a conversation she had with Leila a few months back. Her cousin had been honest with her. Brutally honest with her.

Elena thought back to a common Spanish idiom: *Amor con amor se paga*—Love is rewarded with love. It hadn't happened that way for Elena. Yet. She didn't choose men well—that, or she attracted the wrong ones—and she needed to figure out why. Marc was just the latest in a long line of mistakes she'd made.

Initially, she'd been swept away by his money and good looks. He was charismatic and powerful and important in the world of the über wealthy, and on his arm, she'd felt like somebody. She was more than just a school teacher, more than just eye candy, more than she'd ever hoped to be. She'd felt special, *really* special, for the first time in her life. In spite of all the warning signs, she'd begun to think that Marc Ghetty could be her one and only. Instead of seeing him for what he was, a rich playboy having a little fun with her, she thought she was in love with him. Worse, she thought he just might be in love with her too. He'd definitely said all the right things. And in return, she gave him every piece of herself—withholding nothing—only to find out in a very public and very humiliating way that, to him, she'd meant nothing.

He'd hurt her more than anyone had ever hurt her, and that was saying something, given her history. At least her parents had never pretended to be more than they were. Marc had. He'd lied to her a hundred different ways. But if her cousin thought a few compliments from him on Instagram would be enough to win her back ... Elena jerked her chin to the side. "I have a brain in my head, *prima mía*, and I promise to keep using it."

"So that's a no? You won't go back to him?"

She shook her head decisively. "*Claro que no.*"

"Good, I hate that guy."

Elena grinned at her cousin's vehemence. "*Ya somos dos.*" Only she couldn't quite hate him, and she hated herself for that.

Leila left shortly after, heading home to her fiancé and their two golden retriever pups. Jackson and her cousin would probably sit in front of the fire together tonight, as they often did, and share the events of their respective days. She smiled at the thought. She'd made the right decision—leaving them to build their life together without her there at the Victorian as a third wheel.

Once Leila left, Elena stood alone in Jackson's kitchen, the hum of the microwave filling the silence. She stared at the countertop, tracking a scratch with her finger, and let her mind drift back to Marc—not his charming smile or the way he'd made her feel for those first few weeks, but to the moment she'd seen the truth: a hollow promise in a tailored suit. She'd given him everything, and he'd left her with nothing but a bruised heart and a lesson she couldn't unlearn. Maybe that was the worst part—not just the betrayal, but how it made her question herself, her choices, every flutter she'd ever felt.

Later that night, after throwing away most of her frozen dinner, Elena wandered through her new home. It would be her first night here. Jackson had left the whole place furnished for her, a good thing since Elena didn't own anything.

Yet, she corrected. She didn't own anything *yet*. That was about to change, and the thought made her smile despite the fact that she had just moved, yet again, and this time her only companion was a potted plant Leila had gifted her that would be dead in a week. Two tops.

She had a long journey ahead of her, and step one was buying this house. It was perfect for her. The only thing she didn't like about it was the mangled juniper shrub in the front yard. It would be the first thing to go, followed by the Barcalounger. She'd get all new furniture. Really pretty stuff that was comfortable too. She'd already started saving aggressively, which she supposed Leila was bound to notice sooner or later. So what if her car was a mess and her nails looked less than perfect? She knew how to look good on a budget, and in a year, she'd have enough money for a down payment on a house. On *this* house. It would have her name on the deed, belonging fully to her and not some landlord who could turn her out on a whim.

As for step two? Well, that would be a bigger challenge given her history with men, but one thing at a time.

Chapter 2

G abe stared at the ceiling. Another sleepless night. A quick glance at his phone told him it was two in the morning, and he still hadn't slept a wink. How could he, when he had the distinct feeling that his life was unraveling.

Lexi was growing more and more unhappy each day, and he could no longer deny it. Neither could he deny that he was increasingly struggling to manage Dominick Stone, the school board president. Personally and professionally, he was failing.

Dom Stone had been the sole member of the board to vote against Gabe's initial hiring as the district superintendent last summer. Gabe hadn't worried too much about that, figuring he'd be able to win the guy over eventually, but that was looking more and more impossible by the day. Dom seemed determined to drive Gabe out of Nicolet Public Schools, and Gabe couldn't figure out why. He micromanaged Gabe like some kind of overbearing wife. No matter what Gabe did, Dom found something to criticize.

Last night's board meeting was case in point. Dom had thrown a fit in front of everyone over Gabe's recent hiring of three additional custodial staff—positions the board had approved at their last meeting. Selecting candidates was well within Gabe's purview to do, and the fact that Dom insisted the board should first preview and then approve these hires was in direct conflict with human resource governance standards.

Gabe had stuck to his guns and won the battle, if not the war, but the whole thing had made him want to drop-kick old Dom straight into Tuesday of next week. If Gabe couldn't even hire for approved custodial positions without Dom's oversight, what was he doing in this job, anyway?

Realizing his fists were clenched under the covers, Gabe willed himself to relax. No wonder he couldn't sleep. He was ready to punch Dom's lights out.

"Daddy?"

Gabe sat upright at the sound of his daughter's voice.

"What's wrong? he asked, as he pushed back the covers and set his bare feet on the cold hardwood floor.

She whimpered. "I wet the bed again."

The third time this week. "Oh, honey," he said, scooping her in his arms and feeling the wetness of pungent urine on his hands. She'd really soaked through her pajamas this time.

"Sorry, Daddy."

"It's okay. No, don't cry. It's okay. We'll get you all cleaned up, alright?"

She nodded against his chest. "I don't like it."

Gabe flipped on the light in the bathroom and blinked against the sudden brightness. "I know you don't, but you can't help it, and this won't last forever."

She sniffled.

"It's really common for kids to wet the bed," he reassured before setting her down in front of the bathtub and turning on the water to let it warm up.

"Did *you* wet the bed?"

"I'm sure I did, but I don't remember."

Gabe caught her frown before he pulled the pajama top over her head and threw it on the floor. He helped her undress the rest of the way and checked the water temperature. "Now Uncle Will," he added, "he wet the bed until he was ten."

He turned to look at Lexi and saw that, as expected, she'd perked up at the sound of his brother's name.

"He did?"

"That's what Mimi says. Here—"he helped her climb in "—I'll use the wand to rinse you off waist down, like last time."

"Did Uncle Will cry 'cause he wet the bed?"

"Nah. He knew he'd outgrow it," Gabe improvised as he rinsed her. "Just like you will."

Lexi smiled at him then, something he'd noticed she did less and less these days. He turned off the water and smiled back at his beautiful, six-year-old daughter. "But I'll tell you a secret about Uncle Will," he said, lowering his voice and wrapping her up in a towel like a burrito.

Lexi's eyes danced. "What?"

"He might not wet the bed anymore, but I know for sure he still picks his nose when he drives. Then he flicks his boogers out the window."

"Gross!" Lexi giggled, just as he'd hoped she would.

Predictably, Dom had written himself into Gabe's calendar the following day, taking his only open time slot between three-thirty and four o'clock. From the moment the school board's president had arrived in Gabe's office, he'd had a whole lot to say. If it hadn't been evident before, it was now very clear to them both that theirs was a mutual disliking, and neither felt the need to pretend otherwise. Unfortunately for Gabe, that dislike didn't seem to result in a mutual avoidance, as one might assume.

Dr. Dominick Stone was the longest serving member of Nicolet Public School's Board of Education, and had been president for the last four years. From what Gabe had seen, his hiring a year ago had been the only time the board hadn't bowed to Dom's authoritarian will. Despite the retired neurosurgeon's dissent, Gabe had been hired for the job. The fulfillment of a dream.

At the moment, Dom was busy re-litigating the events from last night's meeting, and since Gabe had nothing new to say on the topic, it was a welcome disruption when his secretary buzzed in.

He picked up the phone while Dom was still speaking. "Hi, Adele."

"I'm sorry, Gabe, but it's Lincoln Elementary again. Poor baby, they can't console her. They're askin' for you to come an' get her now."

Gabe ran a hand through his hair. He glanced at the clock on the wall and stifled a sigh. It was only ten after four. Lexi was supposed to stay at the after-school program until five-thirty.

Turning away from the school board president, Gabe spoke softly into the phone. "Adele, I can't break away just yet." He had another meeting after this one, and it couldn't be rescheduled.

His secretary barely missed a beat. She was excellent that way. "I'll forward my calls to Jennifer 'til I get back. Little Miss Lexi can sit out front with me again and color."

Gabe closed his eyes and pinched the bridge of his nose. "Thanks, Adele. I owe you one."

"Oh, it's far more than one, Gabe. I'm keepin' count, you can be sure of that." She laughed as she disconnected, and Gabe nearly smiled. He'd been lucky enough to nab Adele from the high school office right before the start of the school year. The principal over there had nearly had his head.

As soon as Lexi walked into his office holding his secretary's hand, Gabe could see the salt trails on her cheeks. Thankfully, it was Friday, and he'd have a weekend to recover from the hellish week of seeing his daughter this way. He had a minute before his next appointment—a video call with the state budget office—so he scooped her up in his arms, pink backpack and all. One whiff of her baby shampoo, and all thoughts of work were momentarily forgotten. "Tough day?"

He felt her nod against his neck, and her arms squeezed him tighter.

"Me too."

She said something, but it was muffled, and he tipped his head back. "What's that?"

"Did you cry?"

He shook his head.

"I did."

"I'm sorry, Lex."

"Cuz I missed you." Her brown eyes looked mournfully into his. "I miss Mimi and Papa."

He nodded. "Me too. What do you say we drive over to Bayshore tomorrow afternoon and visit them?"

She perked visibly. "Can we sleep over?"

Gabe hated to give up an entire Saturday. He had tons of jobs to do around the house, not to mention sorting through the nanny applications that had rapidly accumulated in his Indeed account. It had been Adele's suggestion, and she'd helped him post the job only yesterday. Help was coming soon. "We'll see," he answered.

"Please, Daddy," she pleaded.

"We'll see," he repeated firmly. "Let's get you set up to color. I have one more meeting today and then we can head home. What do you say to Adele for picking you up from school again?"

Lexi was silent.

"Lexi, say thank you to Adele, please."

Lexi spoke to the floor as she mumbled a quick thank you. They were going to have to work on this. Lexi's shyness was coming across as rude, and it was downright embarrassing. Everyone would think he hadn't taught her good manners, and he didn't want people to think he was a terrible parent.

"You're very welcome, Miss Lexi." Adele spared him a glance and a smile before returning to her desk.

"Okay, squirt. You remember where the coloring books are?"

She nodded and entered his office to grab the basket of coloring supplies he kept on his back shelf for her.

"Good girl. I'll go get the desk and get it set up right here, just outside my door like always."

"Okay."

He hesitated, looking at Lexi just a little longer as she lifted the basket. She was the spitting image of her mother. Hair the color of dark chocolate with eyes to match. It pained him sometimes, looking at her. He'd never told anyone that before, and he never would. She might look like her mother, but she was all his. Only his.

Multiple times during his meeting, Gabe found his thoughts drifting back to his daughter. Where had she disappeared to these last few months? Everything about her was ... muted. Was her old self still in there somewhere, and would he ever get her back? As the call wrapped up, Gabe heard Lexi laughing. It was more than laughing—it was a fit of the giggles he hadn't heard in far too long, and he was missing it.

The meeting had already gone over the allotted time, and Gabe could see that the meeting's participants, which included several superintendents from Michigan's Upper Peninsula, were getting antsy too. He tuned back in just in time for a question directed at him.

"For Title I this year, Michigan's pulling in about four hundred million from the feds. Nicolet's allocation is sitting at a little more than two million. You'll need your spending plan submitted by June first. Where are you with that?"

Gabe quickly shuffled through his binder, stopping when he found the right sheet. "We're working on it, but two million's cutting it close with our numbers. We're putting it toward reading interventionists, classroom resources, and a new pre-K program. Can we pull some of last year's leftover funds to stretch that?"

The answer was more or less what he'd expected. They could only reallocate up to fifteen percent. More than that would require approval from the Michigan

Department of Education, which they wouldn't get. It was a common theme: Somehow there was never enough money.

The rep ended the call with a reminder to everyone that audits would begin in July. Gabe wasn't worried. As with everything, he kept his Title I records tight.

Lexi's laugh rang through again, and he said his goodbyes quickly before moving toward the door. Peering into the waiting area of the central office, he saw Adele at her desk on the phone. On the other side of the room, his daughter sat beside Elena Torres, who was drawing on a notepad.

Lexi was leaned sideways, nearly in Elena's lap. She giggled again. "He's kinda like a cartoon," she exclaimed.

"That means I'm doing it right," Elena responded without ceasing the rapid movement of her pencil.

Her voice, soft and lilting with that faint accent, hit Gabe like a note he hadn't realized he'd been waiting to hear. He shook his head slightly—where had that thought come from?

"What's your favorite cartoon?" she asked Lexi.

"Doc McStuffins," Lexi said without hesitation. "But I can only watch it at my Mimi's 'cause we don't got a TV."

Elena looked up at Lexi, clearly surprised. "I didn't have one growing up either," she admitted.

Lexi grinned. "We're the same."

"Are we?" Elena asked with a small smile on her lips, her dark eyes catching the light.

Looking at them side by side, Gabe had to agree with his daughter. The two of them, seated closely together as they were, looked like mother and child, and that realization did something to his insides that was not altogether pleasant—or professional. He needed to stop staring.

Lexi spotted him and hopped up. "Daddy, come see the picture Elena drawed of you."

He covered the space between them in three strides. "Let's see what she drew."

Sheepishly, Elena held up the drawing, and his brain noted two things at once. One, his daughter had called Elena Torres by her first name, which was against the rules. Adults were always mister and missus. Two, the "drawing" wasn't exactly flattering. She'd taken the picture of him from the wall in the waiting area and turned it into a caricature where his chin was drawn in an exaggerated square, his brows were so prominent as to cast his eyes in shadow, and his stern scowl somehow amplified his already high cheekbones. They sat like oversized hills on his face. She'd turned his chair into a throne, and he sat holding a scepter.

"I sincerely hope I look nothing like that," he said, his tone flat.

Elena's quick, teasing glance sent an unwelcome jolt through him. He crossed his arms as if that could block it out.

His daughter, the beautiful traitor, dissolved into another fit of giggles, making him grin in spite of himself and earning her a look of delighted surprise from Adele, who was still on the phone.

Elena shushed her, but she was laughing, too, a sound that was warm and unguarded. Gabe supposed her little drawing was payback for their last meeting back in January, which had been rather unpleasant for him. If Elena had tried to conceal her anger with him, she'd failed miserably. He much preferred this version of her. Smiling. Playful. Too playful, maybe. He shouldn't be noticing how her laugh lit up the room.

"Can you draw me next?" Lexi asked the young teacher.

Elena reached over and smoothed a hand over Lexi's hair in a gesture so intimate that Gabe froze. The casual tenderness of it—her slender fingers against his daughter's dark strands.

"Sorry, kiddo. I have a meeting with your *papá*, which he's very late for."

They had a meeting? Since when?

"Aww," Lexi said with a frown

"Tell you what, I'll draw one of you over the weekend and give it to Adele on Monday."

"But how will you remember what I look like? You hadda keep looking at Daddy's picture to draw him. You looked at it *a lot*."

Elena flushed a pretty shade of pink and avoided looking at him. "I'll take a mental picture." She mimed holding a camera in her hand. "Say cheese," she instructed.

"Cheese," Lexi said with a shy smile.

"Click," Elena said. "There. I've got it."

"You're so fun." Lexi blurted before turning away, her shyness returning.

"You're a lot of fun too, *cariña*. Thanks for keeping me company while I waited."

As Elena stood, Lexi turned to her father. "Guess what, Daddy?"

"What?" he asked distractedly, still wracking his brain over what meeting he might be late for with Elena and trying not to notice how her skirt hugged the curve of her hips as she rose.

"You're Elena's *jefe*. It means boss."

He smiled, grateful for the reminder of their roles. "I guess I learned a new word."

Lexi addressed Elena. "Daddy thinks he knows *all* the words, but he doesn't."

Elena grinned. "Ready for me?"

"I didn't know we had a meeting," he confessed. "I'm sorry." He turned to Adele who had just hung up. "Adele, is Miss Torres on my schedule today?"

Adele clicked her mouse. "I don't see anything."

Elena's eyebrows slanted together, and she looked him fully in the eye then, her gaze sharp. "But I got an email a few weeks ago from HR that said we were meeting today for my year-end review. Joanna Bentley sent it."

Joanna hadn't included him on that email or even mentioned the meeting to him, which was unlike her, but he supposed, given the circumstances, he could understand the mistake. She'd just finalized her divorce, and she'd been out of sorts.

Gabe knew he should probably reschedule this meeting so that Joanna could be a part of the review, but it was her mistake, and Elena was here now. From the look in her eye a second ago, she wouldn't appreciate being rescheduled. He knew from their last meeting back in January that, although her overall demeanor was one of warmth, when pressed she could turn fiery.

This meeting would definitely be easier than that last one, and he tried not to think about what it meant that the idea of sitting in a meeting with Elena, just the two of them, made him feel like a teenage boy on his first date to the movies. Ridiculous. He was her boss, not some kid with a crush.

On the outside, he maintained his composure. "Joanna did not communicate that to me. However—" he glanced at his watch, needing something mundane to anchor him "—I do have some time now, if you like."

Elena adjusted the Chanel purse hanging on her shoulder. "If you don't mind."

He asked her to give him a moment so he could pull up her file and give it a quick review. On his way back to his office, he stopped short beside Adele's desk as he heard Lexi speaking again to Elena. She sounded inquisitive. Happy.

"How do you say 'draw' in your language, Elena?" she asked.

"*Dibujar.*"

"*Dee-boo-har,*" Lexi practiced, her voice dreamy. "I like how you talk. It sounds like a song."

Gabe turned to look back at them. He had to agree. Elena's accent was soft and musical and he found himself standing there, caught mid-step, waiting to hear what she might say next.

She glanced at him then, and their eyes locked a beat longer than necessary. Heat crept up his neck, and he cleared his throat before turning away to see Adele taking it all in. She sent him a pointed look.

"I know what you're thinking," he muttered so only she could hear.

"It's what you should be thinking too, *jefe*," she whispered.

"That she should be Lexi's nanny?" he asked, surprised that Adele would have had the same impossible thought. She could never be the nanny, of course, but the thought had come to his mind just the same.

Adele lifted her thick eyebrows. "No, Gabe." She hummed at him—a disapproving sound. "And you call yourself highly educated." She clucked her tongue once before turning away, dismissing him before he could react.

Clearly, he'd missed something.

Gabe got the review meeting started the way he always did. He thanked Elena for coming in, told her how fortunate the district was to have her on staff at the high school, et cetera, et cetera. In the case of Elena Torres, Nicolet High School really was fortunate given the fact that their last Spanish teacher could barely speak the language. He'd also been a total nut job, as he understood it. He'd stalked Erin Hennings, the high school principal, but he'd been no match for her canoe paddle, which she'd knocked him out with one night. The story had made the paper, and he'd made a mental note that Erin was tougher than she looked.

Being from Puerto Rico and a native Spanish speaker, Elena Torres was a dream come true for a small town like theirs, despite the unfortunate incident in January. There weren't many Spanish speakers here on the southern Lake Superior shore, that was for sure.

"Our little district doesn't have much diversity, so I really value how you've stepped in and brought something new to our students this year," he said, focusing on the file in front of him to avoid her gaze. "I've gone through Erin's—Ms. Henning's observation notes, and the way you weave culture into your lessons is a standout. You've made Spanish come alive for our kids."

Elena, who'd been wringing her hands, stopped long enough to thank him before resuming. Her voice was quiet, subdued, and he made the mistake of looking up—catching the way her lips parted slightly as she spoke. He shifted in his chair, irritated with himself.

He might as well get the negatives over with. She was waiting for them anyway.

"One area we could look to tighten up," he continued, "is classroom management. During the observation on February twelfth, things got a little loose. Students were chatting over you, and it took a while to refocus them after Ms. Hennings helped you address the behavior of a student who blew a spitball at the dry erase board."

"It's my toughest class because of him," Elena admitted, her eyes meeting his again, earnest and unguarded.

"Believe me, I'm aware. That young man is well known to me, and the fact that he was willing to misbehave while the building principal was present in the room ... it's pretty telling. Still, I think it's a good focus area for next year. Your mentor, Mrs. Benninger, has some solid tricks up her sleeve for keeping order. She'll be a good resource for you again next year."

He could see the moment she interpreted the meaning of his last remark. All the tension left her, and she smiled—a genuinely happy one, bright and relieved. She had a job next year.

Briefly, he lost his train of thought but quickly regained it. Addressing the elephant in the room, he added, "Despite that viral video after the holidays, I will recommend to the board that we renew your contract for another year. They'll meet to formally approve contract renewals at a meeting in mid July."

She was fully glowing now. "Thank you, Mr. Wright. I—I really appreciate your confidence in me."

They each stood, and he extended his hand to her. Her grip was firm, her hand warm, and he let go a fraction too fast, stepping back. He didn't see her all the way out through the waiting room, but he heard her and Lexi speaking once more, his daughter's voice bright and animated, and he was encouraged. He would find a nanny who could connect with Lexi just like this. With the twenty-plus applicants he had to sift through, surely one of them would make his daughter laugh the way Elena Torres had, and none of them would make him feel this off-balance. That was the plan, anyway.

Chapter 3

Elena sat on the sofa in her aunt's condo, catching up as their dinner baked in the oven for its final ten minutes. They'd attended Mass together tonight, and now they were having lasagna with homemade garlic bread and a side salad, and after nothing but frozen dinners for days on end, Elena could hardly wait. It would be her first meal since she moved to the bungalow that wasn't cooked in a microwave.

Carmen Molina studied her over her glass of Merlot. "She must be a very special girl for you to be feeling this way. I've never known you to take such an interest in a small child before."

"I don't know what it was, *Tía*, but when I went in to wait for my meeting and saw her sitting there, she looked ... she looked so ..."

Carmen waited while Elena hunted for the right words.

"Sad. *Abandonada*. She looked like me when I was her age. Lost. She's six, only a little younger than I was when *papá* left."

"Oh, *mija*."

"I made her smile, *Tía*. I made her laugh. She doesn't do that with just anyone. That's what the secretary said."

"How did you draw her out?"

Elena laughed. "By *drawing* a caricature of her father. I asked to borrow her notepad, and I just started drawing. At first she pretended not to watch, but after a couple of minutes, she was asking me questions and then she was laughing at the features I exaggerated."

Carmen chuckled. "You always did have a talent for that. I still have the picture you did of Samuel. It's up in the attic at Leila's. He thought you were so clever. And you are."

Wrapping her aunt in a hug, Elena said, "I miss my *tío*."

"Yes."

"It's been a long time." Elena broke away. There was something she'd been wanting to ask her aunt, but usually Leila was around, and her cousin wasn't ready for this conversation. "Are you still spending time with your neighbor?"

Carmen's cheeks turned a pretty shade of pink, but she didn't pretend to misunderstand. "He's a good man."

"He seems to be. Have you had him over for dinner?"

"Not yet, but he's coming tomorrow."

"Does Leila know?"

"No. We're still just getting to know one another. If he—if he's who I think he is, I will have to tell her. She will be hurt. She loved Samuel."

"We all did. But in the end, she'll be happy for you, *Tía*. You said he has two daughters?"

"Yes. The younger one lives in Grand Rapids with her son. They live only a few blocks from our old house. The other daughter, Lucy, lives here in Nicolet. I've met her. She's lovely. A bit lost professionally, but very sweet. You would like her."

"I hope I can meet her. I'd like to meet Mr. Jarvi too. I've only said hello to him in the hall."

"You will, *mija*. You will. Now, enough of this. I'm supposed to be the one asking you about your love life," Carmen said with a playful smile.

"Don't worry," Elena said with a roll of her eyes. "You do that plenty."

"Not today, I haven't, even though I desperately want to."

Elena smiled. "What do you want to ask me, *Tía*?"

"I thought you didn't like him."

"That's not a question, and who are you talking about?"

"Mr. Wright." She eyed Elena steadily.

"I like him fine," she dodged.

"You know what I'm asking."

"I don't, actually."

"You were practically spitting fire after that 'morality meeting' in January, and now you are drawing pictures of him with his daughter?"

"He's my boss *Tía*, and I already explained about his daughter."

"So there are no feelings there? Because I know you well, Elena, and—"

"No feelings there," Elena said firmly, sipping her wine.

"He's a very attractive man. I've met him at the store. Very kind too. A good father, I think." Carmen leaned forward. "Listen, *mija*, please don't misunderstand me. I'm not asking about Gabriel Wright because I want you to date him. I'm just trying to figure you out."

"What do you mean?"

"I mean he's single, and he's a good man, and you just don't seem to be attracted to the good ones."

Elena pursed her lips. "You've already talked to me about this, *Tía*. So has Leila."

Carmen raised her eyebrows expectantly. "And?"

Agitated, Elena stood to tuck one foot underneath her and sat back down again. "I'm working on it, okay?"

Carmen reached down to a low shelf on the end table and when she popped back up, she was holding a book. "I'm no psychologist, but I own a bookstore, and I read a lot, and I just read this."

Elena groaned when she looked at the title of the book her aunt had placed in her hands. *Good Girls and Bad Boys — Expert Insights*.

Carmen was animated when she spoke, her hands punctuating her words. "I want you to read this, Elena. It's excellent, and it says lots of girls who've been abandoned by their fathers choose bad boys."

Elena tilted her head with a frown and tried to interject, but Carmen leaned forward, her face mere inches from Elena's. Her words came out in a rapid tumble, as if this were her last opportunity to speak her peace. "They don't realize it, Elena, but they've transferred the wish of being loved by their fathers onto this other man who they know won't love them back, but they think if they can win him over, well then maybe they can heal that original wound and fill that terrible, empty void. Don't you see?"

Elena blinked. "That's completely ridiculous."

Carmen continued on as if she hadn't heard her. "I believe your pattern with men comes from what happened with your father."

Elena set her wine glass down on the coffee table and stood. This was done. She hardly ever spoke of her father, which her aunt well knew. What could her *tía* be thinking? She turned back to her aunt with a forced smile. "I'll check on the lasagna. It must be close."

Carmen stood as well, wringing her hands. "I don't want to hurt you. I want to help."

Elena stopped abruptly and turned, her aunt following her so closely, she nearly plowed into her. "I know you do, but you can't. What happened, happened. He left. *Mamá* couldn't handle it, and I got—" She took a deep breath and lowered her voice. "Look, I'm figuring it out. You aren't the only one reading this kind of stuff, okay? I'm trying." And she really was giving it her best effort. It wasn't easy, as it turned out, attempting to figure herself out.

One thing she did know, and it wasn't to say that there wasn't a kernel of truth to what her aunt had said, but bad boys excited her. They were full of passion. They contained a deeply masculine energy that pulled her in even when she knew better. They were strong, and that strength made her feel safe. Secure. Protected.

But the ones she kept choosing were actually dangerous for her, and she knew that too. They'd each been exciting, all right, but they were terrible at commitment, and that's what Elena was looking for. She'd been ready for a while now. It's what she'd hoped for with Marc, which had been completely stupid. Thinking that a notorious playboy like Marc Ghetty would change his ways and want to settle down with her was as foolish and improbable as someone moving to Nicolet hoping for a tropical climate and then being shocked when it snowed. Anyone with a brain would know better.

She should have known better.

"Take this," Carmen said, handing her the book. "It's worthy of your time."

The easiest course of action would be to take the book, so that's what Elena did. She couldn't promise she'd read it. So far, she'd committed to a few articles on the internet written on the subject. A whole book was a little much.

"Now, one final worry," Carmen said, resting a hand on Elena's arm.

Elena said a quick prayer to Saint Monica. " *Tía*, I really don't —"

"Are you sure you should be taking a second job? Leila told me you got hired at Victoria's.

"I'm only going to tend bar and wait tables a few nights a week, *Tía*."

"I worry you'll stretch yourself too thin."

"Has anyone ever told you that you worry too much?"

"But you are mine to worry over, Elena. It's my job."

Just like that, Elena's irritation vanished. "Oh, *Tía*."

"I made my sister a promise before she died, you know, and I will keep that promise. I am your *Tía*, always, but I will stand in as your *Mamá* as best I can, and that means telling you the truth as I see it."

"I love you. And I'm grateful. I hope you know that."

"I do know. But I also know that sometimes we will butt heads, as mothers and daughters do."

Elena gave her a watery smile. "That's okay. I want to butt heads."

Carmen laughed and held her arms open wide. "Come here."

Wrapped in her aunt's arms, Elena spoke against her shoulder. "*Tía, te quiero mucho.*"

Carmen whispered her love back, her voice thick with emotion.

Over dinner, they talked about Leila's wedding plans, about Carmen's bookstore and café, which continued to thrive. Half the town came in each week, and as much as Leila wanted her mother to retire, Carmen wasn't ready to give it up. Months ago, as a compromise, she'd taken on a manager, Jackson's mother, Virginia. Lately, though, Virginia was working fewer hours at the store. Her daughter, Elizabeth, had just delivered twin boys during the holidays, and she was helping Lizzie and her husband quite a bit on the home front.

"Lizzie and Matt have been working overtime the last few weeks," Carmen said, helping herself to a second piece of lasagna. "One of their brewhouse system thingies died, and they've done just about all they can think of to try to fix it. Virginia says they'll have to replace it."

"That sounds pricey," Elena said.

"It will cost more than one hundred thousand dollars to replace," Carmen confirmed with a shake of her head.

"*¡Uy!*" Elena had no other words. It was a staggering figure that would take her more than three years to make, and she wondered if this situation would have any impact on Jackson. While he had no stake in the brewery, he had recently become business partners with his sister and brother-in-law. They'd gone in on a new sporting goods store that was set to open towards the end of summer. He would be the one running the day-to-day operations, but she knew from Leila and her aunt that his sister and her husband were supplying most of the capital.

As if reading her mind, Carmen said, "With the store set to have its grand opening at the end of August, I know things will be a little tight for them until they can get that revenue flowing. I'm not sure how they'll manage."

Elena set down her fork, no longer hungry, but she told herself this sudden feeling of foreboding was only due to concern for Jackson and his family. That's all it was. They were good people, and she didn't want to see anything bad happen to them.

Chapter 4

It turned out finding a nanny wasn't as easy as Gabe had hoped. Keeping one had proven even more difficult. After two days of interviews and one week of disastrous nannying, he and Lexi were right back where they started. With June just five days away and summer break right around the corner, Gabe was officially desperate. The idea of starting the search all over again depressed him.

It was Saturday morning, and he'd been up since five handling school business. His parents were due in for the day, and Lexi had barely slept the night before, buzzing with excitement. They were the only ones who could rile her up like that. She loved his brother, Will, just as much, but his Air Force career meant he rarely made it home. Right now, Colonel William Wright, a special forces commander, was overseas on a joint op at a naval station in Rota, Spain—the Gateway to the Mediterranean and one of countless places Gabe figured he'd never get to see. Will still had a year to go before rotating back stateside.

Sometimes Gabe envied his brother's adventures. Will had been everywhere, made loads of connections, and could retire with killer benefits whenever he was ready. Last year, he'd made full-bird Colonel, which would have been enough for Gabe, but Will had caught the fever long ago and had no plans to leave before making Major General, at a minimum.

He glanced at the clock at the corner of his desk. It was close to eight, and that meant it was time to get Lexi up. It was important to stick to schedules. It was good for a child to have predictability each day, even on the weekends. Breakfast by eight-thirty, lunch by noon, dinner by six, bedtime at eight.

Rinse and repeat.

Gabe stood, stretched, and basked in his surroundings. The soft morning sunlight streamed through the large window in front of his custom-built desk. Tony, one of his dad's guys, was a master at woodworking. He'd done the desk and all the built-ins too. Gabe sniffed. He wondered how long it would take for the fresh-cut wood smell to wear off. Hopefully never.

He'd put in a few hundred hours helping his dad's crew build this place, not a lot of time, but enough to feel some pride and ownership, especially with his loft office, which had been completely his design.

Gabe walked down the stairs and headed down the hall to Lexi's room. She was already sitting up in bed, wiping the sleep from her eyes, when he opened the door.

"Hi, Daddy."

"Morning, princess. Sleep well?"

"Uh-huh. Mimi took me fishing, and we caught a rainbow, and Papa made me throw it back."

Gabe crossed the room and lifted her easily from under the covers. Surreptitiously he checked her pajamas and breathed a sigh of relief that she was dry. It was the first night she hadn't wet the bed in weeks. "You caught a trout in your dream?"

"No, a real rainbow." She wrapped her arms around his neck and continued the story.

She was animated this morning. Knowing she would be seeing her grandparents soon was all it took to bring out her old self. It made him feel better that she, the real Lexi, was still in there.

"I told him I wanted to keep it and put it in a jar so I could look at all those colors every day, but he said no, so Mimi hid it in her hat, and then she gived it to me."

With one hand, Gabe pushed the curtains away from the window to let in the morning sunshine. "She *gave* it to you, huh? That's some dream. Your papa will feel bad he was so parsimonious."

She squinted at him. "What's that one mean?"

"Stingy." He headed out towards the kitchen.

"I don't know that word too."

Gabe smiled. "Stingy people don't want to give things. They want to keep everything for themselves."

She considered that. "Papa's not *parsmous*. He said everyone should see the rainbow. That's why I couldn't keep it in a jar."

"Parsimonious," he corrected.

"I got real mad at him." She switched gears. "Hey, Daddy?"

"Yes?"

"Mrs. Shreever isn't gonna come back?"

He settled her down on the chair at the counter and then crouched beside her.

"No, baby. She's not coming back."

"She didn't like me."

Gabe worked to keep his face neutral. "What do you mean? She liked you just fine. She just couldn't be your nanny anymore because her own family needed her." He was lying through his teeth and could only hope that Lexi wouldn't be able to tell.

Lexi heaved a large sigh. "She was mean, Daddy. She didn't have a smile."

Gabe rested his elbows on the counter and brought himself closer to eye level with his daughter. "Well, maybe something was making her feel sad."

Lexi looked up at him dubiously.

Gabe chuckled and chucked her under the chin. "She loved being here with you. Remember how she cooked for you and gave you all those worksheets to do?"

Lexi nodded.

"Well, she wanted to take good care of you and teach you things. She was just having a bad week, Lex, that's all. But guess what?"

"Hmm?"

He straightened. "For us, today is going to be a very *good* day. How about we start it out with some protein pancakes with blueberries on top?"

She brightened. "I don't hafta have oatmeal and flaxseed?"

"Let's live on the edge and mix up our Saturday morning. It's time we used that real maple syrup Mimi got us for Christmas anyway."

"Yay!"

Gabe began gathering the fixings while Lexi watched on, chin in hands, from her perch at the counter.

"When will Mimi and Papa get here?"

"About a half hour. Thirty minutes."

"Can we go to the river and look for peepers? Can I bring the blue bucket to catch some?"

"I'm sure we can, but first, we adults need to work on a few things, and then we can have some fun."

"What do you got to work on?" Lexi went to town scratching an itch on her bare shoulder, just under the strap of her white cotton camisole.

Gabe answered as he rummaged through the cabinet containing all the measuring cups. "Your papa is going to check out a few things with the house to make sure it's all up to snuff."

"What's *snuff*?"

What *was* snuff, other than chewing tobacco? "You know what?" he admitted, finding what he needed and closing the cabinet. "I'm not sure."

Lexi giggled. "I guess you don't know *all* the words, Daddy. I'm ..." She squinted her eyes in thought, "... *dis-ta-pointed* in you."

Gabe looked at his smiling daughter and felt his heart squeeze. When she was happy, he was happy, and when she wasn't, well ... "Nice one, smarty pants."

As soon as his parents got there, Gabe knew something was up. Emma and Theo Wright were the kind of people who woke up with smiles on their faces, but as he invited them in, he saw that his dad's eyes were troubled and his mom's were overly bright and red-rimmed.

He closed the door behind them and turned. "What's going on?" he said in a quiet voice, hoping to avoid detection by his daughter who was bounding down the hallway toward them.

His mother hugged him tightly before cheerfully reaching for Lexi. She lifted her easily in her arms and carried her back where she'd come from. "Let's go see that horse drawing you told me about. Is it in your room?"

Lexi was only too happy to oblige, and she chattered on excitedly until her voice faded away in the back of the house.

Once they were out of earshot, Theo placed a firm hand on Gabe's shoulder and asked, "Did you see the news this morning?"

Gabe shook his head. He'd had too much to do and had skipped his usual Saturday morning ritual of coffee-sipping while scrolling the headlines.

His father's voice was grave as he explained, "A navy destroyer was bombed in Rota. A small boat packed with explosives rammed it—blew a hole in it below the waterline."

"What?" Gabe's coffee mug nearly slipped from his hand.

"Fourteen sailors were killed, along with two of Will's airmen and one of his officers. They were all on board getting briefed for some kind of joint operation."

Gabe felt the blood rush out of his head, and he touched his free hand to the wall to brace himself.

"Will—"

"He's safe. He called us. Couldn't say much, of course, but ..."

Gabe went weak-kneed with relief. "He's okay? Why didn't you lead with that?" His brother had been injured on duty in Afghanistan almost two years ago, and Gabe thought he and his parents might crack under the weight of their worry then.

"He's not badly hurt—a few burns—but he's shaken, Gabe. We could hear it in his voice. He lost a friend. Someone you know too."

Gabe hunted for names. He'd met several of Will's military friends over the years. Who had Will said was stationed there with him? And then he remembered. "No. Tommy?"

His father swallowed hard. He tried to speak but couldn't get the words out, so he nodded instead.

"Oh, no." Gabe felt a lump form in his own throat as he recalled the last time he'd seen Tommy Lancaster back in Hawaii when he'd visited Will one summer—the summer he'd met Kaena. He gave himself a mental shake. They were talking about Will's good friend here, not his ex-wife. Tommy tore through life like a freight train, tough as iron with a wit that could make a drill sergeant crack a smile. Dead? The word sank like a stone in Gabe's gut, heavy and final.

This wasn't the first time his brother had experienced the loss of a fellow soldier. Though he himself had been injured in Afghanistan, three of his men had died. Will still wouldn't talk about it. Gabe couldn't imagine how his brother would be affected by this latest loss, especially over someone he'd known so well for so long.

Gabe ran a hand roughly over his face. "Why didn't he call me?" he wondered aloud.

Theo patted him on his arm and stepped further into the house, setting his hat on the counter in the kitchen. "He said he did. Twice. We tried you too."

Gabe, following his father, clapped a hand over his empty back pocket and cursed silently. He'd left his phone on the nightstand in his bedroom. That's what happened when he broke from his routine. Normally he'd shower, do a quick check of his three preferred news sites over coffee, and tuck his phone in his back pocket as he set about the rest of the day. He'd veered from his usual order *one* time and look what happened—He'd missed what might be the most important call of his life. Guilt invaded every corner of his mind, and all he could think was that his brother had needed him, and he hadn't been there. He moved toward his bedroom. "I'll go call him right now."

"No." Theo stopped him. "No, Gabriel. We told him we were coming today, and he asked me to give you this." Theo pulled Gabe into a hug, and after a few thwacks on the back, he squeezed him tighter and added, "I know you want to talk to him today, son, but he said tomorrow would be best. He sends his love."

Gabe held his father and blinked against the sting in his eyes. He felt his dad shudder as he struggled to reign in his own emotions.

"We didn't get his call until after we'd seen it on the news," Theo said, pulling away.

Gabe worked to gain back his equilibrium. "That must've been ... you must've been scared."

"Your mother was beside herself. The images of the ship, a big gaping hole in the port side ... She was terrified for your brother."

Gabe placed his hands on his dad's shoulders and looked him in the eye. "And you?"

Robbed of speech again, his father could only nod. After a moment, he added, "I was strong, for your mother, but ... You know how it is."

Gabe did know. As a dad, he was supposed to be a rock, but a lot of the time he felt like a pebble caught in a stormy sea. He gave Theo a quick, final hug. His father was still solid, toughened by decades of manual labor. He'd always been the strongest, toughest man Gabe knew.

Lately, Theo had been hinting at retiring while he still had his health. It would be a good move—hanging up the tool belt to enjoy life, but Theo was wrestling with how to step back. It was a topic he'd mentioned wanting to discuss today during this visit. Gabe wasn't sure how he'd be able to help, but he'd offered to listen and advise where he could.

They passed most of the morning with coffee in hand, Lexi's laughter ringing off the walls of the living room, their talk frequently looping back to Will. When the carafe ran dry, Lexi grabbed her blue bucket, and they wandered back to the stream at the property's edge to hunt frogs. It wasn't even June yet, but buds had already appeared on the dogwoods along the fence near the road. Soon, the rest of the trees would follow suit. It had been a warm spring, and Lexi was thrilled to discover that all the little critters had hatched or awoken from their long winter slumber.

She was happily building a house for her temporary pet frog as Gabe and his parents settled in on the patio an hour later. They watched her pile sticks, one on top of the other, in the grass.

"This could keep her busy all afternoon," Gabe announced.

"I wonder if she'll become a biologist," Emma mused.

"Maybe," Gabe said, a smile quirking the corners of his mouth. God bless his mother. She thought Lexi was the smartest kid who'd ever lived. When Lexi built with her blocks, Emma imagined her growing up to be a master architect. When she'd first shown an interest in baking cookies, she pictured her as a Michelin award-winning chef.

"All I know is she didn't get her love of critters from me." Emma shuddered. "Now horses, that's a different story."

"She's gaga over them at the moment."

"Just like I was."

"Was?" Theo echoed, eyebrows raised.

Emma smiled. "Like I am."

Emma had grown up with horses, but she'd gone the last twenty years without one, though she talked about getting back into riding once she was retired.

Last he'd heard, both his parents' retirements were slated for the following spring. They still hadn't discussed it today, and if his dad didn't bring it up soon, Gabe would.

"Now, tell us about this nanny," his mother said.

"I could wring her neck," Theo muttered.

They pretty much knew the story. Cheryl Shreever, a woman in her mid fifties with three grown children, hadn't been at all what she'd seemed. Gabe thought he'd be getting a woman who knew how to raise kids with steady patience. She checked all the right boxes. She could cook, she wanted to teach Lexi geography and work on math with her over the summer ... She was everything he'd been looking for in a nanny, and for one glorious week, he felt like he could breathe again. And then he'd come home early one night after a board meeting had been canceled.

Even before he entered the house, he could hear her shrieking at Lexi for getting bath water on the floor. As he kicked off his shoes, she called his sweet daughter a "very bad girl" who was always "ruining everything." He entered the bathroom to see Lexi standing in the tub, shivering and crying, as Cheryl cleaned up a tiny puddle of water on the floor.

It had been all Gabe could do not to drag the woman out of his home by her thick braid. Pretending all was well, he'd lifted Lexi out of the tub and asked Cheryl to wait for him while he got her dressed in her pajamas. Once Lexi had settled down under her covers with a book, he walked Cheryl out to her car, slipped her a wad of cash, and told her not to bother coming back.

Emma frowned at the recounting. "Gabe. What are you going to do?"

"I'll find another nanny."

His parents looked pointedly at one another before Theo spoke up. "Your mother and I were talking. She could come stay with us again this summer. You know we love having her, and she likes being with your mom at the store."

Gabe had already considered that option, but only briefly. He just couldn't part with his daughter for a whole summer, seeing her only on the weekends. Not again. They'd done it last summer, and he'd hated every second. But it was good to know he had a plan B in case plan A failed, which it just might.

"Thank you for that, but I've got it covered. I'll find someone." He crossed his fingers and changed the subject, not wanting them to ask any more questions about Lexi's care. "Let's talk about your plans, Dad. Are you thinking of selling or closing up shop?"

Reluctant to move on from Lexi, Theo hesitated before answering. "I haven't had any bites yet."

"But you probably haven't really spread the word yet, either, and you're the only act in town. Who will fill that void if the one and only construction company closes?"

"That's an interesting question," his dad said, looking at him intently.

Gabe wasn't sure he liked that look. "And what's the answer?"

Theo scratched at his head thoughtfully. "Well, now, I don't know. But it occurs to me that me and you share a last name. Wright construction wouldn't have to close *or* rebrand if you took it over."

Gabe's mind went blank. "Oh, Dad ..."

Theo waved a hand nonchalantly. "Just a thought."

Just a thought? His father had just dropped a bomb on him and acted like it was no big deal. Gabe turned his attention to his mother, who was nodding and smiling. What—they *both* wanted him to walk away from his career and take over Wright construction back in Bayshore? He was slow to respond. "So, if I don't take over the business, then that's it? Is that what you're saying? No more company?"

Theo shrugged. "I can't wait for William. He's married to the military, and for better or worse, it would seem." He wagged his head slightly and Emma rested a comforting hand on his leg. Gabe knew his parents worried incessantly over Will. They fretted over him too. It seemed that a parent could never stop worrying about their kids. He was screwed. A lifetime of anxiety, that's what was in store for him.

Shaking off the depressing thought, he focused on the topic at hand. "Dad, I haven't worked construction since college."

"You built this house," Emma pointed out.

"I helped out on the weekends."

"And did a fine job," Theo added.

"Dad, I'm not sure what you want me to say right now."

"You don't need to say anything at all right now. I just want you to know it's an option. The business is yours if you want it, and if not ..." he shrugged.

"If not, you just close up the only construction company in Bayshore? What will everyone do there, just stop building houses? No, you need to sell it to someone."

Theo's shoulders slumped. "Maybe I will yet."

Gabe pinched his lips together and looked at his mother, who winked at him. He hated disappointing his dad. He was the best man Gabe knew.

Theo Wright—a fine man, a great builder, and an absolutely terrible businessman. How many jobs had he done for people at a pittance because he knew they could use the break?

"*The Lord's blessed me, so that I can bless others,*" he'd say. And it was true. He'd been blessed in a hundred different ways, not the least of which was having met Emma Wright, then Emma Hathaway, who had come to Bayshore long ago on her family's private plane. As they say, the rest was history. And a dramatic history it had been. When she refused to return home with her family, she'd been promptly disowned, and a long estrangement ensued. It had lasted until the birth of Will.

"We don't have to decide any of this today," Emma said. "Just ... be thinking, Gabriel."

Gabe nodded, relieved that he was off the hook for now.

Chapter 5

E lena couldn't wait to get home to soak her feet and get rid of the ache in her arches. She'd known it would be rough to start a second job before her teaching position let out for summer, but she hadn't realized how physically taxing it would be to stand in front of a classroom full of students for seven hours, only to follow that up with another five or six hours on her feet.

Three weeks ago, she'd been hired at Nicolet's fanciest restaurant, Rebecca's, where she now juggled shifts as a server and bartender, depending on the day. Between Rebecca's and the high school, she'd only had one Sunday off in all that time. Without the dream of owning that cute little bungalow, she'd have tossed her apron in the trash by now. But every night when she pulled into Jackson's driveway, the sight of the house steadied her, and the word *home* whispered through her tired bones.

Today was June first, a Friday. School let out June twelfth. She just had to grit it out a little longer—temporary chaos, she could handle.

The night was slower than usual for late spring, but Elena didn't mind. It gave her time to lean on the bar, chatting with Sarah and Olivia, two of her closest friends and colleagues from the school. Sarah, sipping a Shirley Temple, grinned sheepishly. "I'm expecting. Four months," she added before Elena could ask.

Elena's jaw dropped. "And you kept it secret that long?"

Olivia laughed. "She only told me tonight—don't feel too left out."

An hour later, Elena was still buzzing from the news, pouring drinks with a little extra bounce. Her new friend group had become her lifeline in Nicolet. She loved them all, which was a first for her. She was used to women who could dance by her side all night long, only to stab her in the back the next morning. These women were different. Leila had pulled her into their fold a year ago, and they'd clicked fast. Elena knew they'd drop anything and come running if she needed them to. Knowing that gave her a sense of security in a world that hadn't always been kind to her. And now one of them was going to have a baby, which meant she'd get to be an honorary aunt. She wondered if Sarah had told Erin, yet. Probably. Those two were inseparable.

And just like that, as if she'd conjured her up, Erin walked into the restaurant. The woman, principal of Nicolet High School, could fit in her pocket, but she had the personality of a Spanish bull. "Bartender, pour me a drink."

"Rum and Coke?" Elena suggested, wiping down the bar in front of her friend as she hopped up on the stool.

"Perfect."

Elena grabbed a glass and scooped up some ice. "You just missed Olivia and Sarah."

"I know. I wanted to come with them, especially since Ethan's out of town, but I couldn't swing it. I have an unofficial meeting here in a few minutes."

Elena glanced at her watch. "At eight o'clock on a Friday?"

Erin rolled her eyes. "You know Gabe. He's never off the clock."

Pouring, Elena shook her head. "Seriously, this is weird, even for Gabe."

"We're narrowing down my replacement tonight. It's between two candidates."

Elena's heart skipped a beat. Whoever replaced Erin would be her new boss. She doubted anyone could be as good to her as Erin Hennings had been.

"Who are they? Would I like them?" More importantly, would they like her?

Erin bobbed her head from side to side, equivocating as she stirred her drink. "They're both pretty good. I suppose that's the problem. But I get a better vibe from the female candidate."

"What does Gabe think?"

Erin rolled her eyes. "Why do you think we're having this meeting? He thinks if he buys me an expensive dinner, he can convince me to see things his way."

Elena grinned. "Has he only just met you?"

Erin winked. "Don't worry. I'll get my way."

The door on the other side of the restaurant opened, and in walked Gabe the Babe. Elena told her traitorous body to calm down. She couldn't even look at the man without her hormones kicking into overdrive, and it thoroughly annoyed her. Why couldn't she feel indifferent toward him? Especially since she was certain he viewed her as *caos con patas*—chaos with legs. It bothered her that she cared what he thought of her. Between the duct tape incident and that stupid viral video she'd had zero control over, she hadn't exactly covered herself with glory where Gabriel Wright was concerned. She would have expected her embarrassment to have faded more by now, but it hadn't.

Something happened to her when she was near Gabriel Wright. He made her feel off- balance, unsure of herself. Normally, with men especially, she knew how to at least appear confident, and she could flirt her way through any situation. Absolutely. Men were enthralled by her. But not Gabe, not that she wanted him to be. For one thing, he was her boss, but even if he wasn't, even if he were just some guy on the street, she wouldn't flirt with him. There was something about the way he looked at her, as if he could see right through her.

She'd barely made eye contact with him that mortifying day she backed into his car, and then in the "morality meeting," as she'd come to think of it, she'd avoided meeting his eyes at all costs. She didn't want him to see too deeply inside of her. She didn't want anyone to.

"*Ope*, he's here," Erin said, spotting him reflected in the mirror behind the bar. She lifted her glass. "Thanks for this, and wish me luck."

"*Buena suerte*," Elena dutifully responded, forcing thoughts of her boss and her mortification aside. "Oh, wait," she called after Erin.

Her diminutive friend turned.

"Sarah told me the news. Way to keep a secret. And for four whole months."

Grinning, Erin acknowledged the compliment. "I can keep my mouth shut when it counts. And I already called dibs on being godmother, so don't even think about it."

Elena laughed. "I'm sure Benny is *thrilled* about that."

"Benny loves me now. I've completely won him over."

Elena bid her farewell with a smile. Sarah's husband was forced to put up with Erin since she was his wife's best friend, but Elena got the sense he barely tolerated her.

With one final surreptitious glance at Gabe, Elena moved down the bar to refill a patron's glass. Everyone was having babies these days. Jackson's sister had five-month-old twins, Olivia had a one-year-old and was currently filing adoption papers with her husband, Sean. And now Sarah. She'd always thought she'd get her happy ever after someday, but what if someday never came?

Leila liked to think of Elena as the "eternal optimist." If her cousin only knew how things like this terrified her. It was altogether possible that she'd never find a man to love and grow old with. Her track record with men was worse than her track record with house plants. She didn't kill them, but by the end of the relationship, they'd usually given her plenty of reasons to want to.

Gabe carried on small talk with Erin for a few minutes, as they waited to be seated. Seeing Elena tending bar had been a surprise, and not necessarily a pleasant one. With amusement, he watched her turn all the liquor bottles by minute degrees so that their labels were all straight and lined up perfectly. When he'd walked in, she'd clearly seen him and then pretended not to.

He could see her face in the mirror behind the bar and frowned when he noticed the dark smudges under her eyes. How long had she been working two jobs, and why? One question to Erin, and he could get the answer to both questions, but he'd rather be left to wonder than risk Erin misunderstanding his interest in her friend.

Clearly, Elena was spreading herself too thin. She'd had a tough year. He felt himself feeling sorry for her until he noticed her done-up nails as she adjusted a bottle of Tanqueray. The woman wore designer clothes, carried designer purses, and always had a fresh manicure. Obviously, she was living beyond her means and killing herself in the process.

And working as a bartender. His eyes narrowed.

A teacher in his district was working as a bartender. That was just great. At least it was an upscale restaurant. Gabe could only hope Dom Stone wouldn't find out. His opinion of Elena was already low.

Once he and Erin were seated at their table, they made small talk as they waited for the server to take their order. Gabe did his best to focus on their conversation, but it was hard for him not to watch the tired beauty at the bar. His eyes had a will of their own, and he found himself sneaking glances at Elena every few minutes. With her hair pulled casually back in a ponytail, she looked more like a college student after a week of finals than she did a high school teacher. Her skin glowed in the bar lighting, and her teeth flashed white each time she smiled at the three men seated at the bar who continued to find reasons to call her over to them.

There was something about her. Even with fatigue casting shadows under her eyes, she exuded a sort of vibrant energy and a magnetism that pulled at him in spite of his determination not to let it. Even though he'd only ever interacted with her three times, he felt a strange, electrifying connection to her every time he saw her. It was one he recognized and wasn't sure he liked. He'd felt it before, years ago, and he knew from that experience he shouldn't trust it.

Erin ordered the most expensive item on the menu and looked at him with a smile, daring him to make a comment. He didn't. It was worth it to him to let her think she had the upper hand. Gabe liked the guy from Traverse City for Erin's position, and he worked to persuade her over their dinner. "He's the known commodity, Erin. We don't know your candidate from Eve. I have connections in Traverse City, and I asked around. He's got a great reputation."

"My girl boosted grad rates from eighty-five to ninety percent at her school," Erin shot back.

"My guy boosted teacher retention by fifteen percent in three years," Gabe countered.

They went back and forth that way for several minutes, and Gabe was so focused on winning his case, he missed the entrance of two new patrons who stood at the hostess stand, waiting to be seated.

Erin noticed first. "Oh, no," she whispered.

Gabe followed her gaze to the entrance of the restaurant and felt an immediate rush of protectiveness towards Elena. There stood Marc Ghetty, the Silver Fox himself, with a guy who was vaguely familiar but Gabe couldn't place.

Elena didn't need this. She'd been the talk of the town a few months back when she began a high-profile fling with Marc, a somewhat famous playboy and owner of a successful real estate investment firm, who occasionally made the news both in and outside of Nicolet. They'd caused quite a stir when they'd first started dating, but by the time Christmas rolled around, Marc had moved on with some man-eater without breaking things off with Elena first.

If Marc had thought Elena would step aside quietly, he had the surprise of his life when he bumped into her downtown at the ball drop on New Year's Eve. The event attracted hundreds, if not thousands, of people, so they had a fairly large live audience. They had a sizeable virtual audience as well, something Elena hadn't counted on. Someone had recognized Marc and recorded the whole thing, posting it to social media shortly thereafter where it had blown up the internet.

Elena hadn't held back. She called that overrated multimillionaire every name under the sun, in two languages—a skill set Gabe could have used himself four years ago and which must have felt amazing—and then she'd insulted him in terms that couldn't have been misunderstood, not even by a convent full of nuns. Her words hit like a verbal knockout punch, and the clear underdog had won the match. Gabe watched the clip half a dozen times, at least, and he wasn't the only one. It went viral, and on January second, Dom was in his office looking for blood.

Erin sat suspended on the edge of her seat, barely breathing. "She's seen him. Has he seen her?"

Instead of answering, Gabe set out to stall the inevitable. At least this way, Elena could have a minute to prepare herself. "Marc!" he called, standing from his chair.

Recognition flashed in the older man's eyes. His nickname—Silver Fox—was spot on, Gabe had to admit. At the very least, it was much better than Gabe's unfortunate nickname. *Gabe the Babe.* He could murder the person who'd coined it. If only he knew who that was.

"Mr. Wright," Marc acknowledged as he sauntered over, leaving his friend standing at the hostess station. That's when Gabe placed his companion: Jordan Jamieson with the Minnesota Vikings. Marc sure did make the rounds. He was friends with businessmen, professional athletes, and movie stars. Why he stayed so close to tiny, sleepy Nicolet, Gabe wasn't quite sure. He nodded a greeting to Minnesota's star quarterback and received one in return before returning his attention to Marc.

They shook hands and conversed briefly. Marc asked how the district's security update planning was going, and Gabe filled him in. They'd met several weeks back to discuss the second endowment fund Marc planned to gift Nicolet Public Schools for the much-needed updates. It was all in the works, and Gabe wanted it all finalized as soon as possible—for the district's sake, absolutely, but almost as much for his own. They desperately needed the funds, but Gabe couldn't stomach much more of Marc's presence in his life. Swallowing his dislike of the guy was getting harder and harder, but the district couldn't afford to alienate such a wealthy donor, so he had to grit his teeth and play nice.

After a few more minutes, they wished each other a good evening and Marc returned to the quarterback at the hostess stand. Gabe sat without glancing at Elena, and Erin hissed. "He's seen her."

"It'll be okay." Gabe took a leisurely sip of his water. Deliberately, he steered them back to their earlier discussion, but he could tell they were both distracted. Especially when Marc got up from his booth and began making his way to the bar.

Erin's eyes narrowed into slits. "Great. Now he's going over there. Why would he do that? She doesn't want to talk to him." She drummed her fingers on the table before coming to a decision. She pushed her chair back and stood. "I'll be right back."

"Sit," he ordered. "I'll handle this."

"But—"

"I said, I'll handle it." Gabe spoke the words in a tone that he knew invited no argument, not even from Erin. She sank back into her chair, eyes darting between him and the bar, her fingers still tapping out her unease.

Gabe stood, smoothing his jacket as he crossed the restaurant. His pulse ticked up—not just from anticipation of a confrontation, but also from the way Elena's shoulders stiffened behind the bar. She'd seen her ex coming. Her hands froze mid-pour, a bottle of bourbon trembling slightly over a glass, and her jaw clenched tight. She looked like a storm about to break.

Marc reached the bar first, leaning one elbow on the counter with that slick, practiced grin flashing in the mirror behind the bottles of booze. "Elena Torres," he drawled, loud enough to turn heads across Rebecca's polished dining room. "Bartending, huh? Pour me a Scotch, neat—top shelf. You know what I like."

Elena set the bourbon down with a sharp clink, her eyes narrowing as she faced him. "Marc." Her voice was flat, but Gabe, now steps away, caught the anger simmering beneath. "We're fresh out of top shelf. How about a house special instead? It's flashy and hollow—just like you."

A few patrons chuckled, and Marc's grin faltered, a flicker of something—hurt?—crossing his face before it hardened. "Still got that mouth on you, huh? Heard that got you in a little bit of trouble. And how's your car? Still held together with a roll of tape?"

"That's the best you've got? Calling me poor?" Elena shot back, her voice rising enough to carry over the bar's hum. "Take your bank account and shove it, Marc—It won't buy you anything in here."

The bar hushed, heads swiveling—patrons, servers, even the hostess craning to see. Marc straightened, his jaw tightening as the chuckles spread. "Do I need to get your manager?" he asked, his tone clipped, eyes flicking to the growing audience.

"Everything okay here?" Gabe broke in. He'd been hanging back, but now he stepped up beside Marc. His voice was calm, but his body angled toward Elena, a quiet shield.

Elena shot him a look—half gratitude, half defiance. "*Claro*, Mr. Wright. Just peachy." She smirked, but her hands gripped the bar's edge, knuckles whitening.

Marc turned to Gabe, his smile returning, though it was strained. "She's a loose cannon, Gabe—you saw that video. And you let her teach kids?"

"Leave him out of this," Elena snapped, stepping around the bar's edge to close the gap with Marc. Her voice rang out, drawing more stares. "You don't get to waltz in here and play king, Marc. I might live off tips, but you're nothing but a wallet with a pulse."

A gasp rippled through the restaurant, followed by stifled laughs from the three guys at the end of the bar. Marc's face flushed, his eyes flashing with raw hurt and fury. He leaned in, voice dropping to a hiss that still carried in the quiet restaurant. "Keep it up, Elena—you're burning bridges."

Gabe slid between them, his shoulder brushed hers, but neither of them pulled away. "Back off," he said to Marc, low and firm, his gaze locking with the older man's. "You've said enough, and your buddy's waiting."

Marc's eyes darted to Jordan Jamieson, who watched with a raised brow from across the room, then back to Gabe. He took in Gabe's close stance with Elena and hesitated, his jaw working. Forcing a tight smile, he said, "Careful, Gabe. She'll drag you down with her. Don't say I didn't warn you." He shot Elena a lingering look before turning and stalking off.

Gabe turned to Elena, his breath catching at their proximity. He could feel her heat radiating through the thin space between them. She was breathing hard, her fists balled, her dark eyes locked on Marc's retreating back.

"You okay?" he asked, his voice rougher than he'd intended. His hand hovered near her arm before he pulled it back.

She blinked, meeting his gaze, and the fire in her eyes softened, revealing a flicker of vulnerability. "I don't need your help," she said, but the edge was gone, her voice almost a whisper.

"I know." Gabe's eyes held hers. "But I'm here anyway."

Her lips parted, a faint flush creeping up her cheeks, then she broke away, stepping back behind the bar. "*Gracias*," she muttered, grabbing a rag and scrubbing at nothing.

Gabe watched her a moment longer before forcing himself back to Erin, who was staring, wide-eyed.

He sat across from her once more, and she raised her eyebrows—a challenge or a question? He wasn't sure.

"It's handled," he said, picking up his fork, but his pulse still thrummed. Marc's parting words—"She'll drag you down with her"—echoed, and the feel of Elena's shoulder against his lingered. Handled, maybe, but the air felt charged with trouble. What specifically? Gabe didn't know.

By the time he pulled into his driveway, it was nearly ten. Gabe couldn't remember the last time he'd been out so late. His younger self had closed the bars on the weekends. Now, he was lucky if he could stay awake on New Year's Eve to watch the ball drop on TV. When had he become so ... old?

If Will could see him now, Gabe knew what his brother would say. He'd tell him to get back in the game. Except that probably wasn't true anymore. He'd talked to Will twice since his ship had taken the hit six days ago. The first conversation hadn't lasted longer than five minutes. Gabe had brought up the bombing, but Will hadn't wanted to talk about it. The second time, Will had sounded a little better, but still not himself. There'd been no joking. No hint of humor, which made sense. He was still reeling. Still mourning the loss of his good friend. He worried his brother would never be the same again until he remembered he'd had that same fear the first time. Will had recovered from that. He'd recover from this too. He just needed some time.

He paid Anna Davis, the local college student Erin had recommended to babysit Lexi. Anna had watched her a few times now, and Gabe thought Lexi might be warming up to her.

Tonight, as she slipped on her spring jacket, Anna grinned. "We read six books, Mr. Wright, and halfway through that last one, she was out. I even got her laughing a little tonight.

Hope flickered in Gabe's chest. "That nanny position's still open if you want it. You and Lexi would have fun, and I'd make it worth your while."

Anna laughed. "You've already tempted me with more than I'd earn in a year at 906 Pizza. But my plane ticket's set—I'm off to Alaska for the summer with my boyfriend.

"Bummer for us, but good for you," Gabe said, forcing himself to smile. "Enjoy the trip."

After seeing Anna out and locking up, he stopped at Lexi's room. He'd planned just to peek in from the doorway, as he did every night, but movement in the bed told him she was still awake, and he stepped inside.

"Why aren't you sleeping?"

She sniffled in response.

He sat down, and the bed sank under his weight. Reaching out, he stroked her hair.

"Lex, what's wrong?" He heard another sniffle.

"Anna's going away."

"You like Anna?"

Lexi went quiet.

Gabe reached for his daughter under her arms and moved her to his lap. With her arms around his neck, she clung to him, and he thought his heart might break as she heaved sobs against his chest.

After letting her cry for a minute, he said, "Lexi, are you sad about Anna?"

"Mrs. Shreever beed so mean to me, Daddy, but Anna is nice, but now she won't babysit me anymore 'cause she's going to 'Laska. We read so many books, and I fell asleep, and I didn't get to say bye to her. I waved from my window, but she didn't see me, and now she's gone."

"Oh, honey, I'm sorry you didn't get to say goodbye."

"I want her to be my nanny, but she's going to 'Laska."

"I know, baby. I'm sorry."

"I wanna go be with Mimi and Papa in Bayshore."

"I'd miss you too much if you lived with them again. I need you here with me."

She squeezed him tighter.

His voice was thick with emotion when he said, "You're my best girl, Lex."

"You're my best Daddy."

Beginning early Monday morning, Gabe continued his frantic search for a nanny. Kindergarten would be out next week and he had nobody to take care of Lexi. He had nobody to take care of her this week either, and by Wednesday he was no closer to finding someone than he'd been at the beginning.

"Adele, I'll be right back," he said on his way out the door. It was not a good routine—this picking up Lexi after school and bringing her back to his office for the remainder of the day—but what else could he do?

Lexi jumped up and down when she spotted his car, growing more and more impatient as she had to wait for him to reach the front of the pick-up line. When it was finally his turn, he put the car in park and got out. Lexi's teacher released her, and she ran to him, her purple backpack bouncing awkwardly on her shoulders. She launched herself into his arms, and he picked her up.

Lexi's exuberant greetings were the best, and he soaked up the scent of her baby shampoo as he kissed the top of her head.

"Did you find a nanny?" It was the same question she'd asked him yesterday and the day before.

"Not yet, baby girl."

"Is Mrs. Shreever gonna come back?" Another repeat.

"No, Lex. Remember, she's about to be a grandma. She's going to be real busy taking care of her grandbaby."

"I hope she doesn't be mean to that little baby, Daddy."

Gabe chuckled as he closed her door and got back into the driver's seat. He waved goodbye to Lexi's teacher as he pulled back into the traffic loop. "I'm sure she won't," he reassured her, speaking to her reflection in the rearview mirror.

Although, who could say what Mrs. Shreever would or wouldn't do. He'd misjudged her. Big surprise there. He seemed to lack the necessary radar to tell if a woman had good maternal instincts or not. Strike two.

Gabe glanced again at Lexi, who wore a wide grin. "You look happy, kiddo."

"Daddy, this is the best news of my whole life. I thought Mrs. Shreever might hafta come back cause Mimi said you're *dezprit*. I was gonna hafta get a peeper from the creek and put it on Mrs. Shreever's head if she came back so I could scare her away forever and ever."

He laughed. "That's an evil plot."

She giggled. "Can we go home now, Daddy?"

"No, honey. It's back to my office for us, but just for a bit. You can color again, alright?"

Her smile faded, and she sighed dramatically. "Okay. So much coloring is better than Mrs. Shreever."

Friday night came, and Gabe still hadn't found a nanny. He hadn't told Lexi yet, but he'd enrolled her in the summer enrichment program that began on Wednesday of next week. He hadn't told her because he was holding out for a miracle. He sank into the couch, rubbing his temples. As much as he missed Lexi at the moment, he was grateful his parents had picked her up today to stay the night and most of tomorrow with them. He'd head over there in the afternoon, have a little dinner, and then bring her back home with him.

He thought back to last night. Another nanny interview, another bust. This one had credentials out the wazoo—ten years' experience, glowing references—but Lexi had just stared at her feet, mumbling one-word answers before bolting. He couldn't blame her; the woman had all the warmth of a tax form. Twenty applicants down, and not one had brought back that giggle he'd heard with Elena.

Elena.

Her name hit him like a stray thought he couldn't dodge. He'd tried not to think about her since that night at Rebecca's a week ago—the way she'd stood up to Marc, fire in her eyes, or the way her shoulder had felt against his, warm and fleeting. He'd caught himself watching her too long for the rest of his dinner with Erin, feeling that pull he'd sworn off years ago.

But it wasn't just that. It was Lexi—how she'd lit up with Elena that day at the office, sketching and laughing like her old self. And now, with Marc's words—*She'll drag you down*—still gnawing at him, Gabe had to wonder. She was a mess. Two jobs, a beat-up car carrying a woman dressed in designer labels, a viral meltdown—but she had a strength he couldn't ignore, and his daughter had come alive in her presence.

He glanced at the clock—8:30 p.m. Rebecca's would be busy, but not slammed. Lexi was safe in Bayshore, so why shouldn't he swing by? He knew he was thinking crazy—Elena was a teacher, his employee, not a nanny—but he was out of options, and something told him she just might say yes.

Thirty minutes later, he stood outside Rebecca's, the hum of Friday night chatter spilling through the door. Through the window, he spotted her behind the bar, pouring a draft with that same tired grace he'd seen before. Her hair was up, a few strands loose, and those dark smudges under her eyes hadn't faded. When he opened the door and stepped in, she looked up, caught his gaze, and froze for a split second before flashing a tight smile—wary and not altogether welcoming.

Gabe approached, dodging a server with a tray, and leaned against the bar. "Hey."

"Mr. Wright," she said, wiping her hands on a towel, her tone clipped. "What brings you back? Checking up on me after the other night?"

"No," he said, then paused. "Well, maybe. You okay after that?"

She shrugged, avoiding his eyes as she straightened a jar of limes. "I've dealt with worse. Can I get you a drink?"

"No." He hesitated, feeling the weight of the ask. "I need to talk to you. About Lexi."

Elena's hands stilled, her brows lifting. "Is she alright?"

"She's ... not herself," he admitted, voice low. "Hasn't been for months. I've been trying to find a nanny—someone she'll connect with—but I'm not having any luck. I was thinking, remembering how she was with you that day in my office."

Elena blinked, a flicker of softness crossing her face. "She's a sweet kid. I liked drawing with her."

"She liked it too. More than you know." Gabe rubbed the back of his neck, the words sticking. "Look, I know this is out of left field, but I'm running out of ideas. I need someone for the summer, maybe longer. Someone she trusts. I was wondering ... would you consider it? Being her nanny?"

Elena's mouth dropped open, then snapped shut. "Me?" She gave a quick headshake. "I'm not a nanny, Gabe—Mr. Wright. I teach. I bar tend. I don't—" She stopped, eyes narrowing. "Is this because of what Marc said? You think I'm desperate for money?"

"No," he said quickly. Hadn't she just heard him admit that he was the desperate one in this scenario? "It's because of Lexi. You're good with her—better than anyone I've seen. And yeah, I know you've got a lot going on, but I thought ... maybe it could help you too."

She stared at him, and the bar's noise faded into the background. Her lips parted, then pressed tight, and he saw the wheels turning—pride, doubt, something else. "I don't need any handouts."

"It's not." He leaned closer, just enough to catch her citrus scent. His voice dropped. "It's a chance. For Lexi. For you. Just ... will you at least think about it?"

Chapter 6

According to Google Maps, Gabe's house should be coming into view off to the right anytime, but so far all Elena saw was rolling hills lined by a white picket fence on the roadside, and trees of seemingly every variety on the far side across the fields. She'd never been out this way before, and she already loved it. It was a slow, sprawling beauty that made her want to do things like grow tomatoes or churn her own ice cream.

As she climbed over one final, small hill, a white farmhouse came into view. It could have easily been taken right out of her Pinterest board. It had batten board siding, her absolute favorite, with a black roof and black accented windows. Columns of natural wood held up a spacious front porch that matched the wooden garage doors. Together they created the perfect blend of rustic and modern. It was the quintessential modern farmhouse.

Her dream. Gabe's reality.

"*Tienes suerte*, Gabe, but then I will, too, one day." Her luck might not allow her to live on a sprawling field in the country in a home that looked like it came right out of an HGTV special, but she'd be getting two paychecks on Friday, and she already had an appointment for her car's bumper to be fixed the following week. Tomorrow she had a meeting at the bank to open another account. It was to be her house savings account. It was happening. She was making it happen.

Gabe had asked her to think about nannying for Lexi, but it hadn't taken all that long to come to a decision. He'd offered her twice as much money as she would have made at Rebecca's for the summer, and spending her time with a sweet kid like Lexi beat having to pour beer and mix drinks for hours on end.

Elena felt like she'd won the lottery, and she couldn't wait to get started with this new gig.

As if the bucolic, country vibe could intensify further, the pop of gravel under Elena's tires as she pulled into the driveway was almost too much to take, and she smiled. This was going to be the best summer ever. She was taking care of a little girl who already adored her, a little girl who Elena knew—on a deep, subconscious level—needed her. She'd only have to interact with Gabe briefly in the mornings and evenings, which was good. Her anger toward him from that January meeting had faded, but she was still uneasy with him. For some reason, she heard warning bells whenever she looked at Gabriel Wright for too long.

Lexi would be a nice buffer between them, and Elena knew she'd enjoy caring for the young girl each day, even though she was giving up the luxury of late summer morning sleep-ins. But it would all be worth it. She was building her future and helping another person at the same time. Well, two people if she counted Gabe.

Instinctively, Elena knew she could help Lexi. Erin had filled her in a bit on Gabe's story, and even though Erin had been short on details—because she didn't have them herself—she'd shared enough for Elena to know that Lexi needed the love and attention of an adult female. Elena could never replace the mother Lexi didn't seem to have, but she could fill the child's cup for the summer, and she intended to. She'd be helping Gabe, helping Lexi, and helping herself.

Everything she earned over the next few months from the nanny gig would go directly in the new account to help her purchase her own dream house—the bungalow would be hers in a year, if she did it right. In the meantime, at least for the summer, she'd be spending most of her time in this beautiful spot. She squinted. Was that a river on the far end of the property? Elena shielded her eyes from the bright morning sun. Yes, she could see the sunlight sparkling on the slow-moving water. Well, wasn't that just icing on the cake? None of it was hers, but that didn't matter. She was going to enjoy it anyway.

It was a terrible morning. Lexi was throwing the biggest fit of her life, and she wasn't showing any signs of stopping. Gabe had done all he could think to do and was letting her ride it out as he watched out the front window. Elena would be there any moment, and all he could hope for was that his daughter would be set to rights before she arrived. This was not the same Lexi that Elena had met the other day. She wouldn't recognize this wild-eyed, out-of-control version of his daughter. He knew he didn't.

This purple-faced terror no longer wanted Elena or anyone else as her nanny. Her last coherent words to him were that she was going to go live with her "sparkle family."

This was a brand-new development as of last week. One morning, just like every other morning, Gabe had awoken Lexi and lifted her out of bed. While she woke up in his arms, he'd opened the curtains. Normally, this was where she told him about her dreams. So naturally, when she mentioned a sparkle family, he assumed she'd dreamed of them, but she insisted they were real.

"Are these sparkle people a family of dolls or something you saw on TV at Mimi's?" he asked.

"No, Daddy. They're my sparkle family. They live in the woods. I'm going to go there because they miss me really a lot."

This was a first. Lexi had never done much imaginary play. He decided to wing it. "I love that you have a pretend family who misses you and a real family who—"

"They aren't pretend, Daddy," she interrupted. "They're my sparkle family. I have a sparkle sister, a sparkle mommy and daddy, a sparkle *brudder*, and a sparkle puppy."

He looked intently into her brown eyes. "Let me get this straight. You think you have another family—"

"My *sparkle* family."

"So you've said. And you think this family lives in the woods?"

"Uh-huh."

"What color is their house?"

"It's a sparkle house."

"Right. And what are their names?"

She hesitated before burying her face in his shoulder. "I don't want to tell you."

"That's because they don't exist, Lexi. *I'm* your family. And I know I may not sparkle or even shine very often, but I'm still your dad."

She lifted her head and gazed at him somberly. "You're my regular dad; not my sparkle dad."

Right. Of course she had a sparkle dad. Gabe was just her dull, dud dad. This was nuts, but he couldn't help but ask the question. "What's this sparkle dad like?"

"He gives me pizza for dinner, and he does hopscotch with me, and he watches *Doc McStuffins* with me, and we ride horses together."

"Hey, I play hopscotch with you." He hated how defensive he'd sounded. But he had to admit it. He'd been jealous of a fictitious dad.

He still was.

Each morning that she woke up telling him all about her amazing sparkle family, he grew more and more resentful of the fake people who'd captured his daughter's love so quickly and so completely.

This morning he'd given her three minutes of "sparkle time" before cutting her off. He sat her down at the kitchen counter with a slice of avocado toast and explained again that Elena would be coming to take care of her. Even though she'd been using Elena's first name since meeting her, he told her he expected her to show respect by calling the new nanny *Miss Torres*. Gabe was a firm believer that children should not be on a first-name basis with adults.

She grew more and more sullen as he reminded her of the house rules and the schedule she would be following each day of the summer, and when he bent to put away the toaster, he realized she'd been very quiet. Too quiet. He stood to look at her, and that's when it had happened. A meltdown of epic proportions. He had no idea what had set her off.

He reached for her to comfort her, but she flailed her arms, hitting the plate of toast with such force that it slid down the length of countertop like a shuffle puck before crashing to the floor, miraculously unbroken. When the wailing and kicking began, he lifted her bodily from her chair and carried her to her twin bed where she thrashed and screamed and worked herself up into a lather. Gabe's heart thudded in his chest as he stood over his daughter, the demon-child, and realized he had absolutely no idea what to do. After five minutes of ineptitude, he left the room, thinking that perhaps by removing himself as her audience, she would grow tired of her little performance.

She was still going strong several minutes later when Elena reached the door.

What was he supposed to do? Leave his kid in this state with a woman who was a virtual stranger to her or stay until she was calm and be late to yet another meeting?

He made the only decision he could live with. After greeting Elena and giving her the scoop, he excused himself to make a quick call to Adele. His heaven-sent secretary told him everything would be just fine, and he believed her. If Adele said it would be okay, it would be.

She'd make sure everyone had enough coffee to keep them happy as they waited for him and gave him some advice before signing off. "Don't you worry about a thing but that child, Mr. Gabe. Now, you listen to me. Go get a washcloth. Run it under cold water, ring it out, and drape it over the back of her neck. It will ground her and cool that little temper of hers."

"I'm the one who will ground her if she doesn't stop this right now," he muttered, holding the phone between his ear and shoulder as he wet the washcloth under the tap in the bathroom sink.

Adele *tsked* at him. "She doesn't need discipline, she needs help. Put that washcloth on her neck and talk all nice and soft and gentle about anything at all. I don't care if you tell her the weather forecast. She needs to hear your voice. I'll get that coffee goin'. Now, don't you speed on your way here."

Gabe promised no such thing before he hung up, dashed out into the foyer, and made another apology to Elena. He saw the hesitation and uncertainty in her eyes as she listened to Lexi, whose voice carried loudly all the way to the kitchen counter where Elena sat, purse still slung over one shoulder. He wondered if he looked as uncertain as he felt too.

The next five minutes felt like five hours, but Adele was right. She must have been some kind of magician because the cool washcloth trick worked like a charm. Lexi only took it off and threw it on the floor twice. The third time she let him hold it there, and after a big, long shudder, she let herself be soothed.

"There, now. Does that feel a little better?"

She spoke between sniffles. "I'm ... really ... hot. I'm ... really sweaty."

"I know. We'll get you changed into some new clothes, and then I'll help you wash your face."

"Okay."

He hesitated, not sure if now was a good time to instruct her in a life lesson. In the end, he figured it was always a good time. He couldn't help it. He was an educator. "Lexi, you need to remember to use your words. You're too big to throw fits like that. If you're upset, you need to tell me you're upset."

She looked at him silently.

"Elena is here, er, Miss Torres, I mean."

"I don't want her."

"She's sitting in the kitchen. She has a notepad with her. Do you think she drew that picture of you like she said she would?"

Lexi shrugged.

Gabe wondered again what had happened to bring about such a change in attitude. Just this morning, once she'd finished talking about her loathsome sparkle family, Lexi had gone on and on about all the fun things she and Elena were going to do today, and now she didn't care? Didn't *want* her?

Well, that made one of them. He might as well admit it. Even under stress, his body responded to the mere sight of Elena Torres. He needed to remind himself, as many times as it took, that Elena was one hundred percent off limits. Acting on his feelings could mess up both of their careers, and if that wasn't enough of a deterrent, the fact that she was his daughter's nanny should be enough.

The problem was, his response to her was almost reflexive. How could you stop a reflex? He gave a quick headshake. He'd have to figure out a way. He would just have to deny his feelings until they went away. Yes, that's what he'd do. It'd be like when he switched them to a whole foods diet after reading that article in a parenting magazine two years ago. At first, he'd craved all the usual favorites, but he'd denied himself, telling himself every time a craving hit that he didn't want it. It had been tough at first, but soon he found that what he told himself was the truth. He really didn't want any of that garbage anymore.

He'd just use that same type of willpower with Elena. Acting on his baser instincts wouldn't be good for any of them. "I don't want her," he muttered to himself as Lexi washed her face. He'd tell himself that until he truly meant it.

It took ten additional minutes, but Gabe presented a cleaned-up version of his daughter to Elena.

Elena stood from her spot on the stool and smiled brightly. "Good morning, Lexi. It's nice to see you."

Lexi stared, straight mouthed. Gabe stared too. How was this woman still single? *I don't want her.*

Elena glanced at him, looking for guidance.

"Lexi, please say hello to Miss Torres," he prompted.

"Hi." She stared at the floor.

"We're going to have some fun today. I promise." Elena smiled warmly, making her even more enticing.

Gabe rubbed at his temples. The day hadn't even officially started yet, and he already had a headache. "Excuse me," he said, moving around the counter to the place on the floor where the plate had been. "I just need to clean up a bit."

"I already got that plate," Elena said, stopping him in his tracks. "I can get the crumbs too if you point out where the broom is."

He turned around, refusing to look at her again, and gestured at the closet next to the pantry. "Right over there, and thank you. I'll just get my bag and be off then." He grabbed his bag off the table next to the door. "Lexi, if you get hungry, you can ask Miss Torres for more avocado toast. The other half of the avocado is in the fridge. Lunch can be the leftover couscous and chicken from last night along with a banana. Okay?"

Lexi didn't answer, but when he risked a quick glance at Elena, she nodded. "Sounds good. We'll be fine."

"I'm sorry," he said with a shake of his head. "I would show you around, but I'm already late. When I get home, I'll take you on a tour and we'll review some things." *I don't want her.*

"It's okay. Lexi can show me around, right Lexi?"

Lexi only stared at her.

"The extra booster seat is in the garage, but I'd prefer you not go anywhere until I can show you how to secure it in the car." Gabe frowned. And that was another issue. He wasn't altogether certain he wanted Elena driving Lexi anywhere, ever. He drove a Suburban on purpose, for safety. It was a beast of a car, but he knew it was safe for his child. Forget the bumper, Elena's ancient LeSabre probably didn't even have side airbags. He was going to have to figure something out.

"That's fine. We can stay here today."

He nodded. "Good. Thank you."

He kissed Lexi and pulled her into a hug. "Be a good girl for Miss Torres, okay?"

She nodded twice into his shoulder.

During the twenty-minute drive, Gabe rehashed the morning. What had happened to cause his daughter to decompensate like that? He'd read a book on how to handle the terrible twos, and he'd counted himself lucky when the tantrum phase seemed to pass his daughter over. She'd turned six in April. Wasn't she a little too old for fits like that? And wasn't she too old to invent completely fictitious families out of the blue?

He made a mental note to look for a book that could deliver all the necessary insights into six-year-old girls. Maybe he'd buy two so his mother could read the other one. For that matter, maybe he'd get three and give one to Elena. He needed all the help he could get.

Now that he had a plan of attack, he let his thoughts move back to Elena. Seeing her in his home, in his space, had been surreal. She'd been wearing a collared oxford shirt with blue stripes and a pair of jean shorts. Her hair had been styled in a simple braid down her back, and her lips were tinted only with the tiniest hint of color. She wasn't nearly as done up as she was when she was at the school, but somehow, she still sucked all the air out of his lungs. She was just that kind of woman, he realized. Even though she was casually dressed, Gabe hadn't failed to notice how the buttons of her shirt stretched taut across the feminine swell of her breasts, or how silky smooth her bronzed legs were under those shorts.

Gabe swallowed. It wouldn't matter what she had on—leggings, shorts, or a plastic poncho—the woman stirred his blood like no woman had for a very long time.

His daughter's words echoed in his ears—*I don't want her.* He could learn a thing or two from Lexi.

Elena took in her surroundings. She was inside Gabriel Wright's home, and she felt more lost than an octopus in a garage, and no, she didn't care that that particular Spanish idiom didn't translate; it was how she felt. His space was impossibly tidy, especially considering a young child lived here. Where were all her toys? Her bedroom, she hoped.

He'd chosen light, wide-plank wooden flooring in the living room, with neutral-toned furniture and white walls, which was very airy and pretty but made her feel as though at any moment she was in danger of mussing something up.

She looked at her feet, still in her flip-flops, and immediately took them off. Holding them in her hands, she faced Lexi whose eyes were red and still a little wet.

Please don't start crying again, Elena silently begged. What had she been thinking? She didn't know anything about little kids, but she'd thought she could march in here and be a full-time caretaker of a kindergartner? No wonder her aunt had questioned her. "I brought your drawing," she said, lifting the notebook in her hand. "Sorry I'm getting it to you a little late, but I think it turned out. Want to see?"

The girl shrugged.

"Here." Elena opened the notebook to the first page and handed her the sketch. She'd drawn the young girl with impossibly large eyes that twinkled with mischief. She'd exaggerated the arch of her brows and the curve of her impish smile. She looked like a perfect little doll.

As Lexi studied it, Elena thought the corners of her mouth might have twitched, but she couldn't be sure. "What do you think?"

Another shrug.

"Do you like it?"

"You drawed my eyes really big."

"Yes."

"How come?"

"Because I think they're your best feature. They sparkle, like coffee in the sunshine."

That drew an unexpected smile from Lexi. "They *sparkle*," she repeated in a reverent whisper. Turning her gaze from the drawing to Elena, some of Lexi's earlier tension seemed to dissolve away.

Encouraged, Elena asked, "What do you want to do this morning?"

Lexi shrugged. At this rate, the girl's shoulder muscles would be getting quite the workout.

"How about this? Let's get you some breakfast, since it didn't look like you ate very much this morning, and then we can go for a walk outside and you can show me around. I want to see all your favorite spots."

"The river and my swing?" Lexi asked tentatively.

"*Los dos*. I'd love to see both," Elena said, moving towards the kitchen. "Now, what was it your dad said you could have? Avocado toast?"

Lexi trailed close behind. "I wish I could have pancakes again."

Elena's eyes lit up. Pancakes were one of the few things she could make well. "I can make you some. Where do you keep the mix?" She scanned the kitchen, zeroing in on what might be the pantry.

"The mix?"

Elena nodded. "You know, the box with the pancake mix in it?" She pointed to the tall cabinet doors. "There?"

"I don't think we got that." Lexi walked over to the pantry door and opened it.

Elena stood behind her and peered inside. There were bags of dried beans, steel-cut oats, boxes of rice and quinoa, various seeds, nuts, and oils, something called monk fruit, canisters filled with flour and coffee beans, and a whole lot of other things Elena had never purchased and wouldn't know how to cook. There were two types of kitchens out there: ingredient kitchens and pre-packaged kitchens. Gabe's kitchen was an ingredient kitchen on steroids.

"How does your dad usually make pancakes?" Elena asked.

Lexi pointed to a canister of utensils. "He flips 'em with that flipper thingy."

Elena smiled. The kid was adorable. "But what does he use to make them?"

Lexi thought a moment. "Well, he gets out the different flours and that tub up there really high." She pointed at a tub of whey protein powder. "And he puts in that vanilla right there," she said pointing to a bottle of absolute vodka that held a brown liquid along with what Elena assumed were vanilla beans. Of course, the guy made his own vanilla.

"And then he puts eggs in there and then ..." Lexi squinted her eyes, thinking hard. "I don't know what else. Something that's a powder, maybe."

Elena had only ever made pancakes out of a box, and even then, she bought the *complete* version, so all she had to do was add water.

"Tell you what, how about some toast with some peanut butter and jelly?"

Lexi almost smiled. "Okay."

Elena looked for the peanut butter in the pantry. The closest thing she found was pressed peanut flour in a jar. "Where's your peanut butter?" she asked.

Lexi pointed to the refrigerator.

"Oh." Elena opened the fridge and took a step back as she took in the contents inside. This was getting truly frightening. Everything was arranged tallest to shortest inside, with the tallest items found in the back. The produce drawers were full of fruits and vegetables, and not a crumb could be found on any of the shelves. Gabe was the neatest and freakiest of all the neat freaks out there, not to mention the nuttiest of all the health nuts. She'd pegged him for being somewhat uptight, but this was on a whole new level.

Elena turned to look at Lexi, who sat patiently at the barstool at the counter watching her. "I don't see it."

"It's in the door," she said helpfully.

Elena removed a glass jar with a label she didn't recognize. It certainly wasn't Jif. The jam, was right next to it and appeared homemade because, well, of course it was.

After locating the toaster and the bread in a drawer, Elena got to work, but she stopped up short after opening the peanut butter. It had a clear oil at the top of it. She stuck a knife into the liquid to test it.

"You gotta stir it," Lexi instructed.

"Oh. Okay." Elena stuck the knife deeper into the jar only to have it get stuck. Clearly, stirring Gabe Wright's peanut butter would not be a one-handed job. Elena put some elbow grease into it and got the texture in the jar to loosely resemble that of normal peanut butter, but when she went to spread it on the toast, the bread tore. "This is no way to live."

Lexi giggled, a bright little sound.

Elena looked up, warmth flooding her chest at the sight of the delighted child, and let out a laugh of her own. "Oh, you think this is funny?"

Lexi nodded, another giggle bubbling out.

"What kind of peanut butter is this?" She held her gooey knife in the air, pointing it at Lexi. "Do not tell your father I can't make toast with peanut butter and jelly on it, okay? He'll fire me on the spot."

They shared a conspiratorial smile. "I won't tell," Lexi promised.

Elena laughed several more times as she continued to stir. She was making progress with her ward, but not so much with the peanut butter. "Lexi, *cariña*, I don't think this is normal peanut butter."

"It's the healthy kind. It doesn't got so much sugar in it. Sugar isn't good for me."

"Really? I love it," Elena admitted.

Lexi looked momentarily scandalized before tipping her head in thought. "My mimi says sugar is Papa's reason for living. He sneaks candy bars sometimes."

"I think I like him already."

The two of them shared another smile.

The day only improved from there. Elena wouldn't pretend that they were becoming fast friends—Lexi was still cautious and more standoffish than she would have hoped—but they explored the fields around her house, and she showed Elena the river, which, given its name of Apple Creek, was not actually a river at all. Elena wondered what made a river, a river and a creek, a creek. The creek was sandy bottomed and clear and deep enough to splash around in, and suddenly Elena had a need to be in the water. She'd grown up surrounded by the ocean. To say she'd been a water baby was an understatement. Hardly a day went by growing up that she hadn't gone to the beach, even if it was just for a quick dip. It was one of the reasons she knew she could live in Nicolet. Looking out over Lake Superior did the same thing for her soul that standing in front of that vast ocean had done. If only it were a little warmer for swimming.

"Should we wade?" Elena asked.

Lexi tipped her head. "What's that?"

"Wading? It's where we go in, but we don't swim. We only get wet to our—" she couldn't think of the word for *espinillas* "—to this part of our legs below our knees and above our ankles," she said, pointing.

Lexi brightened some. "I like wading."

And so they waded, and Lexi caught three frogs, which she called *peepers*. Elena had been forced to hold one. Pretending that the slimy, cold creature was the most precious thing in the world, she tried not to shudder. Once Lexi had tired of that, they lay in the grass to warm up their legs, which were pink from the icy water of the creek. It was turning into a warm, breezy afternoon, and as they laid there in the soft grass looking up at the budding trees, Elena experienced a complete contentment she didn't often feel. It was a gift when she did feel it, though it was always fleeting. She wished she could hold on to it, but she'd learned long ago to be grateful that she felt it at all.

Chapter 7

By the time Gabe got home, Elena was feeling very proud of herself. Although she hadn't heard Lexi's giggle as often as she would've hoped, she knew the young girl had enjoyed their time together. Elena had pushed her in her tree swing, which was in the middle of the field, they picked dandelions, and Lexi had caught some very large June bugs that Elena could have sworn were dead, but that Lexi claimed were only having a nap. "They like to fly at night, so when it's day, they hafta sleep."

After lunch, they drew together. Elena sketched the Wright's home, which Lexi promptly hung on the fridge, and the little girl drew a family of stick people that she said lived off in the woods. She talked about them as if she'd just seen them all yesterday, which was kind of sweet. Then they'd read a few books before Lexi got distracted and wanted to show off her collection of toy horses. They were playing with them when Gabe got home, and Elena had just mastered the sound of the neigh and whinny when Gabe poked his head into Lexi's bedroom.

"Hey, there."

Elena jumped and dropped her horse. "*¡Uy, me asustaste!* I didn't know you were here."

Gabe chuckled, and his eyes crinkled at the corners. Elena's stomach did a little dip. It was a good thing he didn't often smile, she thought, looking away briefly.

Lexi got up and ran to him. She held him around his waist.

"Hey, squirt." He scooped her up in a hug, and her arms tightened around his neck.

Elena stood and brushed off imaginary dust from her shorts.

"Did you have a nice day with Miss Torres?"

Elena saw her nod against his chest.

"Good. Why don't you play in here another minute while I show her around the house a little so she knows where to find everything tomorrow."

"I showed her everything, Daddy."

"Did you now?"

"I showed her the pantry and the refrigerator and the dishwasher, but she washed the dishes in the sink anyway."

"Wow, nice work," he praised. "I'll just talk to her about a few more things, and then you'll see her again tomorrow, okay?"

"Okay," she said, releasing him as he set her bare feet down on the floor.

"Bye, Lexi. This was fun," Elena said. "Let's do it all again tomorrow."

Lexi treated Elena to a brief wave.

Gabe waited until they were out of the hallway and into the great room before focusing on her intently. "Sorry I didn't check in more than the one time. It got busy. But it sounds like everything went okay?" His voice tipped up in question.

Elena forced herself to hold his eyes and nodded. "It was good."

"Any more tears or ... outbursts?"

"No, none. And like I said in my text, I got some laughs and smiles out of her."

He nodded, still looking serious. "That's good."

"We played in the creek and spent most of the morning and early afternoon outside. Then we were in the rest of the day reading and playing." If she'd expected him to praise her for engaging in wholesome activities, she'd have been gravely disappointed.

"That's nice," he said absentmindedly. "Let me show you a few things. I would have done this earlier if I'd had my head screwed on straight this morning."

He showed her the pantry and kitchen items as well as the medicine cabinet, cleaning closet, and art supplies cupboard, all of which Lexi had already shown her. "And out here," he said, leading her into a pristine garage, "is where all her outdoor toys are."

There were several bins with labels on them. He'd written out things like soccer ball, beach toys, and chalk, and on a shelf above them she noticed colored sand in various ziplock bags.

"What's that?" she asked, pointing to the sand.

"Kinetic sand. It sticks together. I only let her play with it in the grass." He pointed to a collapsed table behind the bins. "Just move this table out there, and she can set up and have at it."

"Okay."

"And here's her extra booster seat." They went out to her car so he could show her how to secure it with the seat belt. "I hope you don't mind, but I looked up your car's safety ratings, and the middle seat will be the safest place for her. I'd prefer to know when you plan to venture out with her. Just shoot me a text, if you don't mind."

Elena's first reaction was to take offense. How dare he imply that her car wasn't safe or insinuate that she couldn't be trusted to drive Lexi around! His next comment settled her down.

"I know that might seem overbearing or controlling, but my daughter is ... she's everything to me, and I just like to know where she is when I'm stuck at work. Helps me worry less." He smiled sheepishly.

All irritation erased, Elena responded with an understanding smile of her own, and told him she'd be happy to do what he'd asked. She also let him know she'd been thinking of taking Lexi to the park tomorrow after stopping by the bank first. She could tell he was reluctant to agree to that, but he just asked her to drive safely. Briefly, she thought about joking with him that she only would now that he'd asked her to, but she decided against it.

They moved back to the garage, and Elena looked around at the shelving that had everything in its place. Did a man like Gabe have any spontaneity? He lived by a schedule. He ate couscous, for heaven's sake. He hung all his shovels in order of size—garden spade all the way down to snow shovel. He, too, was surveying the garage, no doubt finding something out of place, and it gave Elena a chance to look over the man himself. He was what her childhood friend, Lucia, would have called a *bombón*, a real hottie. He wasn't super tall, maybe five foot ten but his broad shoulders made him seem larger than he was, and those cheekbones, well, they might be considered his best feature if not for those deep-set eyes. Elena had always loved eyes like those on a man. They lent an air of mystery. She shivered.

Except that Gabe wasn't mysterious at all. She wondered if he ever got bored with himself. In a way, she felt sorry for him. She hadn't been completely honest with her aunt before. Gabe was attractive, and she did get a distinct little dippy feeling way down low in her belly when she looked at him sometimes, but she knew it could never go anywhere because she would never let it. Plus, he wasn't at all her usual type.

The next day, Elena arrived to a much more tranquil house than she had the day before. Lexi was quietly eating a bowl of oatmeal at the counter in the kitchen when she let herself in.

Gabe came breezing into the kitchen, messenger bag slung over one shoulder. "Hi, Miss Torres," he greeted before stopping to kiss Lexi on the cheek. "Bye, Lex. You two have a good day." He moved to the coat closet where he fetched a pair of shoes. "Elena, I'd like Lexi to have that hummus and sprout pita I put together for her in the fridge. I made one for you too."

Sprouts? That would be a first for her. "Oh, thanks."

He glanced at her and slid his foot into the second shoe. "I won't always make the lunches, but just until you get your bearings, I thought I would."

"Thank you," Elena repeated.

Gabe backtracked to kiss his daughter once more. "Love you, baby girl."

"Love you, Daddy."

He paused to nod at Elena before disappearing into the garage.

As soon as the door closed behind him, Lexi turned to her. "Mrs. Shreever made me lunch every day."

"Did she?"

"She always made us dinner too."

"Oh." Was she supposed to be cooking them their dinner? Elena would have to ask. What would she make them? A box of Mac and Cheese, she could handle just fine, but she had never cooked quinoa or couscous a day in her life. She opened the pantry and noticed the rice and dried beans—she could probably make red beans and rice. Maybe she'd throw that together today and surprise Gabe. She'd watched her mother cook it a hundred times. How hard could it be? She'd start dinner prep at four so everything would be ready at five or five-thirty when Gabe got home. He'd realize then, if he hadn't already, how lucky he was to have her.

"Oh, shoot," Elena said aloud, remembering something.

"What?"

"I forgot to remind your dad that I need to go to the bank today. It will just be a quick appointment. I'll text him."

Lexi shrugged.

Elena's appointment wasn't until one o'clock, which gave them plenty of time to play in the creek again and do some chalking on the sidewalk before lunch.

Elena was drawing a rainbow when Lexi asked, "Can you draw my sparkle house?"

"You mean this house?" she asked.

"No, I have a sparkle house."

"That's nice." She grabbed the blue chalk.

"It's real. It's not pretend."

Elena glanced up to see Lexi staring at her intently. "Oh, really?" It was the best she could do. "What color is a sparkle house?" She put the blue chalk down on the concrete and surveyed her other options. "Yellow?" She held it up with one hand.

"No, not yellow. My sparkle house is purple because I have a purple dress at my sparkle house with matching heels."

"Heels, huh?" Elena repeated with an amused smile. She exchanged the yellow chalk for the purple one and began to draw.

"I have a sparkle mommy there."

Elena stopped drawing and looked up. "You do?"

Lexi nodded.

"What's she like?" Elena asked, remembering the family of stick people Lexi had drawn the day before and starting to put it all together.

"Her hair sparkles, and she makes me cookies with sparkle chocolate chips. They're just little tiny." She demonstrated how small using her thumb and her pointer finger. "And they're sweet, but they don't got any sugar in them, so I won't get cavities."

"That sounds delicious."

"She teached me how to make them with her."

"What else does she do?"

"She drives me to cheer practice, and she paints with me. She paints hearts—big hearts and little hearts—because she loves me."

"I'm sure she does. You're a very lovable girl."

Lexi contemplated that. "Sometimes moms leave."

Elena nodded. Dads left too, but she didn't say so. "Sometimes they do," she said instead. She wished she knew the full story about Lexi's mom, but whether she'd died or left voluntarily, it was clear that Lexi felt the loss regardless.

"My sparkle mommy won't leave."

Elena smiled and placed a gentle hand on Lexi's shoulder. "I'm glad."

"I miss my Mimi."

"Is Mimi your grandmother?"

Lexi nodded. "She has a store, so she can't come here very much. She lives in Bayshore."

"I'm sure she misses you."

"She loves me too."

"I'm sure she does."

Lexi sighed. "I wish I could go to my sparkle house today."

"Where is your sparkle house?"

"It's very far away." She shook her head regretfully. "Through lots of woods."

"Well then, how do you get there?"

"I use my magic with my fingers, like this," she said, swirling her pointer finger up in the air. "But I runned out of magic, so I can't show you. But I miss my sparkle family."

Good grief, there really was an entire family of sparkle people. Poor Gabe.

"Remember, I drawed them yesterday."

"I do remember." Elena got back to work drawing the purple sparkle house. She established the roof line before adding, "You know, I think you are a very lucky girl to have a sparkle family. I never had one of those."

Lexi nodded. "My sparkle family is real. I have a sparkle brudder and a sparkle sister, and a sparkle daddy and mommy and dog. Our sparkle dog, his name is Sharklove, and he throwed up in the kitchen last time."

"Yuck."

"And I have a sparkle pony."

"Wow, a pony?" She added windows.

"Yeah, and in the pool we have a sea lion who goes down the slide and splashes. He's nice to me and lets me pet him."

"Ooh, a pool." Elena picked up the blue chalk and got to work on the pool with a slide.

"Lexi, do you dream about your sparkle family at night?" she asked as she drew.

Lexi's voice took on an edge. "It's not a dream," she insisted.

Not wanting to risk another Lexi meltdown, Elena moved on. "I'll tell you what. Since your magic is broken right now—"

"It just runned out, but it'll come right back, and then I'll go see them."

"Right, since you ran out of your magic for now, why don't we go to the park after I'm done at the bank?"

"The one down at the harbor?" Lexi asked hopefully.

"That could be fun. Maybe you'll see some of your friends there."

"Sometimes my friend Miley goes there, but she's at cheer camp with her mommy for a lot of days. I go to her house sometimes, and her mommy makes cookies with us."

Ah. Just like Lexi's sparkle mom. Elena knew then exactly what was going on, and what was more, she understood it. How many times had she taken mental notes at her friends' homes and then dreamed she had a family just like theirs? Countless times, especially when she'd been young.

Elena decided right then and there that she'd do all the "mom" things with Lexi that she could. They'd make cookies—she'd learn how to bake if it killed her—and they'd go shopping and read books together and ride bikes. She wasn't this child's mother and would never be, but she could stand in as one for the summer, just the way *Tío* Samuel used to act the father figure for her during her visits. Lexi needed someone to show her what it was supposed to look and feel like, even if it did hurt a little.

"We'll still have a great time without Miley. Maybe we'll even see some boats out in the water. We can watch them go by while we eat ice cream cones."

Lexi's eyes grew wide. "Ice cream cones?"

Elena nodded.

"They have lotsa sugar in them."

"It'll be our secret."

"But my teeth might get a cavity in them and fall right out."

What had Gabe done to this child? "We'll be sure to brush them as soon as we get home."

Lexi broke into a wide grin.

Chapter 8

Lexi helped Elena get the seatbelt over her lap and through the slots in the booster seat. When she was in her sparkle car, she didn't need a booster seat.

Elena didn't do it right, but that was okay. Lexi could help Elena do the things she didn't know how to do. Elena was nice and Mrs. Shreever wasn't nice at all. Mrs. Shreever knew how to buckle Lexi in, and she knew how to cook, but Mrs. Shreever never gave her ice cream, and she never went into the creek either. She didn't smile like Elena, and she wasn't so pretty like Elena.

Lexi frowned. She wasn't s'posed to call her Elena. Daddy told her she had to call her something else.

Miss Tires?

That wasn't it.

Miss Teris?

No. That wasn't right either. Lexi sighed. She just wouldn't call her anything. Once, at Daddy's office, she got to call her Elena. They were friends because friends said each other's names. But Daddy made Elena not her friend yesterday in the morning when he said she had to call her *Miss*, and that made Lexi know that Elena was only her nanny and not her friend, and nannies weren't very nice. Lexi didn't want a nanny.

But yesterday, Elena wasn't mean at all. She played with her and didn't make her do her times tables or jography. Elena taught her a frog was called a *rana* in her language. Ranas didn't say *ribbit*. They said *cruá cruá*.

Lexi caught lots of frogs yesterday. She gave one to Elena to hold, and she was scared of the little peeper, Lexi could tell, but she held it in her hand anyway because Lexi asked her to be brave. And now, today, Elena was going to get her ice cream. *Secret* ice cream.

Lexi smiled and stared out the window, watching the trees go by in a blobby blur of green.

Elena was explaining the flavors of all the ice creams when they pulled into the bank's parking lot. Lexi got her backpack that held her paper and colored pencils and took Elena's hand as she helped her out of the car, and they walked across the parking lot holding hands. Miley held her mommy's hand when they walked into school too.

But then something strange happened. Elena stopped walking when she saw two men standing on the sidewalk near the doors of the bank. One was dressed really fancy and had sparkly, silvery hair. The other man looked like he got mad a lot. Elena must have felt scared because she didn't move at all for a really long time. It was like someone put glue on the bottom of her sandals. "Elena?" Lexi asked, forgetting her father's rule.

"Change of plans," Elena said as she turned them both around and back to the car.

Gabe checked the clock above his office door. He'd been in this meeting for over an hour already, and there was no end in sight. He was on a Zoom call being put on by the Michigan Department of Education's Superintendent of Public Instruction along with well over one hundred other superintendents throughout the state. It seemed some much-needed changes were coming to the Michigan Merit Curriculum. Normally, this kind of thing was right up Gabe's alley, but today he continually had to redirect his thoughts back on the task at hand. He didn't even want to think about how many times visions of Elena had entered his mind. This morning, she'd worn next to no makeup and had left her thick, dark hair to cascade in soft waves down her back. She'd looked like a teenaged babysitter, and he'd felt about a hundred years old as he'd explained he'd made her a lunch.

He was doing it again—thinking about Elena when he needed to focus, although he was pretty sure he had the gist. Starting in two years, all students would need a personal finance class to graduate, and along with the economics class requirement, it could count as the senior math experience. Seemed straightforward enough, but the presenter liked to hear himself talk, and so on and on it went.

Gabe's phone buzzed on his desk. Seeing that it was a number he didn't recognize, he sent the caller to voicemail before setting it down. A minute later, it buzzed again. Again, he sent the caller to voicemail.

A minute later, Adele opened his door.

Gabe checked to make sure he was still muted on the call and shut off his camera before swiveling to Adele.

"I've got an EMT on the line, Gabe. He's with Lexi and—"

He shot out of his seat. "What's wrong?" Elena had texted earlier about taking Lexi out. His gut reaction had been to call and say he didn't want Elena driving in that rickety old LeSabre with his daughter, but he hadn't wanted to insult her.

"Hush now," Adele said firmly. "Everyone's fine. Lexi's in the ambulance getting checked. Just a precaution."

"An *ambulance*?" His voice spiked, nearly a shout. "She's in an ambulance? Where's Elena?"

Adele sighed, exasperation edging her tone. "She's there, too, Gabe. I spoke to her. They're both okay. They got rear-ended is all. Elena's phone smashed into the dash and broke, so she couldn't call you."

He fumbled through his messenger bag for his car keys, hands trembling. "Adele, what the hell happened?"

"That's all I know. Now breathe, Gabe. Lexi's fine."

He dropped his head into his hands. "It's just one thing after another."

Adele stepped into the room and spoke softly. "Take a deep breath now, and then you go on and see for yourself. I'll handle things here." She gave him a gentle pat on the back.

He glanced at his watch. "I have that interview in thirty minutes."

"I'll reschedule it. Go."

Before ten minutes had passed, Gabe pulled up to the intersection of Mc-Clellan and Washington. Thirty seconds later he was behind the ambulance demanding to know what was going on. Lexi and Elena were in the back. His daughter grinned as she listened to Elena's heartbeat with a stethoscope. Two paramedics chatted behind them.

When Elena spotted him, she jumped to her feet and looked ready to burst into tears.

Lexi saw him at the same time and was lifted out by a paramedic before she could jump down. "Daddy!"

He lifted her into his arms, cradling her head in his hand and kissed her on the forehead. Moving her to one arm, he wrapped his free arm around Elena as she joined them. He pulled her protectively against him when he felt her trembling. He didn't realize what he was doing until he'd already done it, and he could tell she was as surprised by the gesture as he was himself. Quickly, he let her go. "You okay?"

He'd been asking Lexi, but Elena responded with unfiltered fury. "No—*Me da rabia*. That man hit us really hard!"

Instinctively, Gabe tucked her against him once more and squeezed Lexi even tighter.

Gabe was in no frame of mind to return to work, so he called in for the rest of the day, and the three of them headed to Harbor Park where Lexi played for over an hour. They took turns pushing her on the swings until some children her age invited her to play tag with them. Once she was settled in with her new friends, he and Elena removed themselves to a bench in the shade where they could watch over her and look out over the harbor. The sun cast thousands of glinting diamonds over the surface that remained in Gabe's vision even when he closed his eyes.

Elena sat beside him with only a few inches separating them. He opened one eye and stole a glance at her. Up close like this, her skin looked even more aglow, like soft shiny bronze reflecting the heat of the sun. His fingers itched to lift the small white strap of her tank top that had fallen off her shoulder. Instead, he folded his hands together and began to speak at the same time she did.

"I'm sorry—"

"Please don't be—"

They laughed awkwardly.

"I was just going to apologize that the duct tape failed," he said. "I must not have done a good patch job."

Elena shook her head. "I had it scheduled to go in next week, but I should have had that bumper fixed months ago. When I heard it dragging behind me and slowed down—" she clapped her hands together. "*Bam!*"

Gabe's heart raced, yet again. Just by looking at it, he knew Elena's car would never drive again, though he didn't think she knew that yet. He had to remind himself for the zillionth time that nobody had been hurt. His brain knew it, but his heart was still scared. He could kill the guy in the car who hadn't been paying attention. "What were you going to say?" he asked.

She smiled and met his eyes. He'd noticed she didn't do that very often—look him in the eyes, that was—but this time she held his gaze. "I was going to ask you not to be mad about the ice cream."

Reluctantly, he grinned back at her. "I don't let her eat that stuff, it's true, and it's one rule that I can back up with loads of good reasons, but no, I'm not mad about the ice cream."

"But—" she cut herself off with a slight shake of her head.

He turned to face her more fully. "What?"

"It's just—you're angry about something. I can feel it ..." She searched for the word. "... radiating off you. Are you mad about the accident?"

She was right, but he was surprised she could sense it. He thought he'd been hiding it well. Yes, he was angry, but not about the ice cream and not even about the accident, although it had shaved five years off his life, at least. He was just ... angry in general. He didn't want to need a nanny. He didn't want to rely on his parents so much for help with Lexi. And then there was work. He was dropping balls left and right, but what else could he do? Lexi came first. That was a no-brainer. He was her only parent, but he was also the district's only superintendent, and he owed the community his very best.

He couldn't do it, he admitted to himself in defeat. He couldn't give Lexi and an entire community of people what they needed. There wasn't enough time in a day or enough Gabriel Wright to go around. The realization depressed him.

Nobody at work had said anything—yet—but they would if he continued to have these types of disruptions where his role as dad bled over into his role of superintendent. But he didn't have a choice. He couldn't shut either job off. He was still Dad at work and still superintendent of Nicolet Public Schools when he was at home.

Neither role left any room for him to just ... be. When was the last time he'd read a book just for pleasure? When was the last time he'd spent a day fishing or mountain biking? When had he last sat down with a cold beer and a friend? He didn't even have friends anymore, at least not here in Nicolet.

Before Lexi had come into the world, he'd been Mr. Social. Now there wasn't room in his life for any of those things he used to do, and it made him feel guilty that he missed those parts of himself. He loved being a dad, he really did. And he loved his job. But his life ... it was so crowded; he didn't have any time even for himself. Outside of being superintendent and Dad, he didn't know who he was anymore. He used to know that.

What he wanted was to go back in time and start over. He'd make a lot of different choices than the ones he'd made. To start with, he never would have approached the stage that night all those years ago. But then he wouldn't have Lexi now, and that was unthinkable. How could he regret everything that led to her becoming his daughter? She was his greatest joy in life. His whole reason for living. She was also his biggest complication, and the guilt he felt whenever he allowed that reality to settle into a coherent thought was enough to throw him into a tailspin of self-reproach.

What kind of father thought about his own kid that way? He loved her. He loved her more than his own life, and yet he knew. He knew how easy things would be for him if he hadn't been left to raise her on his own.

"Mr. Wright," Elena said, peering at him. "Where did you go just now?"

He shook himself back to the present and fought the disappointment that she was back to calling him "mister" again. "Sorry, I just have a lot on my mind."

She nodded slowly. "It's hard work, what you're doing with Lexi."

He couldn't keep the defensiveness out of his voice. "We're fine."

She peered at him dubiously. "Are you sure?"

Gabe didn't even try, this time, to keep the irritation out of his voice. "Yes, I'm sure. You think we aren't fine?"

She shrugged delicately. "It's just that I've ... noticed a few things."

"I assure you, everything is fine."

She didn't respond. The silence was loaded with accusation, and Gabe resented it.

"You haven't even been in my life—in Lexi's life," he corrected, "for two whole days. How can you ask me a question like that?"

She fidgeted uncomfortably beside him, but she spoke confidently. "Two days is all I need to know that you're giving a hundred and ten percent, and even you can't keep that up forever."

"Watch me," he challenged.

She continued as if he hadn't spoken. "You feed her the healthiest foods I've ever seen. I didn't know what a chia seed was until I saw a bag of them in your pantry and looked it up. And avocado toast for breakfast? For a six-year-old? And then there's Lexi's vocabulary. Mr. Wright, it's amazing. She hasn't even been six for more than a few months, but she knows more English words than I do. And she's picking up Spanish like you wouldn't believe. She's like a sponge, but that's because you are always teaching her. How many books do you read her every night?"

She didn't stop speaking long enough for him to answer.

"You don't even have a television in your house, at least not that I've seen, and not for the same reasons I didn't have one growing up. You're doing a good job, but I think ..." Her eyebrows slammed together.

"What? What do you think?" And he found he really did want to know despite his earlier frustration that she felt the right to weigh in at all.

"I ... I guess I'm trying to say you're doing a good job, but I'm worried. I'm worried for you both."

It surprised Gabe when he heard himself say, "Well, that makes two of us."

"But you really are doing a good job," she repeated a third time.

"Really?" he asked sarcastically. "If I'm doing such a bang-up job, maybe you could explain to me why she's created an entirely new family for herself in her mind."

"Her sparkle family?"

She knew about them? Lexi must have told her, he realized with a sinking heart. How many other people had she told? What kind of kid, happy in her life's situation, made up an entirely new family for herself? It meant that he wasn't enough. No matter how hard he tried, he'd never be enough for what Lexi needed. For a horrified moment, he thought he felt tears prick his eyes, but just as quickly, it passed. It must have been the pollen.

He sighed. In a way, it was a relief to have someone to talk to about it. He hadn't been able to bring himself to ask his mom what it could all mean. She was already burdened with so much: worry for his brother, worry for him and Lexi ... "She talks about them nonstop," he admitted, "like they're real. Where did they even come from? That's what I want to know. A few weeks ago, boom, they were just on the scene out of nowhere."

Elena squinted her eyes thoughtfully. "They say kids with vivid imaginations have very high IQs."

"Well, then hers is off the charts."

Elena chuckled. "There are worse things."

"I guess." Gabe studied her openly. Her lips were like the petals of a flower, soft and delicate, and oh so enticing.

"So, here is a question for you."

He cleared his throat. "Shoot."

"Am I fired after what happened today? Car accident, non organic ice cream ..."

It wasn't a question he'd expected, and he laughed. "No. You're not fired."

She peered at him apologetically. "One more question?"

He smiled. "Sure, why not?"

"Can she please call me Elena? It's what we both would prefer. Having her call me Miss Torres ... it places *una barrera* ... a barrier between us. She told me that's why she was upset that first day. She wants us to be friends."

Gabe frowned. "I want her to grow up respecting authority. My parents never allowed me to call adults by their first names precisely to remind me that they *weren't* my friends. They were my elders."

"I understand that, but I wonder if you could make this one exception. She needs to be at ease with me if I am to be caring for her so closely each and every day. I will still have an expectation that she treat me with respect, and I'll make sure she calls every other adult the way you want her to."

It made sense. It would have saved them all some trouble if he hadn't laid down the law like that. Had he become too stuffy? Again, he had the sense that he was a doddering old man speaking with a hip—and beautiful—teenager. "Okay. I can do that."

"Thank you."

He looked at her. "You're welcome." The sun reflected off her black hair, and her ruby lips pulled into a smile. She was stunning. And had precisely zero interest in him. He'd known that from the moment he'd met her, and it had caught him off guard, if he was being honest. He didn't think he was cocky about it, but he wasn't unaware of his looks. Women had been throwing themselves at him his whole life. Even the ones who were subtle had ways of sending him clear signals of invitation.

Not Elena.

Even if she were to have a change of heart and wanted something with him, he didn't. He couldn't. His personal life was complicated enough as it was. And professionally? He couldn't date someone subordinate to him without causing himself and that person a lot of grief. He would need to declare a conflict of interest and file the form with the board, blah, blah, blah. And all of that would be just to date her, never mind what could happen if they broke up, which they of course would. His mother had drilled it into his head in high school: *You either break up or you get married. Those are your options.* Since he wouldn't be marrying anyone again—ever—a breakup was a given. And a breakup with a subordinate was a nightmare he wasn't willing to take on. It was a good thing she wasn't interested.

"What are you thinking?" Elena asked him.

"Just reviewing some school policy," he answered honestly.

"I thought so. You had a look."

"I had a look?"

"A serious one." She drew her eyebrows down. "Like this."

He smiled. He wouldn't ever date Elena, but he could enjoy her company. He felt like today they'd made a first step in getting to know one another, and he liked what he saw. Maybe a friendship, of a sort, was in their future. "Like my caricature?" he joked.

"Just so." Her teeth flashed white in the sun. She switched gears, growing serious. "I hope I don't offend you with this question, Mr. Wright, but I feel it's important to know."

Gabe braced himself, his smile fading. Instinctively, he knew what she was going to ask.

"Did your wife, Lexi's mother, did she pass away?"

"No," he answered curtly, and then added, "but she might as well have."

Lexi came bounding over, breaking whatever spell Elena had cast over him that had allowed him to speak of something he *never* spoke of.

He cleared his throat before saying, "You ready for that ice cream?"

Lexi shrieked and jumped with excitement. She turned to Elena. "I getta have that ice cream with all the colors!"

With an eye roll toward Elena, he told Lexi to go say goodbye to her friends. Once she'd bounded off, he turned to her. "You promised her superman? That's like a brand-new thief making a bank his first target. Couldn't you have pushed chocolate or vanilla first?"

She laughed, showing no remorse. "Are you going to let her have it?"

Gabe nodded.

"Doesn't it contain red dye forty?" Elena asked innocently.

He cringed. Red forty, yellow five, and who knew what else. "It will be on your conscience," he told her.

Elena grinned. "You're not nearly as rigid and controlling as I thought you were."

He shot her a crooked smile. "Well now, isn't that high praise?"

Chapter 9

E lena couldn't deny that the situation at the bank and the subsequent accident had cast a shadow over the day. But it had ended on a high note as she'd sat in the sun with Lexi and Gabriel Wright, eating ice cream as the boats went by. Lexi even laughed at Elena's blue lips, and although Gabe had only ordered vanilla for himself, he'd gotten in on the fun by deliberately getting a dollop on his nose. Lexi had laughed and laughed.

Now they were headed back to Elena's rented bungalow, and as Gabe made the final turn onto her street, she realized she was disappointed her time with them was ending.

"Looks like you have company," Gabe noted.

Elena didn't see anyone right away. There weren't any cars in her driveway, but then she spotted the two bikes propped up against the side of the house and their owners, Jackson and Leila, sitting on her porch.

"That's my cousin, Leila, and her fiancé, Jackson. He's the one I'm renting this house from."

"Ah."

She turned to the back seat. "Bye, Lexi, I'll see you tomorrow."

"Bye, Elena." Lexi beamed.

She returned her attention to Gabe. "Thank you. Minus the ambulance ride"—*and spotting Marc at the bank with the president of the school board*—"this was a great day."

He smiled. "No problem. See you in the morning."

Elena hopped out and gave one final wave goodbye before turning and walking up to the front porch. "What are you two doing here?"

Leila beat Jackson to a response. "We were out riding and thought you might be home. We checked the garage. Where's your car?"

"The shop," she said offhandedly, not wanting to get into it. "Have you been here long?"

Leila looked at her watch. "Not long. Ten minutes maybe."

Elena offered them both something to drink, which they declined.

"Let's just sit for a bit out here," Leila said.

Elena pulled up a chair. She looked back and forth between Leila and Jackson. They were quiet. Too quiet. Her stomach flipped. "What's going on?"

"Elena, I ..." Jackson began before hesitating. "I'm so sorry to do this to you, you have no idea. I know you just moved in not that long ago, but..."

Elena's stomach went into free fall.

"... I need to put the house on the market."

No. No, this wasn't happening. Not this house. Not the one she'd just moved into. The one she'd tried to open an account for today so she could save up her money to buy. No.

She tilted her head, her eyes narrowing as if piecing together a puzzle. "I don't understand. I thought we had a plan for me to rent from you, and that I could try to buy it in a year or so. We even talked about a land contract."

Jackson looked tortured as his eyes shot back and forth between her and Leila. "I wish we could still do that, you have no idea, but I need to sell it now, Elena. Lizzie and Matt are low on capital, and they can't meet their obligation to our store for the next few months. I need to fill the gap, and the only way I can do that is to sell the house. If there was any other way ... any other way at all ..." His eyes pleaded with hers for forgiveness, but Elena wasn't in a forgiving mood just then.

She had the sudden urge to stomp her foot as she stood. "Is this because of that *stupid* brewing machine?"

He winced. "News travels fast, I guess."

"*Tía* Carmen told me."

"I'm sure she heard from my mother. She's never been great with a secret."

"Come on. I'm practically family," she said, offended.

"Anyway, it can't be repaired," Jackson continued, " and they're on the hook for a lot of money, and they weren't expecting it, obviously, and I wasn't expecting this." He gestured at the house. "I feel terrible."

Leila looked ready to cry. "We're so sorry, Elena. But listen, we'll help you. We'll get you all moved back into the Victorian with us. It'll take a few hours, tops."

Alarm rose inside Elena until it stuck in her throat. That would be a giant step backwards. She wasn't going to do that, no matter what the circumstance. She wasn't going to be the poor relative that took advantage of her family. She wasn't going to live in Leila's house like some guest, the odd woman out living with a pair of soon-to-be newlyweds. The days of rooming with people were over. She was an adult now. She had plans. Except now those plans had evaporated. Where could she go?

Elena swallowed down her panic and looked at Jackson. "Are you asking me to move out today?" she asked quietly.

"No, no, no. Of course not today."

"When?"

He cleared his throat. "Um, I'm listing it on Monday of next week. So, once it sells ..."

"Monday of next week," Elena repeated, staring at her sandals and her polished toes. Six days. She walked to the edge of the porch, her back turned to them. The house wouldn't be for sale for long, not in this market. She figured she'd need to be out before two weeks was up. Three, tops.

This was impossible.

She shook her head as she fought against the sting in her eyes, and then, inexplicably, she felt hysterical laughter bubble up from way down deep. Nothing about this was funny, but she gave herself over to it anyway and let it out. She laughed and laughed, and then she laughed some more, and finally, when she turned around, she laughed even harder still at the arrested expressions on the two faces staring back at her.

Elena wiped her eyes with the back of her hand. "*Lo siento*. Oh, that was just what I needed." She sighed as she stared off at the scraggly, crooked juniper shrub in Jackson's front yard. If this had been her house, that thing would have been firewood eight weeks ago when she'd moved in. She would have unpacked her boxes first, and job two would have been to take an ax to that mangled thing and put it out of its misery.

But now she was moving—again—and it would never be hers to chop down. Nothing had ever been hers, well, except for her car, which had come out the same year that Rachel and Ross started dating on *Friends*. One thing was certain—it hadn't aged nearly as well as her favorite sitcom. But the car actually wasn't hers either, was it? She still owed a few hundred dollars on it, so technically, it was the bank's, and who knew if it would be worth fixing now that the back end was all pushed in?

And now she didn't even have a working phone. What did she have to show for her life? Absolutely nothing. And now, after what she saw at the bank, she was sweating her job too. Gabe had said the board would vote in July, and he'd made it seem like a done deal, but Marc was friends with the board president? She hadn't known that, and it made her nervous. More than nervous. Nothing in her life felt secure.

The sting behind her eyes returned, and she spoke quickly while she still could, before her voice became so shrill that only dogs would be able to hear her. "You know what's crazy? This isn't even the shortest time I've lived in a place."

Jackson looked at her pleadingly. "Elena, I'm—"

Something snapped inside of her, and just like that, her eyes cleared. "*Don't*, Jackson. Don't say you're sorry again. You either, Leila. Neither one of you has *any* idea what it is to have no home. *Ni idea*. I have no roots. I've lived in dozens of places with a mother who didn't even know I existed half the time. I could never save any money for college because I was too busy trying to keep us from being evicted. Most of the time, giving everything I had to our landlords *still* wasn't enough to keep a roof over our heads."

Jackson's eyes went wide, and she realized he'd misunderstood.

"I don't mean *that*. I'm talking about giving them all my money, from every paycheck, but don't think a few of those landlords didn't try—*viejos verdes*, *todos*. I was stronger than that. I still am. I don't want to move back into your house with you, and I won't. I won't do it. It's your home, not mine, and I refuse to. So, you can sit here on my—*perdón*—*your* front porch and look at me like you feel so sorry for me, but don't. I've been making it on my own a long time, and I'm not about to stop now."

She was breathing hard and couldn't seem to slow down. "I need you both to leave. Please. I'll call you tomorrow, Leila."

Elena didn't watch them go. She marched off the porch and into the garage through the door on the side of the house. She was a woman on a mission, in search of an ax.

Chapter 10

T wo days later, Elena awoke to a car parked in the driveway, just as Gabe had told her she would. He'd leased a brand-new Honda Pilot for her to drive, and the key was waiting for her in the cup holder. It wasn't hers, and she still had massive problems, but Elena couldn't help but feel a small thrill as she started up the engine. Just for fun, she'd pretend it was hers. A brand-new car with leather seats and a sun roof. Life sure knew how to keep her on her toes.

Sometimes she didn't understand herself. She tallied the reasons she *should* be miserable: her car was likely totaled, homelessness loomed before her, her phone was toast, and her top enemy in town seemed chummy with the most powerful person on the school board. As if that weren't enough, she'd murdered an ugly but innocent shrub, another debt to Jackson, another dent in her already strained wallet. It was plenty to freak out over, but right now, with the sun beaming, a good song playing on the radio, and the new-car smell filling her nostrils, she couldn't muster a breakdown. Happiness had ambushed her, so the meltdown would just have to wait.

The day was flawless. Lexi, as usual, kept Elena on her toes, so to burn off some of the girl's endless energy before Gabe got home, Elena suggested a walk in the woods beyond the creek. She'd noticed a path on the other side of the footbridge, but they had yet to explore it together.

"I'll bring my sparkle wand," Lexi shrieked, running to the garage and grabbing a stick.

As they made their way across the field and past the tree swing, Lexi waved her stick wand like a maestro, her sneakers kicking up dust once they made it to the trail on the other side of the creek. "They're singing, Elena—listen!" She giggled, belting out, "Sparkle, sparkle, dance in the trees!"

Elena grinned, catching the rhythm. "Oh, I hear it—Hop like bunnies, twirl with me!" She grabbed Lexi's hand, hopping and spinning with her until they both stumbled, laughing. The trees swallowed up their echoes, a secret just for them. A gentle breeze rustled through, and Lexi slowed, her wand drooping. She pointed to a clearing ahead, her voice soft. "That's the magic door to my sparkle house."

Elena knelt, brushing Lexi's dark hair away from her face. "Are they here?"

"They go lots of places, but my mommy always waits for me right here so I can always find her."

"I bet she really misses you."

"Yes," she responded gravely.

"Can you see her right now?"

"No." She shook her stick. "My wand is broke, so I can't see her right now, but she can see me." She looked at Elena. "She says you're really pretty."

"That's so nice of her. Can she hear us?"

Lexi shook her head.

"Well, we could leave her a note." Elena picked up a leaf. "You can tell her you're coming back with your magic later." She handed the leaf to Lexi, who used her pointer finger to pretend-write on it before tucking it under a rock with care.

By the time the workday was done, Gabe couldn't wait to get home and kick up his feet, but then he remembered that dinner wasn't going to cook itself. Elena, God bless her, had taken a swing at red beans and rice the other night, but the beans were Sahara-dry and the rice crunched like flavorless gravel. He'd choked it down, then fibbed the next day about how much he'd enjoyed it before letting her off the hook by saying he'd prefer she spent her time with Lexi as opposed to working in the kitchen. He could tell she was relieved. So was he, even though it meant endless nights of spatula duty. That had been the one good thing about Mrs. Shreever. The woman was the devil in a pair of orthopedic shoes, but boy, could she cook.

Driving along the white fence that bordered the road, Gabe saw something flicker out of the corner of his eye. Lexi was sprinting alongside him, brandishing a stick like a tiny warrior, with Elena not far behind. He let off the gas and applied pressure to the brake.

His daughter's hair streamed wildly behind her, and her face registered pure joy as she laughed. Elena, laughing too, waved as she closed the gap and caught up to Lexi.

Watching his daughter run across the verdant field was like watching the opening of *Little House on the Prairie*, all wholesome, sun-dappled innocence, a picture of youth and vigor. Elena on the other hand, well, it was a little less prairie and a little more *Baywatch*—minus the slow-mo and red bathing suit, unfortunately. He was ashamed to find that his eyes didn't quite know which running female to lock onto—his adored little girl, or the luscious nanny whose curves could derail a train.

Gabe came to a stop on the roadside, solving his dilemma by looking straight ahead until they were alongside the car on the passenger side.

"Hi, Daddy!" Lexi called, breathless as she ducked through the fence. She was still beaming when she made it to the window. "Elena was pushing me on the swing ... and I went *so* high ... and I saw you coming ... so we ran *super* fast to wave," she panted.

It was a nice welcome to get after a grueling day. Elena sidled up beside Lexi, her smile wide and her cheeks flushed with color. Fatigue drained out of him like a leaky balloon. "You're a sight for sore eyes, both of you. Do you want a lift back to the house?"

Elena and Lexi traded a glance. Lexi flicked her head to one side. "We'll run back."

He envied that energy. When had he last cut loose—really stretched his legs, pushed his limits, felt the wind instead of just deadlines? "Alright, see you there."

"Guess what, Daddy?"

"What?"

"We went to see my sparkle family but nobody was home, so we left a note."

And just like that, his mood tanked. He managed a stiff nod. Elena met his gaze but said nothing. He'd have to talk to her about encouraging this sparkle family business. Lexi was talking about them more and more every day, and he didn't like it. "That's nice," he responded vaguely. "I'll see you both at home." He smiled first at Lexi and then at Elena, her hair windswept and the color still high in her cheeks. He put his hand up in another wave, and she did the same.

He drove on, his eyes flicking to the rearview mirror, reluctant to let them slip from sight. They raced across the field, their dark hair streaming wild behind them, catching the sunlight like ribbons of night. Two souls dancing to nature's pulse, innocent and radiant in a way that made the world feel whole for a fleeting moment. From this distance, Gabe could almost pretend that Lexi was running with her mother, but that scene would never unfold, and the thought pierced him as they faded from view.

He beat them to the house by a good five minutes. After dumping his messenger bag on his desk in the loft, he trudged down the stairs, eyeing the kitchen like a reluctant soldier marching into battle. Dinner again—why did people need to eat every blasted night? He opened the fridge and pulled out a carton of eggs, vegetables, and cheese. It would be omelets tonight. Setting the cutting board on the counter with a sigh, he wondered if humanity would ever evolve past this level of daily grind.

Then his mind drifted to Seb—Seb, who'd never chop another vegetable or wash another dish. His buddy's glass hadn't just been half full, it had been brimming. His default setting was one of carefree ease, and he'd had a grin that remained stuck in place even when life didn't cooperate. Toward the end, the pain meds couldn't touch the pain, but Seb didn't complain. And here Gabe stood, griping over having to whip up a decent dinner for himself and Lexi—sustenance Seb would have given anything to share with his own family one last time.

When Lexi burst through the door, she brought the scent of the great outdoors with her—spring breeze mixed with ozone. She was all bright-eyed enthusiasm as she told Gabe about her day. "And then I poked at a spider with a stick, not to hurt it, I was just playing, and then Daddy, *hundreds* of baby spiders came out."

Gabe looked to Elena, who shuddered violently. "It was awful."

"It was so fun, Daddy," Lexi countered. Abruptly, she stopped talking. She knit her brows together in concentration before looking at him and saying, "*Me gustan las arañas.*"

He took a step back and took in Lexi's proud smile. "Whoa! You're speaking Spanish?"

"That means, 'I like spiders,'" she informed him. "Elena doesn't."

"No, Elena doesn't," Elena said, grabbing a hair brush off the counter and motioning for Lexi to follow her into the living room. To Gabe, she said, "Let me run a brush through her hair and then I'll go. Otherwise, you'll have a tangled mess on your hands with tonight's bath."

Gabe thanked her and watched from a distance as Lexi sat on the sofa be-tween Elena's legs as she worked the brush through his daughter's hair—from the tips first and then all the way up to the roots. Once the tangles were out and Elena continued to brush, the expression on Lexi's face was one of pure bliss. Gabe's heart squeezed painfully as he cracked another egg.

In the end, Elena stayed for dinner. He'd made the rookie mistake of asking what she was having for dinner, and hearing that she had a frozen meal—an absolute nutritional travesty—waiting for her at home, well, he couldn't let her leave. Not in good conscience. He pictured the sodium-soaked, preservative-laden slop she'd have nuked, and shuddered. The woman deserved better than microwaved BHT, and her gushing over his simple omelets, embarrassing as it was, made sense if her baseline was basically thawed out chemicals masquerading as food.

He knew he was quieter than usual as they ate, but he had a splitting headache that three ibuprofens hadn't touched. Thankfully, Lexi kept the conversation flowing, her voice bright. "I showed Elena the door to my sparkle house."

He paused, fork halfway to his mouth, and set it down with a soft clink. Not again. "Were there any peepers in the creek today?" he asked in an effort to steer talk away from the sparkle family.

Lexi shook her head. "I need Mosie. Mosie likes to hunt frogs with me. She's gentle with them," she told Elena.

"Who's Mosie?"

"My Mimi and Papa's dog. She's super smart. You point your finger and say 'bang, bang' and Mosie falls over."

"That's quite a trick," Elena said. "Who taught her that?"

"My Uncle Will. He's far away right now, but Mosie didn't forget the trick. She's a good dog, just like Sharklove."

Gabe's shoulders stiffened. "Who's Sharklove?" he asked, though he suspected he already knew.

Lexi played with her food.

He looked to Elena for the explanation.

"Sharklove is Lexi's sparkle dog."

He pressed his lips into a thin line. Don't engage, he told himself.

After several seconds of rearranging her omelet, Lexi piped up. "When can we get a dog, Daddy?"

On second thought, maybe a make-believe dog wasn't the worst thing in the world. "We aren't home enough to take care of a dog," Gabe said evenly.

"But I miss Sharklove so much."

Gabe set his fork down again, harder this time, the clink sharp against the quiet. "Lexi, Sharklove isn't real." His voice was low and firm, each word weighted.

"Gabe," Elena murmured in soft warning.

"Sharklove *is* real." Lexi shot back.

He leaned forward, forearms braced on the table, hands clasped tight. "No, Sharklove is *not* real. Sharklove is pretend and your sparkle family is pretend. You know that, right?" His hazel eyes searched hers, steady but strained.

"They're real!" Lexi's voice cracked. "My sparkle family loves me and won't ever leave!"

The air stilled. Gabe's chest tightened, his daughter's words slicing deeper than she could know. He pushed back from the table, chair scraping, and grabbed his plate. "I need a minute," he said, quieter now, and headed to the kitchen.

He attacked the dishes, water splashing as Elena brought in the rest. "Thanks," he muttered, eyes fixed on the suds in the sink. She offered to get Lexi ready for bed, and he nodded, grateful for the breather.

Elena left Lexi reading a picture book with the promise that her dad would be there to tuck her into bed in five minutes. The kitchen gleamed as it always did, and Gabe sat at the counter with a glass of water in hand. An open bottle of Tylenol sat beside it.

"Rough day?"

"Yeah."

"Want to talk about it?"

He pursed his lips and gave a curt nod, avoiding her gaze. "This isn't good for her, Elena, this sparkle stuff. I'm all for playing make-believe, but this is ... I can't let this go on."

She slid onto the stool next to him. "Why's it bad for her?"

He faltered. "It just is. It'll hurt her eventually."

Elena bit her lip and worked up her courage. "Does this have anything to do with Lexi's mom?" she finally asked.

Gabe turned, staring at her intently before finally nodding. Then, sensing her next question, he raised a hand. "Not tonight. I'll tell you everything, but I just can't tonight."

"Okay." Elena's throat tightened in a sudden ache for this man and his kid. It cracked open her own buried mess—dead car, home slipping away, all those feelings from childhood she'd worked so hard to overcome. She blinked hard, mortified by the sting in her eyes.

"Hey," Gabe said, peering at her. "You okay?"

She slammed the lid on her feelings about the past. "*Lo siento*. I'm fine. I just feel bad about all of this." She hesitated before adding, "And I have some stuff going on, myself."

Concern entered his eyes, and he leaned closer. Elena couldn't help but smile. Mr. Fix-It was ready to burst into action. Too bad duct tape wouldn't work this time. "It's okay," she said to reassure him, or maybe herself. "It's nothing I can't handle."

"Tell me."

"Well, my car's dead and I still owe on it. I have no phone, and I owe Jackson a shrub."

Gabe tilted his head, curiosity flickering in his eyes. "You're landscaping?"

"I chopped down his juniper the other day," Elena said, keeping her voice light.

He blinked, thrown. "Why?"

"He's selling the bungalow."

His gaze sharpened, searching her face. "What does that mean for you?"

She shrugged. "It means I'm apartment hunting." Her tone was flat, but steady.

"When'd you find out?"

"Two days ago, after you dropped me off."

He let out a low chuckle. "So you took it out on a shrub?"

A smirk tugged at her lips. "*Si*. Like you, I have my moments." She dropped her voice and leaned in a fraction. "Go easy on her, Gabriel."

His smile broke slow and warm.

"What?"

"Only my parents call me Gabriel."

"Oh." Heat crept up her neck. "*Lo siento—*"

"No, no," he cut in, still shaking his head and grinning. "I liked it. And you slipped a 'Gabe' in earlier too—beats that 'Mr. Wright' business."

His words landed soft, unexpected, and her smile bloomed in return. For a second, the kitchen felt brighter, like the clouds had parted just for them.

Chapter 11

The next day, Elena's optimism had fizzled. Panic clawed at her every other minute. *What now? How do I survive? Where do I even live?* At least Gabe had tossed her one lifeline: the Honda was hers for the summer. A temporary fix, but it bought her some breathing room.

She tried to focus on Lexi, sprawled on their picnic blanket with turkey-cucumber pitas, apple slices, and carrots. They'd hauled along Lexi's tea set, using bottled water as "tea." Elena rattled off Spanish words—*manzana*, *zanahoria*, *te*—and Lexi parroted them back, eyes bright. She hadn't exaggerated to Gabe: the girl was a sponge, latching onto words after one try. Why not teach her phrases too? Maybe drag out her old Total Physical Response Storytelling kit from the classroom. They could turn it into a game.

Elena couldn't help but fault the American system of education, delaying foreign language lessons until middle school and high school. Everyone knew kids soaked up languages best when they were young. She thought of herself—bilingual by the second grade at her dual-immersion school in Puerto Rico. Half the day was in Spanish and the other half, English. Knowing two languages was an asset, and it was one she wanted Lexi to have.

Each time her panic surged, one look at Lexi as she sipped her tea pulled her back from the edge. She'd figure it out. A car, an apartment, eventually a house. The dream had felt so close, then *poof*—gone. But she knew she'd get there, and while she wouldn't lean too heavily on her family, or even Gabe, knowing they were there, a quiet safety net, softened the sting.

Back at the house, Lexi lay quietly on the living room floor and arranged her toy horses in a neat row, their plastic manes catching the late afternoon light through the large picture window. Elena dried the delicate tea cups from their creek-side tea party, stealing glances at the clock on the microwave. It was six o'clock. Maybe she should whip up something for dinner. Gabe was usually home long before now, and if she was hungry, she knew Lexi must be too. After drying her hands, she took her new phone out of her pocket to see if she'd missed a text from him. Nothing.

It wasn't like she had anywhere special to be once she was done here, but she still found herself fretting. Just when she'd decided to give him a call, she heard the sound of the Suburban crunching up the driveway.

She quickly pinched a little color into her cheeks before hanging the dish towel on the dishwasher handle and waiting for Gabe to walk through the door. Lately, she felt like this before he came in. It was some kind of nervous anticipation, and she didn't know why. A sharp knock at the door interrupted her thoughts. Gabe wouldn't be knocking on his own door, would he?

"Lexi, stay put, okay?" She opened the door to find a towering man on the porch, broad-shouldered and handsomely rugged, with golden-wheat hair and eyes that crinkled with a mixture of surprise and warmth. He took up the whole doorframe, his presence commanding yet gentle.

"Can I help you?" Elena asked, tilting her head.

"Oh." He took a step back. "I'm sorry, I'm looking for Gabe."

"Uncle Will!" Lexi's shriek pierced the air as she bolted around the corner from the living room, ignoring Elena's instruction. She launched herself at him.

He lifted her easily and hoisted her into a bear hug as he stepped inside, his boots thudding against the hardwood.

"Lexi, my sweet girl," he murmured, voice thick with emotion. "You do my heart a world of good." He pulled back, holding her at arm's length. "Let me look at you."

Lexi grinned, leaning back in his arms, glowing under his gaze. "I'm six now."

"I know. I sang to you on the computer, remember?"

"And you got me a present."

"The tea set." His eyes flicked to Elena, who pointed at the tea pot she'd just dried that now gleamed on the counter.

"I'm Elena, Lexi's nanny," she said, offering a smile as she tucked a strand of hair behind her ear.

Will shifted Lexi to one hip and extended a hand, his grip firm but warm. "Will. Good to meet you." He studied her for a beat, his brow furrowing slightly.

"What?" she asked, smoothing her hair again, suddenly self-conscious under his scrutiny.

He bobbed his head, a faint smile tugging at his lips. "You remind me of someone I knew a while back. That's all."

"Oh." Elena's curiosity piqued, but before she could ask more, the faint crunch of gravel sounded again.

He smiled. "Listen, I thought Gabe would be home by now, and I wanted to surprise him, but—" The muted sound of gravel popping outside made him turn to look out the sidelights on either side of the door. "Speak of the devil."

"Daddy's gonna be so surprised!" Lexi squealed, wiggling free and landing on her feet with a thud.

"He sure will, kiddo. Thinks I'm still in Spain." Will's voice softened, a shadow crossing his face.

"What's Spain again?"

"A far away place, Lex."

"Is it through the woods?"

"Through the woods and across an ocean. A world away."

Gabe pushed through the door from the garage. Stepping into the house, he worked to loosen his tie, but when he spotted his brother, he froze. "Will?"

Will stretched out his arms. "Hey there, Shorty."

Gabe didn't hesitate. He crossed the room in three strides, ignoring the dirt he might track in on his shoes, and pulled Will into a fierce hug. "I didn't recognize the car. What are you doing here?"

They held on a moment longer, the kind of embrace that carried years of love and shared history. Elena averted her eyes, feeling like an intruder on their reunion. Even Lexi seemed to know the two men needed a minute. She moved silently to her side, leaning against her as she looked on with solemn eyes.

"I can't believe you're here." Elena caught the tremor in Gabe's voice.

"I know," Will said, clapping Gabe's shoulder as they parted.

"How? Did you get leave?"

"Nah." Will's tone shifted, quieter now. "I'm out. For good."

Gabe blinked, processing. "Out? Like, retired?"

"Medical," Will said, glancing at Elena and Lexi. "We'll talk later."

Gabe wiped at his eyes with the back of his hand, chuckling softly to cover it. "Yeah, okay. You good, man?"

"I'm good, Shorty."

"Mom was worried sick," Gabe added, shaking his head.

Will cleared his throat. "Last scare, I promise."

They stood there, grinning like a couple of boys, and Elena couldn't help but smile too. Men were interesting creatures. Why didn't they just cry in each other's arms and be done with it? Nobody would think less of them. Okay, well if she were being honest, she might have in the past, but the raw emotion running between them softened something inside her, and she realized that her taste in men had been well overdue for a recalibration.

Gabe finally turned to her, as if remembering she was there. "Oh, Elena, this is my brother, Will."

"We've met." Will winked at her.

"Of course." Gabe ran a hand through his hair. "Elena's a teacher at Nicolet High, but she's helping out with Lexi this summer. Did I mention that?"

Will nodded, and his gaze lingered on Elena, curious. "Is that an accent I heard?"

"*Si*. I'm from Puerto Rico," she said, lifting her chin with a touch of pride.

"*¿De Puerto Rico? ¡Qué chévere!*" Will's Spanish was heavily accented but earnest, and his grin widened when he saw her eyes light up in surprise. "*Hace tiempo que no hablo con alguien de la isla.*"

"*¡Mira eso! No esperaba que hablaras español.*" She laughed, switching back to English. "Where'd you learn that?"

"I've been stationed in Rota, Spain for a bit. And I have a good buddy from San Juan who taught me a few words years ago. Nothing I'd repeat in front of the kid," he added with a grin. He paused, his expression softening. "You're far from home. You must miss it."

"*Quizás un poco.* The ocean for sure."

"Hmm. An islander in the Upper Peninsula." Will's tone carried a hint of intrigue as he glanced between her and Gabe. "Interesting."

Gabe shot him a warning look, but Will just chuckled. "Lighten up, Shorty."

Elena didn't have time to consider what she'd missed during that exchange, because in a flash, Will lunged, catching Gabe in a playful headlock. Lexi gasped, then giggled, bouncing on her toes. "Daddy, no wrestling in the house."

Will released him, ruffling Gabe's hair. "My fault, Lex."

Gabe straightened his tie in mock indignation, his eyes danced. "Watch out girls, next we'll be throwing punches."

Elena's jaw dropped. This was Gabe—Mr. Duct-Tape-and-Order—horsing around like a teenager. The contrast between this Gabe and the Gabe she'd thought she'd known was jarring, and she couldn't deny it was more than endearing, seeing him so playful and unguarded.

"Do you have brothers, Elena?" Will asked, brushing at his own shirt.

"I'm an only child."

Will clapped his hands together. "Then you're in for a real treat. Siblings 101, lesson one: lock up the good dishes when we get going."

She laughed, instantly liking his easy charm. "Can't wait for lesson two."

She eyed them up briefly. They were of similar build, and upon closer inspection, they did resemble one another a bit. Will's features were more rugged and time-worn than Gabe's, but he was just as attractive. He was quite a bit taller than Gabe, which should have made him appear imposing but somehow didn't.

"For now," Will added, jerking his thumb toward the door, "I think I'll head out and get my stuff."

"Stuff?" Gabe asked.

"Can I crash a few days?"

"Stay as long as you want," Gabe said, his face lighting up. "Did you eat yet? I've got chicken for the grill tonight—it'll stretch."

"Sounds perfect." Will paused, glancing at Elena. "You staying for dinner?"

"Oh, I should probably—" Elena started, thinking of the sandwich and un-packed boxes that awaited her at the bungalow.

"Pleeease, Elena!" Lexi tugged her arm, eyes wide. "We can show Uncle Will how fast you spin me on the tire swing."

Elena hesitated, looking to Gabe. His expression was open. "Only if you want," he said softly.

"Of course she's staying," Will said, already halfway to the door. "Be right back."

"I'll help," Gabe said, following him out, leaving Elena with a smiling Lexi and a warmth she hadn't expected to feel.

Gabe trailed Will to the silver Ford F-150 parked in the driveway. The evening air was heavy with the scent of pine and cooling earth. "New wheels?"

Will nodded. "Just leased it."

When Will moved to lower the tailgate, Gabe caught his arm, his grip firm but gentle. "Hold up. What's really going on?"

Will's tone was neutral, but his gaze slid to the gravel beneath their feet. "Like I said, I took a medical retirement."

Gabe's eyes dropped to Will's hands where pinkish-red scars crisscrossed the knuckles and fingers like a roadmap of pain. Will had downplayed the burns over the phone—second degree and no big deal, he'd said. But these scars looked angry. Permanent. "Medical retirement," Gabe repeated, searching his brother's face. "What does that mean? You were discharged?"

"No." Will's voice held a forced calm, like he was measuring each word. "It means I qualified for retirement after twenty-one years of service."

Gabe crossed his arms. "Come off it, Will. Even I know a retirement can't process that fast."

"It was expedited." Will's tone sharpened, but he still wouldn't meet Gabe's eyes.

"Why?"

Will looked at him then, shooting him an exasperated look, the kind he used to give when Gabe was a kid tailing him and his buddies around Bayshore. "A medical issue, okay?"

"What issue?" Gabe pressed. He stepped closer. Will looked leaner than he had on their last video call three weeks ago—his cheeks looked downright gaunt compared to how they normally looked. It was like the weight of something unspoken was carving him hollow.

"Does it have to do with these?" He gestured to Will's scarred hands.

Will yanked his hand back, flexing his fingers as if to prove they still worked. "No."

"Are you sick, then?" Gabe's voice cracked, betraying the worry clawing at him.

"I'm not sick, Gabe. And that's all your getting for now."

"What do you mean?" Gabe shot back. "I've gotten exactly zero, and I want to know."

"And you will, okay? For now, just lay off." He dropped the tailgate and hefted out a suitcase, the edge catching briefly as he pulled it out. "Just, give me some time."

Gabe grabbed the two duffle bags left in the truck bed, their weight grounding him as he wrestled with the urge to push harder. Will wasn't like this after Afghanistan. Back then, he'd spilled everything he could. Gabe remembered all the late-night calls, stories of dust and chaos, and even the parts that had hurt Will to talk about. This silence was new, and it scared Gabe a little.

Instead of moving back toward the house after closing the tailgate, Will set down his suitcase and rested his forearms on the edge of the truck bed. His voice was weary when he spoke. "I need this, Shorty. I need some normal—Lexi's laugh, your bad grilling, this place." He gestured at the expanse of field and the woods beyond. "It's just like you said it was. I can breathe here."

Gabe exhaled, the tension in his shoulders lifting. "Good. Stay as long as you want."

"Thanks."

"One more thing?"

"Last thing," Will granted, his eyes wary.

"I'm sorry about Tommy." Gabe had said it before, over the phone, but it felt different now, face-to-face, the loss heavier in the quiet of the evening.

Will went still, his face unreadable for a long moment. "Yeah, me too."

They stood there, neither one moving toward the house. The cicadas hummed, filling the silence, and Gabe cleared his throat, shifting gears. "Mom and Dad know you're here?"

"Nope. I need a few days to, I don't know, find my feet." He inhaled deeply, holding the air as if it could cleanse him, and then let it go. "This place is like a postcard. Exactly what I need."

"I wish I could take some extra time off," Gabe said, regret tugging at him as they started toward the porch. "But I'm on thin ice with the board president as it is."

Will snorted, clapping Gabe on the shoulder with his free hand. "Still a pain in your butt?"

"Worse."

"Someone oughta knock him down a peg."

"It'll work out." It was his daily mantra.

"Lexi's here to keep me company. We'll hang out and have some fun." Will's grin returned. "You said she turned shy, but I don't see that."

"She's coming out of it. Elena's been good for her."

Will stopped short, a sly glint in his eye. "Speaking of Elena, what's the deal there, Shorty?"

Gabe adjusted the duffles. "She's great with Lexi. Better than I'd hoped."

"That's not what I'm asking, and you know it."

"That's all that really matters," Gabe said firmly.

Will's eyebrow arched, skeptical. "Right. So you just happened to hire a nanny who looks like she stepped out of every man's fantasy, and there's nothing else to it?"

Gabe's stomach twisted. He knew where this was going. "She's good for Lexi, Will. That's the story."

"Come on, man. She's a dead ringer for—"

"Don't." Gabe's voice was low, cutting through the evening air. He didn't want to hear her name. Not tonight. "You know I can't talk about her."

Will's grin faded, replaced by something else, and Gabe saw a flicker of understanding. That's when he knew. Will had lost someone over there, and not just Tommy.

"I get it," Will said quietly. "More than you know."

After clearing the table from dinner, Gabe suggested they leave the dishes so Lexi could show Will the tire swing before bedtime. Elena offered to stay behind and help clean up, but Lexi claimed she *had* to go with them. Normally, Gabe wouldn't leave the kitchen looking the way it did, but he could see that Will was restless and needed to stretch his legs. He had a million questions for his brother, but none that he could ask at the moment. Will had asked for time. Gabe could give him that. Tonight, they'd keep it light by focusing on Lexi. The cleanup wouldn't take long to do anyway, since dinner had consisted of grilled chicken, a salad, and saffron rice.

It had been simplistic, but excellent, and Will praised him as they crossed the field of dogwoods toward the tree swing. "You've gotten better at grilling, Shorty. A lot better." He drew Elena into the conversation. "This guy has always known his way around a kitchen, Elena. One Christmas when he was ten or eleven years old, Santa left him a Chef's Knife from William Sonoma. It was his favorite gift that year, and that night he made us a big stir fry. No ham dinner for the Wright family that Christmas."

Elena smiled and shielded her eyes against the sun, still surprisingly high in the sky for seven o'clock. The days were long in Nicolet this time of year, and yet each year it always came as a surprise to Gabe.

"I don't cook very well," Elena admitted with a shrug.

Gabe felt his lips twitch. From his limited experience, this was an understatement.

"Me neither," his brother said easily. "I dated a foodie once. That was pure bliss. I think I gained five pounds in the first couple of weeks."

Gabe listened as Will and Elena chattered on, getting to know one another. Lexi chimed in here and there as she scampered around them. Will asked Elena about her background, and she gave a quick synopsis. Nothing she said was particularly revealing. It was more what she didn't say. Gabe had always gotten the sense that Elena hadn't had it easy growing up. Her mom had passed within the last few years—he knew that from an earlier conversation—and it didn't sound like she'd had a father who'd been in the picture much, if at all. He wondered how she'd turned out so well. She was a hard worker, and minus her viral video and ax-wielding incident, she seemed to take the twists and turns of life pretty well.

Since that day at the park, they really hadn't spent any kind of meaningful time together, and they certainly didn't converse openly the way Elena and Will were now. Instead, they kept it about Lexi, which was the way it should be. Still, Gabe found himself wishing he and Elena could have the ease that she and his brother had with one another. Whenever he interacted with Elena, he felt stilted and stuffy—superintendent, father, employer. He wasn't just Gabe. He hadn't been "just Gabe" for a long time, but tonight, with Will here ... he felt a glimmer of his old self. It was pretty hard to appear the serious boss with a brother who insisted on calling him "Shorty." He'd seen Elena fighting a smile more than once this evening at the sound of the nickname.

"Has he always been a health nut, then?" He heard Elena ask.

Will chuckled and then looked around to make sure that Lexi wasn't listening. "Don't be fooled. Somewhere in that house, my brother has a stash of Twizzlers and Pay Days, guaranteed."

Elena looked at Gabe in surprise. "Is that true?"

Gabe only smiled. That might have been true years ago, but not now. If Lexi had to eat healthy, so did he. Gabe watched as the wind grabbed Elena's hair and whipped it over her face. He resisted the urge to reach out and smooth it away.

"The other thing you should know about Shorty here," Will went on, "is that he's a major overachiever. Always has been. He's the best dad there is, but I gotta tell you, brother, there's no reward for feeding your kid the weirdest food."

Will had always understood him better than anyone, so Gabe knew Will was aware of what drove him as a parent, and it had nothing to do with the general need to overachieve. The truth was, every day he woke up trying to be a better dad to Lexi than he'd been the day before because Lexi deserved no less than that. For her sake, he wanted to give her the best of everything, but he wasn't in it for the recognition, and he didn't want the praise. "The healthy kid is the only reward I need," he said, watching Lexi up ahead as she stopped to pick a dandelion. He felt Elena's eyes on him, and he turned to look at her. She smiled, and he felt a full-bodied suffusion of heat course through him. Man, she was pretty.

Gabe saw Elena to her car an hour later, the porch light casting a soft glow on her smile as she waved goodbye. Back inside, he tossed Will a stack of sheets for the guest bed. "Make yourself at home, but don't expect turndown service," he teased, earning a mock salute from his brother.

"Lexi, bath time," Gabe called, heading to the bathroom. Evenings with his daughter were his sanctuary, a quiet pocket of time where the world's noise faded away. Some of their best talks unfolded over bubbles or bedtime stories, her small voice unraveling big ideas.

Tonight, as he ran the water and tested its warmth, Lexi sat on the edge of the tub, clutching a rubber frog. "Daddy, why don't frogs walk like us?"

He grinned, pouring in a capful of bubble bath. "Good question. What's your guess?"

She squinted, thinking hard. "They hop 'cause they're practicing to fly. Like, if they jump enough, maybe they'll get wings someday."

Gabe chuckled as he helped her into the tub. "That's a solid hypothesis, kiddo. Know what that word means?"

"A really good guess," she said without hesitation, splashing the frog for emphasis.

Now, where had she learned that? Were they already teaching kindergartners the scientific method? He marveled at his daughter, and not for the first time. At six, she was already piecing the world together in ways that left him awestruck. "Smarty pants," he said, tweaking her nose. "You're smarter than I was at your age."

Once she was scrubbed and tucked into her pink pony pajamas, Lexi scampered to the living room where Will was sprawled on the couch and flipping through a magazine. "Uncle Will, read me a story," she demanded, thrusting a picture book into his hands.

Will raised an eyebrow, taking the book. "This one, huh? *The Loon's Song*?"

"It's my favorite," Lexi said, as she climbed into his lap. "Daddy got it at Luca's Book Café."

Gabe leaned against the archway and watched them. He'd picked the book up on a whim, drawn by its watercolor loons gliding across a lake, but its gentle story of a lost bird finding home had hooked Lexi—and him—fast. Honestly, anything was better than those *Berenstain Bears* books she sometimes asked for, where Papa Bear bumbled through life, saved by Mama Bear's sighs and wise words. Gabe wasn't that kind of dad, and he didn't love the stereotype, but Lexi adored that little treehouse family, and that made it tolerable. Barely.

Will opened the book, his deep voice soon settling into the rhythm of the story. Lexi nested against him, her eyelids already drooping, and Gabe was filled with a mix of gratitude and relief. Will was here. He was safe, and Lexi was happy. For tonight, that was enough.

With Lexi tucked in, her goodnight kisses still warm on their cheeks, Gabe unlocked the liquor cabinet by the stone fireplace. He poured two glasses of scotch on the rocks, the clink of the ice cubes echoing in the quiet. After handing one to Will, he sank onto the sofa while Will claimed the chaise lounger. They sipped their drinks in silence, each gazing out the window where dusk bled into night. It was June twenty-first—the official start of summer.

Gabe swirled his glass, the amber liquid catching the lamplight. Summer always sparked something in him—energy, hope, life bursting at the seams. Good things seemed to be waiting around every corner. But last summer had been different. Seb's death in March had left him grieving through long, hollow months. If the sun shone at all last summer, he hadn't noticed through the fog of his grief. Lexi had stayed back in Bayshore with his parents, which had been best for her but in hindsight, not so great for him. Taking care of her would have forced him to at least put on a good face. Without her, he'd wallowed. He was much better now, but sometimes he still got that awful feeling in his stomach when Seb would come to mind. Cancer was a terrible way to die, and it had stolen his best friend in weeks. Seb had deserved so much better.

Seb had made only two requests of him. The first, Gabe honored immediately. He left his position as principal of Bayshore High School and filled Seb's role as interim superintendent for the district as his friend faded away in hospice care and died a month later.

The position was supposed to be his permanently—everyone said so. Instead, it had gone to the daughter of a school board member. Gabe could have taken back his principal job, but it would have meant displacing a colleague who'd earned her shot, and he couldn't do it. The truth was, he'd needed an out. Everywhere he looked in Bayshore, he saw his friend's ghost. And then there was Seb's wife, Marni, and their newborn baby boy. He could hardly look at them, and so his second promise had gone unfulfilled.

And then the position had opened in Nicolet—an escape hatch—and he'd taken it. But with each passing month, he doubted himself more and more. Nicolet was home, but Bayshore was in his blood. His parents were there. His memories. His roots.

Will's voice cut through the silence, low and teasing. "At the risk of sounding like a woman, what're you thinking?"

Gabe chuckled, the knot in his chest easing. "Too much."

"Give me the short version."

Gabe exhaled and let it spill—Seb, the move, the doubts, all of it and then some. Will leaned back, listening with that steady focus Gabe had always leaned on. His brother could push his buttons like no one else, but when it mattered, Will was a rock.

"Alright," Will said, stretching his legs across the chaise, ice clinking as he sipped. "Let's break it down."

They started with Seb, swapping stories that pulled laughter from the pain. Like the time Seb shaved Jimmy Milligan's eyebrows at a sleepover, earning him a lifetime ban from the Milligan house. "Poor kid," Will said, wiping his eyes. "Good thing they grew back."

On Nicolet and the doubts, Will waved a hand. "Bayshore's not going anywhere. If you want to get back there, you will."

"Easy for you to say," Gabe muttered.

"It is," Will admitted with a grin. "I've learned life's too short to overthink, Shorty. One step at a time."

Gabe snorted but didn't argue. Will shifted gears. "About Lexi's imaginary family—let her have it. Elena's right—she'll outgrow it."

"I hate them, Will, and they're not even real."

"Tough. She's a kid, and this is what she needs right now." Will leaned forward. "Speaking of Elena ..."

"We weren't," Gabe said, his voice as dry as the scotch he was drinking.

"She's something else, Gabe. You're crazy not to make a move."

"She's my employee."

"She's the district's employee," Will corrected.

"You know what I mean. I'm her boss. It's against the rules, kind of."

"Break the rules for once."

Gabe swiveled his head in a slow no. It wasn't his style. "Anyway, she's not interested."

Will arched an eyebrow. "How do you figure that?"

"I've got good radar."

"Your radar's off, man. She's just good at hiding it. No dad around growing up, had mom issues—she's probably just as tangled up in the head with love as you are. You could help each other out." His grin turned wicked.

Gabe sipped, the ice cold against his lips, and stayed silent on the topic of his radar. "I guess you two covered a lot of ground when you veered off together tonight." He'd been pushing Lexi on the swing and tried not to feel jealous as they'd walked to the creek side by side, heads close in conversation.

"Calm down. She didn't say all that much, but I know how to read between the lines." Will sat back and hesitated. "Listen, I wasn't going to bring this up, but ... I saw Kaena. She was singing at Poppy's Bar when I visited Tommy back in Hawaii last year."

"A year ago?" Gabe set his glass down, slow and deliberate. "And you're just telling me now?"

"I didn't think it'd be helpful."

"And now it is?"

"Yeah. Do you want to hear it or not?"

Gabe reclaimed his glass and leaned back, cushions creaking under his weight. He didn't, but now he had to. "Fine."

"Long story short, she's doing good. Happy. Her dad passed and left her the house. She lives there with her boyfriend now."

The words landed like a punch. Kaena was living in a literal paradise with her new man—surfing by day and singing by night. Carefree as ever. His fingers gripped the armrest until his knuckles grew pale.

"She asked about you and Lexi," Will added.

"So, she *does* remember her daughter."

Will ignored his sarcasm. "I said you were both doing great. Played it up a bit."

"Thanks," Gabe muttered.

"She looked good, Gabe."

"I don't want to hear that."

"Called herself a monster, and of course I didn't argue." Will paused. "She's still that free spirit, you know? That's why it never would have worked. I told you that once. Maybe, in a way, it's better she left when she did. Lexi doesn't remember her."

Gabe's laugh was sharp, bitter. "Yeah, well, I do remember. She left me, and she *abandoned* her kid. Signed away her rights like it was nothing. What kind of mother, what kind of wife, does that?"

"Listen, I'm not defending her. But Lexi has no memory of her, Gabe. Isn't that better than the alternative?"

"Is there a point to this story? How does this help me?"

"The point is, she's moved on." Will's voice was quiet, but firm. "You need to do the same."

"You don't get it." Gabe leaned forward, elbows on his knees, glass dangling between them. "You don't know what it's like to lose—"

Will stood, draining his scotch in one swallow.

"Will—" Gabe followed his brother as he crossed the living room to the kitchen. "What the hell just happened?"

"I'm tired." He rinsed his glass.

Gabe's eyes dropped to Will's hands and the painful scars that marred them. And these were only the visible ones. "You lost someone," he said quietly, "and not just Tommy."

Will turned, water dripping from his fingers, his expression inscrutable. "We'll talk about it tomorrow." He brushed past Gabe as he headed for the guest room.

Gabe set down his own glass and stood rooted next to the sink. Tomorrow, he'd push again. For now, the weight of their words tugged at him like a rusted anchor snagged in his ribs.

Chapter 12

The next week zipped by, a blur of summer days that kept Elena's mind busy—mostly. At night, her worries crept in, nibbling at her peace. She'd never be truly homeless, not with her aunt's couch as a fallback, but her apartment hunt was hopeless. Every lead took her to a dead end. During the day, she was able to push it all aside, pouring her energy into Lexi and her work for Gabe.

Will's presence at the house was a bright spot. They'd fallen into an easy friendship, swapping stories over coffee or Lexi's tea parties without digging too deep into old wounds. One morning, as Lexi set up her toy horses on the porch, Will leaned against the railing and grinned at Elena. "*Oye, maestra, ¿cómo se dice* 'hammer' *en Puerto Rico?*"

Elena laughed, setting down her mug. Will loved comparing the language differences between Spain and Puerto Rico. "*Martillo*, same as in Spain. And your accent's getting better, *soldado*."

"*Gracias*," he said, winking at Lexi, who clapped and demanded, "More Spanish!"

Elena obliged, teaching her "*caballo*" for horse, her heart lifting as Lexi mimicked her with a giggle. Moments like these, with Lexi's trust growing, felt like small victories. The girl who once hid behind Gabe now tugged Elena's hand to share secrets or begged for piggyback rides.

Will stretched and pushed away from the railing, glancing at the house's sturdy frame as he moved around the porch. "You know, this place is solid—two-by-six construction, not the usual two-by-four. Makes for better insulation, deeper window jambs. It gives it that rich, classic vibe." He tapped the doorframe, eyes alight. "Solid core doors inside, too. Gabe didn't skimp."

Elena raised an eyebrow, half-teasing. "You sound like you miss it—building things."

"I do," he admitted, his voice softer. "I worked construction before I enlisted. That's what I thought I'd be doing in the service, but they threw me into special forces instead. Turned out I was good at leading, not just hammering nails."

"Your dad has a company, right?" Elena asked, catching the spark in his gaze. "Why not get back into it?"

Will's smile was slow, knowing. "I've been thinking about it." He knocked on the frame again, like he was testing a promise.

He'd finally called his parents a few days ago to tell them he was back, and they'd sped over from Bayshore to Nicolet, their reunion spilling late into the night. Elena hadn't been there to meet them, and she was curious about them.

"They want me to come home," Will told her the next day, "but I need to hide out here at Gabe's a little longer."

"Hide out?" she asked.

"Once I go back"—he swept his hand—"there goes my privacy."

"I've driven through there a few times," she told him. "Small town."

"*Very* small town," he agreed. "And I love it there, I really do, but ... I'm not ready to leave yet."

Elena's lips curved into a fond smile. "*Bueno*. I'm not ready for you to go, and Lexi definitely isn't ready."

Sometimes Elena felt like she'd known Lexi forever. No barriers remained between them, and Lexi's giggles—free and spontaneous—filled the house. Gabe said she was her old self again, and Elena took quiet pride in knowing she'd helped make that happen. Having Will there added another layer to the dynamic and made it all even more fun.

Every moment with Will and Lexi deepened Elena's bond with them, while her connection with Gabe stayed frustratingly distant. Their interactions were like a hesitant dance—each step forward met with a subtle retreat, a rhythm she couldn't quite master. Lately, he seemed even more far away, and she wondered why. Was it work pressing down on him or guilt over time lost with Lexi? Was it her? His piercing glances often had her wondering if he disapproved of her or if she'd done something wrong, but then he'd smile—eyes crinkling at the corners—and the air would hum, charged with an unnamed energy that stole her breath.

Still, one thing shone through her uncertainty: Will's presence was good for Gabe. The older brother unlocked a side of him she hadn't known existed, like a musty room aired out by a flung-open window. Gabe's dry humor came to life in Will's orbit, and his laugh—deep and unguarded—rang out more often, a sound that stirred her despite their distance. She'd seen it just that morning: Will had swiped Gabe's keys and dangled them high with a smirk. "Jump, Shorty," he'd teased, calling him by the nickname Elena still didn't quite understand. Will had Gabe in height, but not by much.

Gabe lunged, pinning Will's arm in a swift tussle until the keys hit the floor. "You may be taller, but I was always faster," he shot back, his laugh edged with triumph. Their roughhousing was a messy, lively echo that always coaxed a grin from her, even as she lingered on the edges, murmuring "*hermanos locos*" to herself with a shake of her head.

One Thursday at the end of June, while Lexi played in the backyard, Elena and Will lingered over their lunch at the patio table. "The house has been shown five times already, and it sounds like there's an offer coming in as I speak," she confided, burying her face in her hands. "Where am I going to go?"

"What about your cousin?" he asked with a mouthful of sandwich.

Elena hadn't touched much of her own sandwich. "She offered. She always offers."

"So, then what's the problem?"

Elena tried not to stare at his hands and forearms as he reached into the bag of potato chips, one of many contraband food items he'd snuck into the house. Obviously, the guy had been burned pretty significantly, but Elena didn't think it was her place to ask him about it. "The problem is, she's offering out of obligation. She's engaged. What engaged couple building their life together wants someone living with them? I'd be there and in the way every morning at coffee, every night at dinner, and all night long every single night."

"Good point." He took another overly-large bite, leaving a blob of mayonnaise on his upper lip.

She tried to imagine him in a pair of fatigues, barking orders at his troops, and couldn't. If Elena had felt any romantic interest in Will, it would have disappeared in that moment. "You've got a little something here," she pointed at her own mouth.

He had the grace to look embarrassed as he wiped it with a napkin, but it only smeared. "Thanks. What about your aunt?"

Elena wrinkled her nose. "Is this how all soldiers eat?" She handed him her own napkin.

He grinned and gave his mouth another self-conscious wipe. "Hey, I have impeccable manners compared to some."

She raised her eyebrows skeptically but didn't argue. "I have an offer there too," she said instead, "but my aunt's condo has only one bedroom, so I'd be on the couch."

He shrugged. "Stay here then."

Elena laughed. "Yeah, right."

"Why not?"

The truth was, she'd thought of that—for about half a second—and dismissed the idea completely before it could take hold. "Gabe doesn't want me around any more than I already am," she blurted before she could stop herself.

Will treated her to a puzzled stare. "Why do you say that?"

"I can just tell."

"You're wrong."

"I'm not wrong."

He set his sandwich down and stared at her long and hard. "Elena, I'm telling you, you're wrong. Gabe is—"

She leaned in, somehow knowing he was about to reveal something important, but then he shifted his gaze. "Never mind, just trust me on this one."

She didn't ask him what he'd been about to say. She was focused instead on asking a question she'd been dying to get an answer for. "Will, what happened with Lexi's mom?"

Will dropped his napkin on the table and leaned back in his chair. "Kaena."

A pretty name. Elena immediately disliked her. "Tell me about her."

"Where to begin? She did a real number on him. Lexi, too."

Chapter 13

G abe stopped at the sound of his ex-wife's name. He stood in front of the screen of the sliding glass door in disbelief. Will was talking about Kaena? To Elena? He ought to make his presence known right now and stop his brother from revealing anything more, but he was frozen in place.

"They met in Hawaii when I was stationed there," his brother explained. "Gabe came to visit me. He was a lot different then. You wouldn't have recognized him. Younger, obviously. And carefree." He laughed. "Man, did the ladies love him, but he never got too invested, you know? Kaena, she was different from the beginning. He fell hard. Shocked the heck out of me, to be honest. But she was this totally free spirit, and it was never going to work. She left when Lexi was two. I tried to warn him, but he was a goner from the moment he laid eyes on her."

Damn those eyes, Gabe thought. He wished they'd never spotted Kaena that night at the ocean-side bar, although he couldn't quite wish for that, could he? Because he'd gotten Lexi out of the deal, and he couldn't imagine life without her.

"*Pobrecito.*" Elena's soft voice was full of pity, and it curled his stomach.

He slid the screen door open a little harder than he'd intended.

Guilt flashed in their eyes as he closed the door more gently behind him and joined them at the table. He pulled out a chair, jaw tight, and sat, letting the silence stretch.

Will watched him. "Shorty—"

"We'll discuss it later," Gabe cut in, eyes fixed elsewhere.

"Daddy!" Lexi shouted when she spotted him. She dropped the hose she'd been using to fill a bucket, which Gabe had no doubt was teeming with frogs—and ran to him, fueled by enthusiasm and wild energy. It was a welcome distraction.

Later that night, once the house was quiet, Gabe sat alone on the sofa, glass of water in hand, with nothing to distract him as he let his thoughts drift back.

He rarely let himself think about that night, but when he did, the memories were vivid. He could still hear the waves crashing at that beachside bar and the first note Kaena had sung on stage.

He hadn't been able to tear his eyes away. She was a Hawaiian goddess with an angel's voice, and her skin glowed in the sunset's fiery blaze. She was the most exquisite female he'd ever seen in real life, and she was looking straight at him. He nodded, a twenty-six-year-old playing it cool. Her smile back was electric.

She owned his attention since the moment she took the stage, and Will didn't miss it.

"Yo, Gabe," his older brother said, waving a hand in front of him once he realized Gabe had completely tuned out his story.

Gabe blinked. He turned away from the stage and looked at his table companions. "My bad." He took a swig of Corona.

Will grinned. "She's hot, I'll give you that." He turned to his buddy, Tommy. "He's always had a thing for exotic beauties."

"Not me, man," Tommy said, eyeing up a bottle blonde at the bar. "I'm going for that one." He stood. "Wish me luck."

Gabe barely glanced up. Barbie wasn't his type. The goddess on the other hand ... "I'm taking that one home tonight," he told his brother, "or I'll die trying."

Will laughed and clapped Gabe on the shoulder. "Yeah, that's not happening, Shorty. Control center's closed for the night."

Gabe pulled a face. He'd forgotten that. Hickam Air Force Base was locked down tight as a drum at night. "You're the special forces commander. You're telling me you can't pull a few strings?"

Reaching over and tousling Gabe's hair, Will laughed. "Can't risk national security just so you can have a little fun, Shorty."

"It'd be more than just a little fun," Gabe said, grinning. "And who put you in charge, anyway."

"The U.S. government, and I've got the stripes to prove it." Will smirked, leaning back in his chair like he owned the place.

Gabe resisted the urge to push him over and took another swig from the bottle. "Climbing the ranks to Lieutenant Colonel doesn't change the fact that Mom still calls you 'Willy.'"

Tommy slumped back, interrupting their bickering. "Husband showed up," he muttered, as Gabe glimpsed Ken glaring over at them from the bar.

"Just as well," Will said, signaling for the bill. "Time to roll—We gotta be up at zero dark thirty tomorrow."

"Not yet," Gabe pleaded, locking eyes with the singer again. Her slow, knowing smile hit him like a wave. "I need her number."

Will stood, pulling his wallet from his back pocket. "I'm not waiting."

Gabe flagged a waiter for a pen and napkin. Quickly, he scribbled his name and number.

"What are you doing?" Will leaned over to look and groaned. "What are you, some bar fly? Where's your self respect?"

Ignoring him, Gabe pulled a twenty from his wallet and rolled it up in the napkin. "Be right back."

Gabe strode to the stage. Mockingly, Will called after him, "A whole twenty? Watch out, Shorty. She'll take one look at that big bill and jump right off that stage and into your high-rolling arms."

Gabe heard their laughter behind him as he dropped the money and napkin into her tip jar. She nodded, her eyes sparkling her thanks, and he grinned back.

He took his share of ribbing on the ride back to base, their laughter loud and boisterous as he gave as good as he got. "Fifty bucks says she calls," he said, "and I'll throw in a hula dance if I'm wrong."

She called.

Three days later, Gabe was a tangle of emotions as he eyed his brother's suitcase resting next to the door. He was sad to see him go.

It was Sunday morning, the first day of July, and Lexi was busy playing horses in her room as Gabe made the coffee. Will said he'd sit with him over a cup before hitting the road. As he watched the coffee drip into the carafe, Gabe thought back to the first time Will had left home. His mother had cried, and Gabe had wanted to. He'd been ten years old and had idolized an older brother who'd always been good to him. Having Will close by had felt like a security blanket, and Gabe could remember those first few days without him—how adrift he'd felt.

It wasn't all that different from the way he was feeling now, even though his brother was only going to Bayshore, which was less than an hour away, and Gabe and Lexi would be following close behind on Tuesday. They were spending the week of the Fourth of July as a family for the first time in a long time. It had only been ten days since Will's arrival in Nicolet, but Gabe had gotten used to having him around, and he couldn't help but wish it wasn't coming to an end.

True, it had bugged him a little how easily his brother and Elena had gotten on together, and he'd found himself retreating from her as if he were some kind of sulking child. Early on, and very briefly, he'd wondered if there was something brewing between his brother and his nanny, but he'd quickly dismissed the idea. They acted like long-lost siblings more than would-be lovers, and that soothed Gabe's wounded pride somewhat, but he was still jealous. And he was still hot that Will had stuck his nose in and told Elena about Kaena. Will's apology had tamped down the inferno, but the embers still smoldered. He'd cool off eventually, but not today. Now it was his turn to get into Will's business. He'd been patient enough.

When Will joined him in the living room, Gabe told him he was done waiting. "Later is now, Will. Spill it."

His brother gave a resigned sigh. "I guess I'll be talking about this soon enough with Mom and Dad anyway. Might as well practice on you." After a tentative sip of coffee, Will set his mug down on the coaster and looked Gabe in the eye. "I've been a mess," he said candidly. "Even before the ship was bombed"—he lifted a hand as if to stave off any questions—"which I can't tell you much about since it's still classified."

"But you can tell me *some* things."

Will agreed. "But I think I need to start with Afghanistan."

Gabe knew the story, more or less. Will and ten of his men had been on a covert mission to disrupt a Taliban weapons cache just outside of Kandahar when their Black Hawk was shot down. Three of Will's men had died in that mission. They hadn't died in the crash, however. Miraculously, everyone on board survived. They'd died later, on the ground, taking enemy fire for nearly two hours as they'd waited for help to arrive. Gabe knew all that, but what he hadn't known was what Will said next.

"I relived those hours every night for months. *Months*, Gabe. No exaggeration. It got to where I would do anything I could think of to keep myself awake. I was ... afraid," he admitted sheepishly "to fall asleep. I was so sleep deprived, making stupid mistakes and feeling like a shell of myself. But then, I got some help, and it got better. It got *a little* better," he clarified. "But when they bombed the Sleuth, and then Tommy ..." he looked at Gabe helplessly as he swallowed a few times. "Shorty, I think it broke me. I'm broken, and I don't know ..." He lifted his hands, palms up in baffled surrender. "You know I'm not that guy. I'm not weak. But when I was walking through the flames, holding on to Tommy with my sleeves on fire ..."

"You carried Tommy out?"

Will gave a quick nod and blinked several times rapidly. "He was already gone."

Gabe couldn't imagine. He could only shake his head and stare at his brother in sympathy.

"I lost more than Tommy. There were others. There was ... a woman. I think maybe you guessed that already. It wasn't serious, but I thought it might—" He cleared his throat. "We'd only been on a few dates, but she was sweet. She was so sweet." Will swiped a hand over his face. "Anyway, I'm done. I can't go back to that life. My doctor, the shrink, she signed all the documentation. So that's that. They gave me a medal." He laughed bitterly. "Go figure, I get an award for bravery and then early retirement for being such a coward. Which is it, huh? I don't know."

Gabe knew. Will was an American hero, and he told Will so. His brother gave a brief nod, not accepting the compliment but not really rejecting it either. Will explained that his insomnia was worse than ever since the bombing. Unable to sleep more than a few hours a night, he was running on fumes. He claimed it was a little better at Gabe's house than it had been at Rota, but not by much, and he'd wandered the house at night and had even walked the property a time or two.

If only Gabe had known, he could have kept his brother company. He wasn't sleeping well these days either, but for different reasons. He fell asleep just fine, but for the last five nights, he'd wake up after an hour or two in a muck sweat, and that would be it. Elena Torres was tormenting him in his sleep, and they definitely weren't catching rainbows in jars in these dreams. What's more, the dreams were so real, so vivid, that he could hardly look her in the eye in the light of day.

He wanted her. He admitted it. His body was screaming out for her. During the day, he could control it, but at night—He didn't know what to do about it.

He refocused on his brother. Being up at night over a woman was hard enough. Gabe couldn't imagine being up at night reliving the memories Will had been reliving. A wave of guilt washed over him for thinking about his own lack of sleep. "I'm sorry, Will. What can I do?"

His brother's lips curled into a tired smile, though it reached his eyes. "You're already doing it, Shorty."

Chapter 14

W ill had done it. He'd talked about the bombing to someone other than a therapist, and he hadn't crumbled under the shame of admitting his weakness. There was hope. As he lifted his heavy luggage into the back of his truck, he felt lighter than he had in some time. There was just one more thing left to say to his brother before he took off, and it wasn't until his car was loaded and the engine was running that he came clean.

"You did *what?*" Gabe thundered.

Will shushed him before looking across the driveway at Lexi who was splashing happily at her water table. "She's about to be evicted—more or less—and her family's tied up for the week. She'd be all alone. How could I *not* invite her?"

"By *not* inviting her," Gabe snapped.

"Lexi wants her to come. She thinks it'll be fun."

Gabe's expression shifted to disbelief that Lexi knew anything about the plan.

"I told her it was a secret," Will added, brushing off a twinge of guilt. This was for Gabe's own good.

Gabe lowered his voice. "Lexi thinks she has a whole glitter family out in the woods, too, Will. I don't think she's the best person to consult on this kind of thing. You shouldn't have involved her."

"*Sparkle* family," Will corrected. "And inviting Elena was the right thing to do." It was also necessary. Will knew his brother better than anyone, and he'd grown close to Elena during his stay. It was obvious: Gabe and the nanny were meant for each other, but their brief daily interactions weren't enough for them to see it.

They needed some time together: a week in Bayshore, with Gabe free from work and more relaxed. But Elena would never go unless she thought Gabe had issued the invitation, hence the white lie he'd told her. They'd leave tomorrow, Monday, which meant Elena would be expecting Gabe to firm up plans today. If Will couldn't persuade his brother to do that, it wouldn't take long for Elena to realize she hadn't been invited by Gabe at all. His brother had to call her, and he needed to be convincing. He told him so.

"No," Gabe said, doubling down.

"What's with you anyway? You act so weird around her. Especially the last few days."

Will watched the color creep up Gabe's neck. He was definitely on the right track. "C'mon, Gabe. While we're all celebrating, she'll be sitting by herself in the house that's being sold out from under her."

Gabe looked at him, speculation gleaming in his eyes. He wagged a finger as he spoke. "I know what this is. You have the hots for her."

A slow smile spread across Will's face. "That's true for one of us, Shorty, but I'll give you a hint—it's not me."

Gabe hesitated before looking at his feet. "All the more reason not to have her come along."

Will suppressed a grin. "At least you can admit it now."

Heaving a sigh, Gabe looked up. "All that does is humiliate me. It doesn't change anything." He ticked off his fingers. "She doesn't see me that way, she's my child's nanny, and she's my subordinate at work and off limits."

Will counted off on his own fingers, "She's been hurt by men and is understandably cautious, she loves your daughter, and you wouldn't be the first high-level school administrator to marry a teacher."

Gabe looked thunderstruck. "Marry! Who said anything about marrying?"

"Well? Isn't that what you're looking for?"

"Hell no."

"Alright, listen, here's the truth." Will had known of one sure-fire way to get Gabe to agree to his plan, but he only wanted to use it if all else failed, and it had. Even if Gabe had agreed to let her come along as a guest, he'd never be able to convince her that it was his idea. If Elena caught even a hint of reluctance by Gabe, she wouldn't come. Here it was. His final tactic. Will schooled his features, hoping he looked grave. "I love Lexi, you know I do, but she requires a lot of focused attention, and I need you this week. I need Mom and Dad—time to talk to you all about some tough things without Lexi underfoot all the time."

"About what happened? Or about what your next move is?"

"About everything. It's Independence Day, Gabe. My first Fourth of July in twenty-one years where I'm a civilian, not a soldier. I'm trying to figure out my next chapter, and I need my family for that. And here's another thing: I know Elena needs the money. She's in a bad spot, Shorty. It's win-win for everyone. I could even help to pay her for the week since I have the feeling she won't come as a guest. She's got this thing about being a burden to people. But if she knows she's needed, that's different. If you tell her we need her for the week, and you're sorry for the last-minute ask, I bet she'd say yes. I *need* her to say yes, Gabe," he urged, laying it on as thick as he dared.

Gabe's face softened with regret. "Why didn't you just say so from the start? Of course I'll ask her."

"Thanks." And for good measure he added, "It's hard to ask for help some-times."

Guilt poured over Will as Gabe gripped his shoulder, his voice steady. "I know it is, but I'm really glad you did."

That night, as he was staring at the ceiling of his childhood bedroom, Will admitted something to himself. What he'd said to Gabe, the reason he'd given, it might have felt like an exaggeration in the moment, but the truth was, he did need his family for the next few days, and for all the reasons he'd mentioned. It would be great to finally be home, but like the Carhartts that still hung in his closet from high school, he knew life in Bayshore wouldn't quite fit anymore. He could no more squeeze back into that old life than he could into those pants, and he didn't know what to do with that.

Will felt the contents of his stomach turn over, and then the sweating began. He flipped on the lamp beside his bed and planted his feet on the cold floor. With a resigned shake of his head, he grabbed the pills from the drawer of the nightstand.

Chapter 15

Monday came quickly, and before she knew it, Elena was on her way to Bayshore. With Leila and Jackson vacationing out of town and *Tía* Carmen visiting a friend in Grand Rapids for the week, Elena would've been rattling around Nicolet with nothing much to do except fret about apartments that no landlord would be showing over the holiday anyway. The chance to escape to the beautiful little town of Bayshore with Gabe and his family sparked a quiet excitement inside of her. Maybe it was the idea of a week away, or maybe, she admitted to herself, it was knowing she'd be spending so much time with *him*. Gabe. Her feelings toward him were shifting in her mind, and she didn't think she could deny or ignore it anymore.

The drive started chatty, with Lexi going a mile a minute about her purple sparkle heels and the blueberry picking she hoped to do during their visit, her little voice filling the Suburban. Elena had gotten good at making the right "mm-hmms" and "oh, wows" to keep her going, letting her tune out just enough to rest her brain. But ten minutes in, Lexi yawned, curled up, and dozed off, leaving the car in a silent hush. Elena tried tossing a few questions Gabe's way—simple stuff about the route, the weather—but he seemed distracted, his answers short, his eyes trained on the road like it held some big secret. So she let it go, settling into a semi-comfortable silence where she let her thoughts drift.

As they rolled into Bayshore, Gabe came alive again. "My parents live up there on the bluff," he said, pointing out her window at a ridge thick with trees. "In a minute, you'll see the house through the leaves."

"What color is it?" she asked, leaning toward the glass and looking up.

"Red."

And there it was—a flash of red peeking out from the lush green. "That's way up there," she noted, thinking of the island she'd called home where hills like these inspired stories of old-time *jíbaros* chasing goats in the Cordillera Central. And just like that, Elena's stomach rumbled. *Jíbaros* were hard-working Puerto Rican farmers found on the island's hilly interior, but thinking of them also brought her favorite sandwich to mind. The *jíbarito* was a tasty Puerto Rican sandwich created as a tribute to the tireless *jíbaros*, and Elena hadn't had one in ages. Maybe she could get *Tía* Carmen to make her one when she got back from her trip.

She glanced at Gabe who shot her a smile. "You should see the road that leads up to the house. I slid down it a time or two on my way to school growing up. And over there—he pointed to a small marina hugging the shore—"that's where I spent my time every summer when I wasn't working a construction site. My best friend had a boat, and we didn't even have to take it out to have a good time. We'd just sit in the harbor drinking beer and watching the town go by."

Elena pictured him—young and tanned, sitting in a boat full of girls, and a smirk tugged at her lips. *Pobrecito*. All that charm, and where had it gone? She stole another glance at him now, his profile sharp against the sunlight, hands steady on the wheel. Some of it was still there, she admitted. And knowing a bit about his ex-wife—how she'd left and what a mess it had made—had softened her toward him. Any lingering grudge she'd had left over after that morality meeting, where she'd pegged him as a high-and-mighty *engreído*, had disappeared. The more she learned about him, the harder it was to cling to that opinion. He wasn't just the superintendent anymore. He was Gabe—complicated, kind, and a little too good looking for *her* own good. A small thrill zipped through her.

"Daddy, can we pick blueberries tomorrow?" Lexi's sleepy voice piped up from the back, punctuated by a yawn.

Elena turned, smiling as the girl rubbed her eyes and waved.

"We're here, Elena."

"We are, *cariña*."

"Like I said, it might be early for blueberries, kiddo," Gabe replied, "but we had a warm spring, so we'll check. Maybe we'll get lucky."

"I like picking blueberries," Lexi told Elena, perking up. "We know the best spots."

"Where?" Elena asked, trying to picture Gabe doing something so ... earthy.

"Kinsey Plains," Gabe answered. "In the middle of the Sandstone Rocks National Lakeshore."

"Oh," she murmured, nodding like it all clicked. The truth was, she had no idea where half the places she heard about in the U.P. were located. She'd driven through Bayshore a couple of times, marveling at the brick storefronts and old homes. The sandstone cliffs loomed in the distance, ferry boats dotting the water with tourists on board. She'd never taken the tour, but she wanted to one day. Her *mamacita* would have enjoyed something like that.

And there it was, that rootless ache that never quite went away. As much as she was looking forward to a week with Gabe's family, it felt a lot like stepping into someone else's life. Even Lexi felt different here. At home, Elena was her favorite by default—the only one there. But in Bayshore, with doting grandparents, Uncle Will, and Gabe all vying for her attention, where would Elena fit? She worried Lexi might push her aside, a silly fear to have about a six-year-old, but real all the same.

Gabe had sworn she was needed for this trip, though he hadn't really said why—just offered her fifteen hundred dollars for the week and apologized for the short notice. She'd jumped at it, no hesitation. Now, though, she wondered if she should've paused and thought it through. These people, this place—it was all unfamiliar, and Gabe ... he left her unsettled in the best of circumstances. She was *aware* of him now, every move, every word, and it left her off-balance.

Gabe turned, navigating the Suburban up a steep hill that dead-ended and turned into an equally steep driveway that wound its way to the top of the bluff. The red house came into view, and Elena forgot to breathe. It was a stunning home, the exterior a deep, rich crimson that was softened by crisp white trim framing the windows and doors. The house sprawled across a well-manicured lawn, and the wide, welcoming porch was adorned with rocking chairs and flower baskets that invited a visitor to sit and rest and watch the hummingbirds at the feeder near the steps.

"We're here!" Lexi chirped again. "I can't wait to show you my room, Elena. It's got purple color on the walls and unicorn blankets."

"I can't wait to see it," Elena said, catching Gabe's eye. He smiled, soft and quick, and her stomach flipped.

"And Mimi has cookies and Daddy hasta let me eat them, 'cause that's the rule," Lexi went on, "and Papa tells so many jokes, and we eat dinner together every night, and in the summer we eat on the patio where we can see the lake, and Uncle Will's here, too, and Mosie, and it's gonna be so fun. We'll be happy every day."

Elena shared another look with Gabe, her lips curving into a grin that mirrored his. "I can't wait."

As Gabe pulled up to the house, the front porch door swung open, revealing his parents' beaming faces. Clearly, they'd been watching for their arrival. The moment Gabe parked, Lexi's door flew open, and her grandmother leaned in, unbuckling her seatbelt and sweeping her into a warm hug in one swift motion.

"There's my granddaughter," the woman gushed. "What took you so long?"

Elena looked on, a silent observer. This family, this warmth—it wasn't hers, but she'd borrow it for a week.

Lexi giggled as her grandmother passed her to the arms of her grandfather. "Daddy was on the phone with work and he was really yelling. He had a mad voice, and it took a long time to get to leave our house to drive here to see you because his phone kept ringing and every time he was just madder and madder."

The older woman responded with a hum of disapproval, and Elena watched as mother and son met eyes. Some kind of silent communication passed between them, but Elena wasn't sure what was said and what was heard. Having spent a fair amount of time in Gabe's home, Elena had picked up on a few things. Nothing specific, but it was obvious that Gabe's work wasn't always smooth sailing. Elena would never want his job, that was for sure. Gabe was in the impossible position of trying to keep everyone in the district and community happy. She wondered what that did to his own happiness.

"Yelling?" her grandfather asked. "Not *my* son," he said with a wink directed at Elena before he set Lexi down and extended his hand. "It's good to meet you, Elena. We've heard a lot about you. I'm Theo, and this here's Emma."

Elena greeted Gabe's parents with a warm smile and marveled at how youthful they looked—far too young to have grown sons. Emma was radiant, her auburn hair gleaming in the sunlight. Beside her, Theo's bright eyes sparkled with vitality.

Lexi's grandmother smiled. "We've talked on the phone, but it's wonderful to meet you in person, Elena. We're thrilled to have you here for the next few days." She glanced at her husband. "We hardly ever get company, right Theo? And now we have a houseful."

Theo chuckled and tugged at his waistband. "Emma here's been baking up a storm, too. I'm in real trouble."

Lexi tipped her head up to look at her grandmother. "Did you make cookies, Mimi?"

Emma tousled Lexi's hair. "You know I wouldn't bake cookies without my cookie monster here to help me. You and Elena can enjoy some on the porch later."

Elena laughed. "Please, I'm here to work. No special treatment."

"Nonsense," Emma said, waving a hand. "You're a guest in our house, and we want you to feel right at home."

Theo nodded. "Now, you go on and head inside. Emma will show you your room while us men handle the luggage."

"I'll show her, Papa!" Lexi chirped, darting toward the porch. "Come on, Elena!"

Elena followed Lexi and Emma into the house while Gabe and his father unpacked the car.

Excitedly, Lexi pointed things out to her. "This is the chair where I do my coloring, and this is where Mimi does the laundry, and over here is where Mosie sleeps ..." She looked around. "Hey, Mimi, where's Mosie?"

"Your Uncle Will has her down at the beach to tire her out," Emma answered. "Maybe we should take you there too," she teased, giving Lexi a gentle pinch on the cheek. To Elena she said, "Mosie is our dog."

"She's a mutt," Lexi explained gravely. "Papa rescued her 'cause nobody wanted her, and Daddy says she's so far on the end of ugly, that she turns back to cute again." Lexi's brow furrowed. "I don't get it, but he always says it, right Mimi?"

"He does," Emma agreed with a smile.

"You'll love Mosie, Elena. She sleeps with me and the unicorns. I like to snuggle her."

Elena loved dogs. It had been a recent discovery when Jackson gifted Leila two lab puppies at Christmas. Those two were the sweetest, and she missed them. "I can't wait to meet her."

Lexi and Emma showed Elena her room, which overlooked the small marina they'd passed on their way in. Elena could see the sandstone cliffs rising off to the right of the bay, their rugged edges stretching toward the horizon where Lake Superior's deep blue merged seamlessly with the sky. The day, already clear and warm, promised to become sun-drenched, stirring inside of Elena the irresistible longing to step onto the beach and feel the sand beneath her feet. Maybe she could take Lexi there for the afternoon and look for Will.

It wasn't long before Gabe delivered her suitcase, and after taking some time to freshen up in the en suite bathroom, Elena was ready for action. She made her way back down to the kitchen where she found Emma and Lexi working some batter at the kitchen counter. "Cookies?" she guessed.

"Uh-huh," Lexi answered without looking up.

"Can I get you anything, Elena?" Emma asked. "Lunch will be ready at noon, but if you're hungry now, I could whip up a light snack."

Elena thanked her, but declined the offer. "I was thinking I might explore a bit with Lexi, but it looks like she's content right now," she said, her voice tinged with hesitation. "Is there anything I can do to help?"

"Lexi's set for the next hour or two, so you're free to take some time for yourself," Emma replied, glancing up from the measuring cups with a warm smile. "I hope you don't mind having some down time here and there. We don't get to see Lexi as much as we'd like."

Elena leaned against the kitchen counter, her fingers fidgeting. "I wasn't sure what this would look like," she admitted. "I still don't know where I fit in here, so will you tell me when I'm needed?"

Emma set the cups down and gently took Elena's hand. Her eyes were kind. "I can appreciate that confusion. I think what we should do is come at this the way a family would. We'll all pitch in wherever we're needed, and when we want to take a little time for ourselves this week, we'll let each other know. Does that sound okay to you?"

Elena nodded and smiled when Emma gave her hand a squeeze before turning back to her preparations. "I think while you're baking, I'll just explore a little. How close is that beach you mentioned where Will has the dog?"

Emma lifted her hands enthusiastically. "Oh, that's a great idea. It's only a ten-minute walk from here. You'll take a left at the end of the road and walk down the rest of that hill to—"

"I'll go with her," Gabe's voice interrupted from behind. Elena turned, breath catching as she saw him standing there—swim trunks, a faded tee clinging to his shoulders, a towel slung around his neck. The casual ease of him—so different from the buttoned-up superintendent she knew.

"Oh, are you swimming?" She hated how her voice wavered.

"Thought I would," he said, his hazel eyes steady on hers. "You?"

"I've never been." She winced as the words slipped out, knowing how stupid they sounded.

"You've never been swimming?" Theo chimed in, stepping into the kitchen, his eyes twinkling with mischief. "Didn't you grow up on an island surrounded by water?"

"Theo!" Emma admonished.

Elena's cheeks burned, but she caught the tease in his tone. "I meant in Lake Superior. I tried once, but it was ice cold."

Theo waved a hand. "It's warm this time of year—practically a bath."

She chuckled in spite of her embarrassment. "I've learned 'warm' to a Yooper means barely above freezing. You're either all crazy or a pack of liars."

A rumble of laughter erupted from Theo's chest, and his shoulders shook as he nodded. "Smart girl. Took Emma years to toughen up. My sweet southern belle wouldn't dip a toe in any water unless it was an eighty-degree swimming pool. But this place has a way of growing on you. By the end of this trip, you'll be diving into Superior like it's nothing."

"I doubt that very much," Elena shot back, still smiling, though her pulse ticked up as Gabe stepped closer, his presence a quiet heat at her side.

He kissed Lexi's head, murmured goodbyes to his parents, and then led Elena out the front door. The late morning air was thick with summer—warm pine and lake water—and they walked in silence until the driveway's end. Gabe was the first to speak.

"I wasn't yelling."

She blinked, turning to him. "What?"

"Lexi said I was yelling earlier. I wasn't. Just wanted you to know."

"Oh," she fumbled, caught off guard by the intensity in his eyes. "It's fine if you were."

"I know, but I wasn't. I just stood my ground, that's all." He looked away, jaw tight, like it mattered more than it should.

"Okay," she said softly, then shifted gears so the frown lines around his mouth would ease. "It will be nice to see Will again."

Gabe nodded, hands in his pockets. "It's been a while since we were home together."

"Do you guys still have a lot of friends here?"

"Some. Most leave after high school. The lucky ones come back."

"Lucky?" She tilted her head, curious.

He glanced at her, something flickering in his expression. "There's not much work here. People want to raise families where they grew up, but they can't always make it happen. The lucky ones can come back."

"Is Will staying?"

"I'd bet money on it. Roots, and all that."

"What about you?" She regretted it the moment the question left her lips. Too personal. Too close.

He stopped walking, turning to face her fully, and the weight of his gaze pinned her in place. "What about me?"

"You left," she said, quieter now. "Do you ever think about coming back?"

She could see his uncertainty as he studied her, but his answer came firm. "No." A beat passed, and he surprised her by adding, "I didn't plan to leave, but after Seb died, this place ... it didn't fit anymore."

"Seb?"

"My best friend." His voice roughened. "Everything changed after that."

"I'm sorry. Does Nicolet fit?" She kept her tone gentle, probing.

He started walking again, slower now. "I don't know. Does it fit for you?"

She matched his pace, their shoulders nearly brushing. "In some ways. Maybe we're alike, you and me—two people without a home."

He stopped again, head snapping to look at her dead on. "You think that?"

"Don't you?" she challenged, ignoring the thudding of her heart in her chest.

He didn't answer right away, just looked at her—too long, too deep—until she felt exposed, raw. "Maybe," he said finally, and that one vague word carried more weight than she'd thought possible.

The beach stretched before them, the morning sun still low and golden in the sky. Kids with buckets dotted the shore. Gabe hadn't been here in two years, but the memories hit hard—summers with Seb, chasing waves and chasing girls, and Seb spotting Marni that first time. She'd been new to town the summer they turned seventeen, all confidence and curves, and Seb had been a goner. One look, and his buddy was toast. Two years later, at the age of nineteen, they'd tied the knot. Seb had been on the receiving end of a lot of teasing, and naysayers had come out of the woodwork, but Gabe had always known that Seb and Marni were the real deal. Now Seb was gone, and Marni was a widow he'd barely spoken to since the funeral. He didn't have an excuse, and he wouldn't blame her if she never wanted to see him again.

It wasn't hard to spot Will down the beach since Mosie was the only dog there. The poor girl couldn't swim, but that didn't stop her from splashing in the shallows of the water. Gabe kept Elena close as they made their way down the beach, small talk spilling out to fill the silence, but her words—"two people without a home"—looped in his mind, gnawing at him.

He hadn't thought of it that way, but her words had struck a chord. This was what had been niggling at him for months. Bayshore had always been home. He'd never imagined a scenario where he would willingly leave it. But after the events of last summer ... Well, he'd thought a fresh start some place new would help, but the same unsettled emptiness he'd felt here had simply followed him to Nicolet. His dad's old saying crept in: *Wherever you go, there you are.* A man couldn't run from himself, but without realizing it, he'd attempted to do just that.

"Hey!" Will's shout carried across the sand. "Thought you'd never show!"

Gabe threw his arms wide. "Here we are!"

The dog, hearing Gabe's voice, quit her splashing, freezing for a fraction of a second before taking off like a dart toward them. Tongue lolling and ears flapping, she was a blur of sand and slobber.

"Incoming!" Will hollered.

Elena instinctively grabbed Gabe's arm, her fingers warm against his skin. He stepped in front of her, bracing himself as the dog launched herself into him. Elena shifted to his left just in time, and the impact sent him sprawling, air whooshing from his lungs as he hit the packed sand with a grunt. Mosie loomed over him like a predator guarding its fallen prey, and if death by licking were a real thing, it was all over for him.

Face scrunched and eyes closed, Gabe pushed against the dog's chest and told her "no" in as firm a voice as he could muster, but if anything, it only spurred her on. A shadow blocked out the sun, and Gabe opened his eyes to see Will lifting Mosie off him by her collar. Eyeing up his parents' dog as he wiped at his face, he scolded her. "They need to teach you some manners, you crazy mutt." But his words fell on deaf ears, and Mosie's tail wagged even faster, like a metronome on speed. Elena hauled him up, her grip lingering, and Gabe worked to catch his breath and restore some of his dignity while the dog pranced excitedly around his feet.

As he wiped the wet sand off his clothes, Elena released his arm and let out a peal of laughter. Soon she was snorting and doubled over with hysterics. Will joined in, the two of them clutching each other as they abandoned themselves to the hilarity.

Gabe used his shirt collar to wipe at the remaining goo on his face. "Go ahead. Yuk it up at my expense."

That made them laugh even harder, and Gabe felt his frown morph into an outright scowl. He'd just saved Elena from being leveled by the ugliest dog known to man, making himself look like a complete fool in the process, and this was all the thanks he got? Elena laughing at him with her hands all over his brother?

"I'm sorry," she gasped, shaking out his towel and stepping close to brush sand from his back. Her touch was light, but it burned through his shirt, and he froze, caught between wanting her to stop and wanting her to keep going. "It was just so funny." Her voice trembled with suppressed laughter.

Will grinned at him and clapped his shoulder. "Lighten up, Shorty. You're on vacation."

Gabe could actually taste the disappointment of a missed opportunity—the chance to lean into the moment and laugh with Elena. He asked himself what the old Gabe would have done, but he already knew. He wanted a do-over but knew it was too late to reverse course, so instead he stalked away. "I'm going for a swim," he told them over his shoulder. Their laughter followed him, tugging at something inside of him that he didn't feel like naming.

As he put distance between himself and them, their laughter faded, and so did his frustration. It was a perfect day in Bayshore, just like always this time of year. Will was right. He was on vacation, and it was time to start having some fun. For the next four days, he didn't need to be the superintendent of Nicolet Schools. He didn't need to worry about budgets, or board meetings, or policy changes. He didn't need to think about doing the grocery shopping, cooking meals, paying bills, or cleaning the house. And he definitely didn't need to think about the phone calls he'd received from Dom and Joanna that morning, or how he would handle the bomb they'd dropped in his lap.

It could wait. All of it could wait. It was only Monday, and for the next few days, he was going to relax. Lexi was happy and hadn't said a word about her sparkle family yet today, at least not to him. Will was home, most likely to stay, and a beautiful woman would be living under his parents' roof to make the whole experience extra sweet.

Elena made him feel things he didn't want to fight against feeling anymore. And today, for the first time he'd wondered if she might just be feeling the same way. Why not test the waters? He was taking a break from his life, from his responsibilities and always having to play it safe. It was time to get reacquainted with his old self, and what better place to do it than his old stomping grounds. A place he knew so well, he could navigate its streets blindfolded.

A familiar voice said his name, breaking into his thoughts and stopping him in his tracks. Gabe looked up to see a face he'd known since he was seventeen. "Marni?"

She stood up from her towel, leaving behind a woman he didn't recognize and two young children. Shading her eyes, she stopped just short of him, neither of them attempting an embrace. "I wondered if I'd see you this summer," she said simply.

"I just pulled into town."

She looked around. "Is Lexi here?"

"She's back at the house with my folks. I'm here with Lexi's nanny and Will." He gestured behind him at Will and Elena who were fast approaching.

She nodded and followed his gaze. "I remember him. It's been a long time." She looked at him then, and he wondered if she was referring to Will or to him.

She looked good. She'd chopped her blonde hair into one of those pixie cuts. It suited her. Seb would have thought so, too, but then Marni could have shaved her head, and Seb still would have thought she was the prettiest girl in town.

When Will and Elena stopped in front of them, Gabe made the introductions.

Elena smiled warmly and Will stepped forward to shake Marni's hand. "It's good to see you again, Marni."

Marni smiled softly. "Likewise."

They stood awkwardly before finding relief in the distraction of focusing on the two little boys playing in the sand, and in an instant, Gabe knew which one was Seb's. He had the same blond hair, the same nose, same chin.

"That's Sebastian in the green hat," Marni informed him, unnecessarily.

"He's adorable," Elena chimed in.

Gabe swallowed hard. "How old is he now?"

"Fifteen months."

He rubbed the back of his neck. "It's scary how time flies."

"He doesn't know you, Gabe."

"I know."

Her voice took on a sharp edge. "Why?"

Gabe looked her in the eye, his voice steady but heavy with regret. "I'm sorry, Marni. I'm really sorry. I don't have an excuse."

He watched the anger leave her body as quickly as it had arrived. She'd always been quick to forgive. He didn't deserve it.

"Come meet him."

Later that evening, after a full day of sunshine and activity, Elena sat on the four-season porch with a mug of chamomile tea cradled in her hands. The smooth water of the bay glinted in the setting sun. Emma settled in the chair beside her.

"How is it? she asked, nodding at Elena's cup of honeyed tea.

She hadn't had chamomile tea in years, and the taste of it reminded her of her childhood. Chamomile tea had been her mother's cure for whatever ailed her growing up—*gripe*, *tos*, *resfriado*. "It's perfect."

Emma rested her own mug on the table between them. "Lexi's down for the night. Thanks for letting me take over. Bath and story time were my favorite with my own boys too. I don't want to miss a moment while she's here." She sighed. "I'm already missing so many moments as it is."

Elena nodded in understanding. "It must be hard."

"Yes. At least I have someone running the shop the next few days. I run a little store for tourists, I'm not sure if you knew that. Anyway, it's all under control, and I can be fully present for this visit." Emma reached for her cup and took a careful sip.

The house was very quiet, and Elena wondered what Gabe was doing now that Lexi was asleep. "What's ... everyone doing tonight?"

"Theo was tired, so he's in bed reading. It's hard this time of year when the sky stays light until eleven, but he won't make it that long. Will is down at one of the pubs with some friends, and last I checked, Gabe was in the shower." She took another sip. "Hmm. You know, I've replaced my evening glass of wine with this, and I have to say, I like it so much better."

Elena looked at her own cup of honeyed tea. "I don't drink much anymore either."

Emma studied her with a knowing look. "Because of that TikTok movie or whatever it is you kids call it?"

Elena's mouth hung open on a silent *o*. "You *know* about that?" When Emma nodded, Elena resisted the urge to cover her face with her hands. "How?"

"Will showed me." Emma's lips twitched. "Quite the exposé on that poor man's ... assets."

Elena winced. "It's not to say I don't regret it, because believe me, I do, but that 'poor man' had it coming."

"Oh, I don't doubt that a bit, dear. I was gratified to have Will translate the parts where you were speaking in Spanish. It provided a more, shall we say, enhanced experience." She laughed. "You know, I had a man just like that once. Arrogant. Cocky. God's gift to women."

"What happened to him?"

"Last I heard, he was on his third marriage. I got lucky when I met Theo here one summer vacation, and I never looked back."

She told the story of Theo working next store to the vacation home her family had rented for the summer after her second year of college. "I watched him nailing those shingles down, and I was the smitten kitten in every way. There was an empty seat on my family's flight home."

Elena leaned in toward her. "No way."

"Oh, yes. I refused to leave with them at the end of summer." She clucked her tongue. "So headstrong. I was cut off without a cent for marrying a 'common laborer,' but once William came along, they were ready to invite us back into the fold."

"That's good. Family's too important to take for granted."

"I agree. At any rate, I'm glad you didn't settle for that billionaire. You're worth more than that."

"Let's not elevate him too high. He's only a millionaire, you know. Just your run-of-the-mill multimillionaire."

Emma laughed. "Hundreds of millions is what I heard."

Elena grinned and felt a warmth spread in her chest. She rested a hand there. "Thank you for saying I'm worth more."

"I knew right away how special you are, and I'm so glad that Gabe stood up for you."

Alarm ran through Elena's veins.

"He and that awful neurosurgeon sparred for a week over that morality clause written into teacher contracts. It's a good thing the rest of the board agreed with Gabriel. One of the few times they've shown some sense. I really don't know what goes on over there in Nicolet."

"*Espera, espera*, wait. Gabe stood up for me?"

"Of course he did." Emma stilled. "Oh dear. Have I just revealed a secret?"

"Gabe defended me to the board?" Elena asked, needing this to be clear.

But Emma was already shaking her head. "I'm so sorry. I've already said too much. Oh, Gabriel will be upset with me, as he should be. But yes, he did defend you, Elena. I thought you knew. I'm so sorry to have spoken out of turn like this." She looked at her innocent mug of tea. "I may as well be drinking wine for as loose as my tongue has become."

"He never said a word to me."

"I guess I don't know why he didn't, but I'm sure he had his reasons."

Elena set down her tea and buried her head in her hands. "I'm so embarrassed. I thought Gabe was the one who—I owe him an apology." She grimaced as she replayed it all. "I wish I could go back to that night with Marc and have a little self-control. I was just so angry."

Emma looked at her with sympathy. "Clearly, I can understand about wishing for a tad more self-control, given my blabbermouth tendencies. Regret is hard, especially when our pasts come back to haunt us."

Elena wasn't ready to move on, but she figured there was nothing more to say to Emma about the Marc incident and Gabe's hand in helping her keep her job. She'd ask him about it tonight if he came back downstairs. For now, she allowed herself to ask a question she'd been wanting an answer to all day. She figured Emma owed her one after the bomb she'd just dropped on her. Leading into her question, she said, "Gabe introduced me to someone named Marni today down at the beach."

Emma sipped her tea. "Marni Moore. She was a classmate of Gabriel's. Married his best friend, Seb. He died last spring."

"I heard that today. What happened?"

"Brain cancer. He had a Glioblastoma, and it was diagnosed late. I'm not sure there's a worse kind of cancer than that. It ravaged him. I knew that boy from the time he was born. His mom was one of my closest friends. Still is, but it's different now. I'm not so sure she'll ever recover. It's hard being the one whose son was taken away. I feel grateful but guilty that my two boys are still alive and well, and I think she feels cheated."

Having seen the effects of pancreatic cancer up close and personal, Elena had to disagree with Emma's analysis, but now wasn't the time. Besides, she rarely talked about her mother's death. "And Marni?" she asked.

"She's doing okay. The baby keeps her busy. She and Gabe had a friendship in their own right. In fact, more than a few people speculated that Gabe would slide in to fill Seb's shoes eventually, but I knew that would never happen. Gabe loves Marni like a sister. That's why it hurt her so much when he pulled away. I still don't understand it. I've tried talking to him about it, but we all grieve differently, I guess."

"Hmm." The thought of Gabe and Marni together brought an unexpected jab of jealousy. Elena thought of the pretty blonde and her cute little son, and was ashamed to admit that she felt threatened. But that didn't make any sense. Gabe wasn't hers and never would be. She didn't think about him that way. Correction: She didn't *use to* think of him that way.

After saying goodnight to Emma, Elena waited another half hour on the porch for Gabe to appear downstairs, but it didn't look like he'd be coming back down. She loaded her cup in the dishwasher and headed up the stairs to bed herself. She slept for an hour before voices woke her, and she threw the covers back to look out her open window. Gabe and Will were seated on the bench at the end of the yard that overlooked the bay, and they were having a heated discussion. Elena couldn't make out their words, only their tones. Abruptly, Will stood and marched toward the house, and she quickly stepped to the side of the window in case he looked up.

She waited several minutes until she heard a door close down the hall, then peeked out her window again. Gabe was still seated on the bench. Not letting herself think about it, she grabbed a sweatshirt, pulled it over her head, and crept down the stairs in her bare feet.

Chapter 16

G abe sat on the bench, the night air cooling his skin as he stared out at the bay, the water a dark mirror under the fading lavender sky on the horizon. The bottle of Corona beside him was still cold, barely touched, and for a moment he could almost hear Seb's voice ribbing him about wasting a perfectly good brew. He'd grabbed it from the fridge more for something to hold than something to drink. The stars winked overhead, brighter here in Bayshore than anywhere else, even Nicolet. The ache in his chest flared. Seb should be here, and Marni too, just like the old days. But instead, Seb was six feet under, and apparently Marni was over at the pub—a single woman out on the town.

Footsteps whispered through the grass, and Gabe's head snapped up, his pulse kicking before he even saw her. Her bare feet gleamed with dew, and her sweatshirt slipped off one shoulder. Elena paused beside him, her dark eyes catching the starlight, and his breath hitched.

"You mind if I sit with you here?" she asked, her voice tentative. He'd noticed this about her. When she was tired or timid, her accent thickened and her speech patterns betrayed her roots. Standing there, barefoot and wearing an old sweatshirt, Elena Torres had never looked more beautiful.

He blinked, recovering enough to grab the bottle and pat the bench. "Plenty of room." She settled beside him, closer than he'd expected. Her shoulder brushed his, warm and soft, and every nerve in his body lit up, hyper-aware of the scant space between them. He swallowed, gripping the bottle tighter. "Nice night," he said, low and rough, just to fill the silence.

"Yes," she murmured. Her hair fell against her cheek, and his fingers twitched with the urge to push it back, to feel the silk of it against his skin. He didn't move. Couldn't.

"Everything okay between you and Will?"

He exhaled, grateful for the distraction. "Yeah. He's got a good buzz going, so it probably wasn't the best idea to get into it with him."

"Get into what?"

"He saw Marni out at the pub. Invited her and Sebastian to the cookout on the Fourth."

"Is that a bad thing?"

"Not bad, just ... complicated." He rubbed the back of his neck, frustration bubbling up. "Will plows ahead sometimes, doesn't think things through. It drives me nuts."

She didn't respond, and he felt her stillness beside him, like she was waiting. He couldn't stop himself from venting. "I can't believe he was at the pub anyway. He's supposed to be here with us, dealing with stuff. And Marni's got a kid at home. What's *she* doing out so late?"

It wasn't the late hour—it was barely eleven-thirty—but the thought of Will and Marni laughing together, carefree, while he sat here missing Seb. It gnawed at him. "And then he invites *my* friend to our cookout without even asking," he muttered, shaking his head. "I don't know what he's doing."

"Do you have feelings for Marni?"

Elena's question hit like a curveball, and Gabe's head snapped toward her, eyes wide. "For *Marni*?" A laugh slipped out before he could stop it. Marni was family, a tie to a past he'd barely made peace with. She wasn't the one who set his pulse racing. That was Elena. He must be losing his edge if she could think that Marni was the one who did it for him. He laughed again.

Her gaze faltered and hurt flashed in her eyes.

Too late, he realized how his laugh had sounded. She thought he was laughing at *her*.

Abruptly, she stood and turned to leave.

Panic surged, and he lunged forward, grabbing her arms as his beer slipped, glugging into the grass. Her breath hitched, and he froze. Their faces were mere inches apart in the dark, and only their ragged breathing broke the silence. "Elena, I'm sorry," he said, softening his grip but not letting go. "I wasn't laughing at you. Please don't go."

She stayed, but her shoulders were tense, her face half-hidden in shadow. He rubbed where he'd grabbed her, then dropped his hands, cursing himself.

"No," he said, serious now. "Marni was a close friend—*is* a close friend, but no. I've never had those kinds of feelings for her. I ..."

"What?" she prompted when he didn't finish, her voice barely audible. Her eyes, dark and searching, held his, and he saw the hurt lingering there, mixed with something new—curiosity, maybe.

He looked down, the weight of his confession pressing on him. "I messed up our friendship. And I let Seb down. I made a promise. I promised I'd take care of her and Seb Jr., and I didn't. I ran away instead."

"Why?" Her question was gentle, but it cut deep.

His throat tightened, and he moved his head in a slow arc. "Because she was the one holding me together. After Seb died, I fell apart—came completely unglued. I'm the man, you know? The trusty best friend, and I couldn't handle it. She was so strong, and I couldn't let her keep carrying me. It wasn't supposed to be that way. I couldn't keep being a burden to her like that."

"Does she know this? That you felt this way?"

He shook his head again, and silence stretched between them, heavy and raw. Then her hand found his, warm and steady, and something in him cracked open. Slowly, she eased back onto the bench, her hand still in his, tugging gently. He followed, sinking beside her, the weathered wood creaking under their weight. Their joined hands rested between them, a fragile bridge in the dark. "Is this okay?" he asked, his voice rough.

"Yes."

Their voices overlapped as they both spoke again.

"Elena, I—"

"Emma said—"

He chuckled faintly. "Sorry, go ahead."

"Emma said something earlier ... about you standing up for me with the school board."

He shifted uncomfortably. "Did she?"

"Did you?"

He nodded, meeting her eyes. They were wide, searching, and he couldn't look away.

"Why didn't you tell me?"

He let out a slow breath. "I figured the less I said, the better. You were embarrassed, and I wanted to help. Knowing the entire board was discussing what happened wouldn't have helped you."

"But you let me blame you. That awful meeting." She shook her head. "I was terrible to you."

He shrugged, but her gaze didn't waver, and he felt exposed, like she could see right through him.

"Why did you do that?" she pressed.

"It was about protecting you," he said, the words slipping out. "That's all."

Her pulse jumped—he could see it in the flicker at her throat—and she studied him, her lips parting slightly. His eyes dipped there, just for a heartbeat, then back up.

"You did that at Rebecca's too, with Marc." She stared out over the dark bay. "I'm not ... *delicada*. Fragile," she said, her voice low.

"I know you're not." His chest ached with how true that was. She was strong, but she still brought out all his protective instincts. "I know you're not," he repeated, "but I wanted to anyway. It was the right thing to do. I couldn't sit back and say nothing. I couldn't *not* fight for you."

The air thickened, electric, and she turned to him and leaned in—just a fraction, but enough to make his heart slam against his ribs. He wanted to close the gap, to kiss her right there under the stars, but he held still, barely breathing.

"What did you tell them?" she whispered.

He dropped her hand abruptly, the memory and sudden reminder of his role crashing over him. She was his employee, a teacher under his watch, and he was the superintendent. He couldn't cross that line, not like this, not today. He forced a wry smile to cover the jolt of unease. "It was me against Dominick Stone. I told the board it wasn't worth chasing. The situation was personal, not professional. It was outside of school hours, you didn't put it out there, and you've got a right to a life. I said if they held it against you, they'd have to hold it against Ghetty too, and he's their cash cow. The legal team backed me up—said it'd be an uphill battle to discipline you. They let it go. No suspension, no termination, no record."

Her shoulders eased, relief softening her face, but she kept looking at him, like she was waiting for more. "You didn't have to do that," she murmured.

He reached for her hand again, couldn't help it, and squeezed it briefly before letting go once more. "I'd do it again," he said, his voice rough with everything he wasn't saying. He stood, needing distance before he forgot why he had to keep it. "We should get to bed. It's late."

Chapter 17

S unlight slanted through Elena's window, soft and low, rousing her at seven. After a shower, she pulled on army-green shorts and a white tank top before being drawn downstairs by the smell of coffee and sizzling bacon, not to mention the need to see Gabe again. She'd dreamed of him last night. It wasn't the first time, but it was the first time she could accept the reason why. She had feelings for Gabriel Wright. Gabe the Babe. Superintendent of Nicolet Schools. Lexi's father.

What was she thinking? She didn't care. His hands on her arms, his rough "I'd do it again"—she shivered just thinking about it. They'd held hands, and not for nearly long enough, but somehow it had been one of the most intimate moments of her life. But then he'd pulled away like he'd burned himself, and she didn't know what that meant.

The kitchen was alive: Theo at the griddle, flipping pancakes; Emma slicing strawberries, both in robes; Gabe at the table, coffee in hand, Lexi coloring beside him. A family, simple and whole. A family beginning their day together in the kitchen. It made for an ordinary yet poignant picture. One she'd longed to have herself for years and years. It might be only temporary, but she was determined to enjoy *this* family as much as possible and savor every moment.

Spotting her, Lexi hopped up from the table and ran to her, wrapping her arms around Elena's waist. "We get pancakes! Papa makes 'em so good. Then blueberry picking, and we getta ride in the side-by-sides, and then we go to the restaurant in Brule Harbor that's got the cream soda that's pink. And then we'll go swimming and then we hafta buy food for the party tomorrow with everyone coming to eat hamburgers that Daddy hasta grill 'cause Papa never does it right."

Elena laughed, scooping her up. "Where did all of this energy come from?"

Lexi took her literally. "I already ate a pancake. Papa flipped it too soon, and it broke, so I got to eat that one with jam on it."

"Jam, huh? That's a new one."

Lexi wiggled down, tugging Elena back to her chair. "Come see my coloring."

Feeling Gabe's eyes on her, Elena greeted him softly.

"Morning," he said, his voice rough with sleep. He held her gaze a beat too long, then looked down at his coffee, his jaw tight. Was he thinking about last night too?

Heat crept up her neck as she sat beside Lexi. After she made all the right sounds over Lexi's coloring page, commenting on how masterfully Lexi had colored the tail of yet another horse and how perfectly the pasture was colored just the right shade of green, she offered her help to Theo and Emma.

Theo wouldn't hear of it. "You just pour some coffee for yourself and let us cook for you. We live for mornings like these."

Emma walked over with a mug and pointed to the cream and sugar across the kitchen. "Doctor it up however you see fit, but I'm telling you right now, if you've never had real maple syrup in your coffee, you've been missing out."

"I'll give it a try," Elena promised. Maple syrup in coffee and jam on pancakes? Interesting, but she supposed she'd like that better than the reverse. From her spot near the coffee bar, Elena asked, "What's a side-by-side?"

Incredulous, Lexi looked up from her coloring book. "You don't know what a side-by-side is? That's silly!"

"She wouldn't ask if she knew, now would she?" Theo retorted, flipping a pancake. "Be a good girl and tell her."

"You ride trails with 'em," Lexi told her.

"They're like a cross between a four-wheeler and a jeep," Gabe added without quite looking at her.

Elena's stomach flipped. "Are they fast?"

"Mine'll do ninety," Will said, as he strolled into the kitchen. He clapped Gabe on the shoulder before heading to the cupboard for a mug.

Elena paled.

Emma added a spoon to the fruit bowl and laughed. "We stick to thirty or forty, tops, dear. You'll be fine."

"Ride with Shorty," Will said, winking at Elena. "He drives like an old fart."

Theo pointed the spatula at him. The griddle hissed. "Watch it, now."

Elena saw Gabe's grip tighten on his mug until his knuckles whitened. "Better than getting wrapped around a tree," he shot back.

Will grinned, leaning closer. "When are you gonna learn to live a little?"

"Right around the time you learn some self-control."

"Is this about inviting Marni? I'm only looking out for her, Gabe." Will froze, his eyes widening as he caught Gabe's flinch. "Aww, Shorty. I didn't mean—"

Gabe stood. "You have something you want to say to me? Say it."

Elena's breath caught and Lexi's marker froze. Her eyes flicked to Elena, wide and uncertain. The brothers sparred often, but normally it was playful and fun-loving. This was different.

Emma set her knife down with a soft clink, her eyes narrowing. "That's enough. Outside, you two. Sort it out before breakfast gets cold."

Theo let out a rueful chuckle from the griddle. "Take it easy, boys. We've got a big day ahead."

Gabe scrubbed a hand over his face. "Fine." He glanced apologetically at Elena before following Will out.

Minutes later, they returned, Will's hand on Gabe's shoulder. Whatever passed between them outside had smoothed the edges, at least for now. The air between them felt easy again, and Lexi looked back and forth between uncle and father and beamed once she was satisfied that all was well in her little world. She let her marker resume its happy squeaking across the coloring book page, and Elena let out a breath she hadn't realized she'd been holding.

It took another two hours to eat, clean up, and get everyone ready to leave. They packed empty gallon-size ice cream containers for the picking, plenty of water and snacks for themselves, bathing suits, towels, sand toys, sunblock, and bug spray. By ten o'clock, they were off.

Chapter 18

The July sun climbed higher over the Kinsey Plains, casting golden light across the dusty trail as Gabe guided the side-by-side through the winding path toward the blueberry fields. Elena sat beside him, her green shorts riding up slightly as she shifted, her hair in a loose ponytail that danced in the warm breeze. In the back, Lexi giggled, belting out a nonsense song about "berry bears" with Emma, whose laughter rang out clear and bright. Will drove alongside them with Theo, occasionally revving his engine just to make Lexi squeal.

Gabe stole a glance at Elena, her cheeks pink from the sun, her lips curved in a contented smile as she turned periodically to answer Lexi's chatter. His grip tightened on the steering wheel, his pulse kicking up at the sight of her—so close, so effortlessly a part of this moment with his family. "You surviving back there? He called over his shoulder to his mom and Lexi.

"Barely!" Emma shot back, grinning. "This one's got more energy than the three of us combined."

They parked near the field's edge, the air thick with the sweet scent of ripe blueberries and pine. The hum of cicadas broke through the quiet as Gabe lifted Lexi from her seat, spinning her once before setting her down. Immediately, she spotted a thick patch of berries and began to pick and eat. Elena climbed out, brushing past Gabe as she reached for a pail, her arm grazing his chest. The brief contact sent a jolt through him, and he caught her eye. Her lips twitched like she'd felt it too.

"Think we can fill these before Lexi eats the whole field?" she teased, her voice light.

Gabe smirked, running a hand through his hair. "She's a machine."

"Bug spray's over here!" Will called, tossing the can to Theo, who fumbled it dramatically, earning a cackle from Emma. "And sunblock, Lexi—don't make me chase you down!"

Once everyone was prepped for the elements, the picking began. Lexi flitted between bushes, chattering about bears, while Theo and Emma worked a row over, bickering playfully about who'd found the better patch. "These are prize-winners," Theo bragged, holding up a giant-sized berry. "You're wasting your time over there, honey."

"Keep talking, Theo," Emma retorted, popping a blueberry into her mouth. "Mine are sweeter."

Gabe and Elena fell into step, side by side, until Gabe stopped and bent down low. Moving a fern out of the way, he uncovered a plant heavy with dark, purple berries. "Found the mother lode right here," he said, voice low as he picked and held up a plump berry. Her eyes flicked to his, a spark dancing there.

"That's a really dark blueberry," she murmured, stepping closer.

"It's actually a huckleberry," he corrected. "I like them even better 'cause they taste sweeter."

"I wonder if I've ever had one."

He held it out, and when she reached for it, he pulled it back again with a grin. Her brows shot up, but she didn't retreat—instead, she leaned in, letting him feed it to her. Her lips brushed his fingertips, and his eyes locked on hers as she chewed. Silently, he cursed himself. He just couldn't stop himself. No matter how many times he swore they couldn't be together, moments like this kept pulling him back to her. It was like he was stuck in a riptide he was too weak to fight.

"Good?" he asked, his voice rough.

"*Perfecto*," she said softly, her gaze unwavering. She never used to look at him like this, almost seeming to avoid eye contact with him. What had changed? The air crackled between them, and for a heartbeat he thought about kissing her—right there, consequences be damned.

"Hey, lovebirds!" Will's voice cut through, sharp with mischief. "You picking berries or staging a romance novel?"

Elena flushed, stepping back with a laugh, while Gabe shot his brother a look. "Mind your own!" He hollered back.

Theo chuckled from fifty yards away. "He's got a point, Gabriel. Your buckets have less than Lexi's."

"Quality over quantity," Gabe fired back, but his eyes slid to Elena, who was grinning into her pail, and his chest tightened. Something had definitely shifted between them, and pretending otherwise was getting harder by the minute.

By one o'clock, their buckets brimmed with fruit, and the group piled back into the side-by-sides, dusty and sun-warmed, and headed for Brule Harbor.

At the diner overlooking Lake Superior, they slid into a booth—Lexi between Emma and Theo on one side, and Will, Elena, and Gabe on the other. Gabe's left thigh and Elena's right brushed under the table. The contact was accidental at first, but neither moved away, and Gabe felt the heat of her leg like a live wire.

Emma handed Lexi a crayon for her to color the kids' menu. "Draw me a bear, sweetie. One that doesn't eat all our berries."

Will grinned over his menu. "You think it was a bear who ate all our berries, Mom? Take a look at that purple mouth on your granddaughter and try again."

Lexi giggled, scribbling fiercely.

"It's a wonder she has an appetite," Gabe observed. "Get ready to eat half her burger," he told his brother.

"Are you letting her get a burger?" Will asked innocently. "It's probably not organic grass-fed."

"Shut up."

Once their food came, Gabe watched as Elena coaxed Lexi into eating her carrots with a story about a rabbit detective. She was good with Lexi—better than good—and he thought again about how seamlessly she fit here with his family. With him.

Elena caught him staring, and instead of looking away, she held his gaze, her fork pausing midair. "What?" she asked softly.

A faint smile tugged at the corners of his mouth. "Nothing. You're just ... good at that."

"She makes it easy," she deflected, but he could see his comment had pleased her.

"You've got the magic touch," Emma chimed in, winking at Elena. "Gabe's lucky to have you for the summer."

Her knee pressed against his under the table, deliberate now, and his hand flexed on his thigh, itching to reach for her. He didn't want to think about how temporary this arrangement was—not when he thought about how her mere presence had infused his world with new life.

"Pink cream soda's here, little miss!" The waitress announced, breaking the spell, as she set a glass in front of Lexi, who cheered. Elena laughed, reaching across the table to help Lexi with the straw, and Gabe exhaled, running a hand over his jaw as he came to terms with the truth: a summer arrangement wasn't going to be enough anymore. They needed her too much, he and Lexi both.

He was in real trouble.

So was she.

The midafternoon sun glittered on the lake as they reached the beach, the water stretching out, endless and blue. Lexi bolted for the shallows, splashing with abandon, while Theo and Emma set up chairs on the sand. "You kids go swim," Emma called, waving them off. "We'll keep an eye on the princess."

Will smirked, peeling off his shirt. "Last one in's a rotten egg!" He sprinted for the water, cannonballing in with a splash that made Lexi shriek with delight.

Gabe barely heard them, his focus on Elena as she waded deeper, the water rising to her ribs.

"I thought you didn't swim in this lake?" he called after her.

She glanced back at him, a playful challenge in her eyes. "I changed my mind. You coming, or are you just gonna stand there?"

He grinned, following her, the pull between them much stronger than the lake's gentle waves. They stopped where the water reached her shoulders, and her hair fanned out on the surface. She tilted her head, studying him. The air buzzed with what they weren't saying.

"You're staring again," she said. Her voice was teasing but her eyes searched his.

"I can't help it," he admitted, stepping closer. The water rippled between them, and her breath hitched, her hand brushing his under the surface—tentative, electric. Neither pulled away this time.

Emma's voice carried from the beach. "You two look like you're plotting something out there!"

"Are we?" Gabe said to Elena, his eyes not leaving hers. She smiled, small and knowing, and his heart slammed against his ribs. He was falling hard, and from the way she looked at him, she wasn't far behind.

He dove in, needing to completely submerge himself in the icy water. He stayed under as long as he could before coming up for air. When he did, he opened his eyes to see Elena popping up beside him. He reached for her, his thumb brushing her arm absently, and Elena's lips parted, a question—or maybe an invitation—hovering there. Gabe fought the urge to close the distance, to hold her in his arms and taste the lake water on her skin.

His fingers curled around her arm. She froze, her breath catching as she looked up at him, droplets clinging to her lashes, her skin warm under his touch despite the chill of the lake. "I wish I could kiss you right now."

A brief flicker of surprise flashed in her eyes as she searched his face. Had he said too much? His cheeks warmed, but then she whispered, "I wish you could too."

"Daddy! Elena! Look at me!" Lexi's voice pierced the moment, and they stepped apart, the spell broken but not forgotten. Elena turned to cheer Lexi's clumsy doggy paddle, while Gabe ran a hand over his face, stunned by the realization that he'd fallen in love with Elena Torres.

Chapter 19

"**W**e need to put letters on it," Lexi advised Elena the next day. It was only nine in the morning, and they'd already been outside for an hour playing. They'd gone on a nature walk, jumped rope, and were now getting ready for a round of hopscotch, or Lexi's version of it. Mosie, exhausted, napped in the shade of the giant birch tree in the front yard. Elena didn't think the pooch would run off, tired as she looked, but she'd secured the tie-out to the tree just in case.

It had been a long time, but Elena was fairly certain *numbers* went into the hopscotch boxes. "What do the letters mean?"

Lexi ignored her as she continued to write capital letters in the boxes. She said them out loud as she wrote them. "*F, H, L* ..."

When she'd finished lettering each one, she returned to the starting point and carefully chalked out a series of letters. Elena watched in fascination. Lexi's mind was a wonder.

P...R...A...D. "Prad? What does that mean?"

"It means, 'Start here and come this way,'" Lexi said, improvising in the way that only little girls with strong imaginations could. "C'mon, Elena. You go first."

Elena obliged, throwing the rock and hopping to where it had landed, picking it up on one foot before continuing to the end, turning around, and hopping back. Lexi clapped enthusiastically, and Elena grinned. It didn't take much to impress a six-year-old.

Lexi chatted endlessly as they took turns. She told Elena all about how her sparkle dad played hopscotch with her all the time. True to her word to Gabe, Elena didn't feed the fantasy, but neither did she discourage it. She showed brief interest and then switched the subject. Lexi didn't seem to notice, rolling with the conversation wherever it led. Elena couldn't be certain, but she thought Lexi was talking about her make-believe family less and less. It was the first time she'd referenced them since arriving in Bayshore.

After another several rounds, Lexi was tired out—finally. Elena could feel a blister had formed on her big toe and was ready to take a break too. They went inside to pour some lemonade before sitting on the porch together to sip as the day heated up and the sun climbed higher and higher in the clear blue sky.

Today was the Fourth of July, and it was a perfect day for all the celebratory activities yet to come. Once the Wright family came back from their outing, they'd head downtown for the parade and then scramble back to prep for the party, which would begin at three o'clock. They'd wrap up by early evening and head back down to the water's edge for the fireworks. According to Theo, they'd need to set up their chairs and blankets along the shoreline well before eight o'clock to secure good seats for the display.

"People come from all over for our fireworks," he'd boasted. "We have the best show around. Even better than Nicolet's." Theo had spent years on the July Fourth Spectacular Committee and had only been retired from it for three years. It seemed he missed being on the front lines of the fireworks display, but Emma was happy to have him finish out his stint with all his limbs and fingers intact.

"When will they be back?" Lexi asked before sucking more lemonade from her straw.

"Anytime," Elena answered.

"Where'd they go?"

"For coffee," Elena reminded her.

"But they drink coffee here."

"I think they just wanted to do something special together today," Elena said.

"But what if we miss the parade, and I don't get any candy?"

"I promise, we won't miss the parade. They'll be back with plenty of time for us to walk down there and get a good spot."

Lexi nodded, accepting this before slurping the remainder of her lemonade.

Gabe told her they had some things to discuss as a family when he'd asked if she could watch Lexi for the morning. She'd have laughed if he hadn't looked so serious. Watching Lexi was the whole reason she was here. Or that had been the intention. This was the first time she'd been alone with Lexi since they arrived.

Yesterday had been the best day ever. She'd loved everything about it. Every stolen glance from Gabe, every "accidental" touch—all of it sparked promises of something more. His whispered wish to kiss her as they'd stood in the lake's cool embrace replayed in her mind, sending shivers across her sun-warmed skin. She couldn't get enough of him, and she knew there was no going back to the cautious distance they'd kept in Nicolet. She felt it in her bones—their connection had shifted forever. They'd had no chance to be alone after the swim yesterday, and she hoped today would be different. Gabe wouldn't let much more time slip by without kissing her. If he did, she just might scream—or steal that kiss herself.

Practical concerns lingered, of course. Elena wasn't sure about the school district's policy on this sort of thing, but Gabe, ever the rulebook guy, didn't seem all that concerned about it. Continuing as Lexi's nanny wasn't awkward exactly, but getting paid for it might feel strange if she and Gabe became something more. She pushed the worry aside. They'd figure it out together.

Elena's heart buzzed with a giddy hope she couldn't tame. She'd always dreamed of her own family someday. This week, she'd been content to bask in the Wrights' warmth as a temporary guest. All her life, she'd slipped into other people's families—weekend sleepovers, borrowed moments—trying them on like hand-me-down coats. But Gabe, Lexi, the whole Wright clan? They fit like they'd been tailored just for her. She knew she was racing ahead, imagining a future she shouldn't be thinking about, but for once, that familiar ache in her heart—the one that only family could soothe—for once, it didn't hurt.

It was only three o'clock, and Gabe had already put in a full day's worth of activities. Early morning coffee, the parade, party prep—but he wasn't remotely tired. Just the opposite. The Fourth of July afternoon pulsed with vibrant energy that he could feel deep in his bones. Lake Superior's waves, swelling under a warm westerly wind, mirrored Gabe's surging optimism.

His morning conversation with Will and his parents had exceeded any expectations he could have had, leaving him buoyed by excitement for what lay ahead. And then there was the promise of things to come with Elena. A grin tugged at his face. He didn't think he could keep from smiling if he tried. At the grill in his parents' backyard, he flipped grass-fed burgers with a practiced hand, the sizzle of meat mingling with the distant pop of early firecrackers.

The lake below shimmered with a thousand glints of sunlight, as if sharing in the holiday's festivities.

The bluff hummed with activity. Theo draped red, white, and blue bunting along the porch railing, while Emma arranged a table with potato salad and blueberry pies. Lexi ever spirited, dashed around the yard with a sparkler she'd begged Will to light "just this once" before dark.

Elena stepped out of the house, balancing a tray of lemonade pitchers. Her dark hair was pulled into a messy bun that somehow made her look even more beautiful. She wore a simple white sundress with tiny red flowers—patriotic enough for the occasion, but it was the way it hugged her curves that caught Gabe's eye. He nearly burned a burger watching her set the tray down and laugh at something Lexi shouted about "sparkle stars." Not even that word—*sparkle*—could dampen his spirits.

"Eye on the grill, Shorty," Will teased, sidling up with a beer in hand. "You're gonna set the whole bluff on fire."

Gabe flipped a patty with a smirk. "Says the guy who's already drinking a beer."

"Hey, it's three o'clock, and I'm retired. Live a little." Will's grin widened. "You've got it bad for her, Shorty. Lucky for you, she feels the same way."

Gabe perked up. "Did she tell you that?"

"She didn't have to. It's written all over her face. And look how she got all dolled up for you too. That's a new dress, you know."

Elena's laugh floated over from the lemonade table, light and infectious, and Gabe followed the sound with his eyes. Her sundress swirled around her ankles as she chased Lexi across the grass.

Early on, her spending had grated on him—the way she dropped cash on designer brands and manicures while her car coughed its last breath. Gabe still didn't understand it. "She must drop a small fortune on clothes," he mused aloud.

Will tilted his head, brows quirking. "Elena thrifts everything she buys." He pointed at the table behind the grill. "That dress? Probably cheaper than a package of burger buns."

Gabe paused in the act of flipping another patty. "All those fancy outfits?"

"What, you thought she was going out and buying Gucci on a teacher's salary?" Will chuckled. "Man, you've got her all wrong. She's smart with money."

A pang of regret stirred in Gabe's chest as he realized he'd judged her without a second thought. He needed to stop doing that. "Guess I don't know her as well as I thought."

Will clapped his shoulder. "You'll get there."

Will's grin faltered as he glanced down the driveway. "Marni's here." He set his beer on the table and looked at Gabe. "You sure it's cool I invited her?"

"Yeah, it was the right thing to do."

"You saying I was right, Shorty?" Will asked, the grin returning.

Gabe's shoulders rose in a lazy shrug. "Actually, no, I didn't say that."

Will turned with a soft laugh, already striding off. "Be right back."

Marni stepped out of her car, and Gabe watched as Will took a covered dish—probably her famous baked beans—while she got Sebastian out of the backseat. She waved tentatively as she spotted him. Gabe felt the familiar lump in his throat, but this time the guilt was mixed with relief, and he let the feeling wash over him. He was finally going to make amends. He hadn't seen her since the beach, and their brief talk then had only scratched the surface of what needed to be said.

Spotting the toddler, Lexi dropped her sparkler in the grass—prompting a quick stomp from Emma—and ran to meet the little guy, the two of them colliding in a giggling heap. Gabe smiled. Since the day Elena entered their lives, Lexi's vibrant spirit had slowly reemerged. Here in Bayshore, her transformation was complete. He was changing too—felt lighter than he had in years. Undoubtedly, Will's return had helped remind him of who he once was—who he wanted to be again.

Marni, making sure Seb had Emma's supervision, approached the grill, her smile small but genuine. "Smells good, Gabe."

"I'm glad you came." He wiped his hands on a towel and glanced at Will who had set down Marni's dish next to the others and was now watching them. "You gonna help me flip these or just stand there looking pretty?"

Will snorted and rolled his eyes, but he took over the grill and shooed them away. "You two go talk. I got this."

Gabe led Marni to the edge of the yard. Other cars were pulling up the drive now, and soon they'd lose their chance at privacy. He could see she was as nervous as he felt, but she was still the first to speak.

"I wasn't sure about coming, but Will insisted. Said it'd be good for us to, you know, catch up."

"I was mad at him."

She chuckled. "I'm sure you were."

"But he was right."

She nodded.

"I owe you an apology, Marni. A real one. I've been a lousy friend since Seb—since Seb died. I didn't know how to be there for you, but I should've tried harder."

Her eyes softened, but a flicker of old hurt remained in them. "Losing him ... it broke us all in different ways. I just missed you." She gestured behind them where Lexi and the toddler played under Emma's careful watch. "Sebastian doesn't even know who you are. You're his Uncle Gabe, you know? Seb must be rolling over in his grave knowing that you're a stranger to his son."

When Gabe spoke, his voice was rough with emotion. "I'm here now. I want to fix it. I want to be here for him, for you. I want to keep my promise to Seb."

"Gabe." She smiled tenderly. "Making that promise was a gift to Seb. He needed to hear it so he could let go. He was so worried about us." She reached out a hand, cupping his cheek. "But I don't need you to take care of me. I have so many people to lean on. My parents are still here. My sister lives just down the road now, which is a whole other story. All I need is for you to be my friend. Sebastian needs you to be his uncle and a strong man in his life. But I don't need you to hold me up. I never needed that."

Gabe nodded, accepting that. "But I still wish I could have been stronger for you. I let you down."

She leaned forward slightly and her lips parted. "You let me down, but not because you weren't strong enough. You let me down because you disappeared for all the wrong reasons. You should have asked me what I needed, Gabe. Then you would have known that all I wanted was someone to grieve with. That's it. Someone who loved Seb as much as I did." She laughed as she wiped at a tear. "He always said you were the brother he never had. He loved you so much."

Gabe pulled her into a quick, fierce hug, the kind they used to share without thinking. "I'm sorry," he murmured into her hair. "No more disappearing."

When they parted, Marni wiped her eyes and laughed softly. "Good. Because I'm holding you to that."

Will ambled over, Sebastian perched on his shoulders, Lexi trailing behind with a fistful of daisies. "You two about done? These kids are starving."

"Who's manning the grill?" Gabe asked in alarm. A glance told him who. "Not Dad!"

Will chuckled. "He's got to learn sometime, Shorty."

Gabe excused himself to rescue the meat. Once everything was back under control, he glanced over at Marni and Will. They hadn't budged and were engaged in a conversation that Gabe couldn't hear, but he could see the smiles they each wore, and he wondered if something wasn't stirring to life there. Later, he'd have to consider how he would feel about that.

Elena joined him at the grill, brushing his arm as she peered at the burgers. "Everything okay?"

"Yeah," he said, meeting her eyes. "Better than okay."

She smiled, warm and steady, and handed him the flipper. "Don't burn my lunch, Mr. Wright."

He chuckled. The weight of the past had lifted and hope for the future, despite some unanswered questions, shone bright.

The cookout rolled into late afternoon, and the backyard filled with neighbors and old friends dropping by. Laughter and the clink of glasses carried on the breeze as the sun dipped lower. Gabe kept stealing glances at Elena. His job at the grill, and her work refilling drinks and helping with the kids, prevented them from talking as much as he would have liked. She fit here with his family, as if she'd always belonged. Every time their eyes met, she'd smile, and he knew she felt it too.

As dusk settled over Bayshore, the group migrated downtown for the fireworks. Emma and Theo had gone ahead with the car to carry all the camp chairs. They'd promised to have everything set up and seats saved so he and Will could take their time walking down with Marni, Elena, and the kids. Gabe carried Lexi on his shoulders, her hands sticky in his hair from the watermelon she'd gorged on, while Elena walked beside him. Will and Marni trailed behind with Seb asleep in his stroller. They were chatting about something that made Marni laugh—a sound Gabe hadn't heard in forever. His heart was full, and that was something he hadn't experienced for a long time either.

As they neared the main drag, the crowd thickened. Every few steps a familiar face stopped them—a neighbor or an old friend—and each time Elena waited patiently as Gabe exchanged greetings. At this rate, they'd miss the start of the fireworks.

Will caught his eye. "Hey, Shorty. Let's cut through the park. It'll be less busy."

Gabe tilted his head in agreement, and they veered left, the park's stillness beckoning them. It was a longer path to the shore, but quieter, save for a small line at the ice cream shop.

Elena nudged Gabe, her voice teasing. "You know half the town."

He chuckled. "And now, so do you." He reached for her hand and craved a moment alone. He lifted his eyes and tilted his head as far as he could. Lexi had been awfully quiet. "You still awake up there, kiddo?"

She yawned. "Can I get down, Daddy?"

He paused, reluctantly releasing Elena's hand to lower his tired daughter to the gravel path. He knew she'd want to be carried in his arms next, but that would have to wait. "Will," he called, glancing back at his brother. "Can you take Lexi for a minute? We'll catch up."

Will winked and scooped Lexi off her feet as she giggled.

"Be there in a minute."

"Take your time," Will teased.

Gabe hung back with Elena, who laughed softly, a nervous edge to it. Her eyes flickered with something unspoken, and the pulse jumped at her throat. He took her hand, guiding her off the path under the broad canopy of a sugar maple, its leaves rustling softly, casting dappled shadows around them and lending an air of privacy. His gaze locked on hers.

"You should know," she began, her voice trembling, "Lexi thinks you're going to buy her a pony. She told me at the parade when the Clydesdales walked by."

"Did she now." His voice softened, and his fingers traced her jaw. He kissed her—soft at first, then deeper, her lips warm and yielding, tasting faintly of lemonade and summer. Her hands slid to his chest, fingers curling slightly as she leaned into him. Her warmth anchored him, and the scent of coconut sunscreen wrapped around them. His heart pounded, every nerve alive with the certainty that they belonged together.

She eased back, her smile radiant, fingers lingering on his arm. "About time," she whispered, eyes dancing.

They rejoined the group, Will's knowing smirk greeting them when they did.

A familiar face caught Gabe's eye from across the park. Joanna Bentley stood near the ice cream stand, her sharp gaze cutting through the distance. She'd spotted him—worse, she'd spotted Elena beside him, their closeness unmistakable. Her lips pressed into a thin line, and even from far away, Gabe could see her gears turning.

He hadn't told Elena about the phone call from Dom before they left Nicolet. Dom's threat to push the board against renewing her contract, citing the old video as a lingering optics issue, had prompted the "yelling" that Lexi had overheard. Joanna had been in on that call, her silence deafening. Now, seeing her here, Gabe's stomach twisted.

Trouble loomed—for Elena and for him. In a little more than two weeks, the board would meet to vote on staff renewals. Normally, it was a formality based on his recommendations, but with Dom in the mix, Gabe knew Elena's renewal was going to be complicated. If Joanna talked about what she'd seen, it would be even worse. He, himself, could very well be reprimanded. The good news was that he had some time to figure it all out.

"Gabe?" Elena's voice pulled him back. "You okay?"

"Yeah," he lied, forcing a smile. "Just thought I saw someone."

She studied him, unconvinced, but let it go as a premature firework exploded overhead. The colors were muted in the daylight, but the red and gold still shone through. Lexi squealed and Elena smiled. He smiled back, shoving Joanna and Dom to the back of his mind. Tonight he'd hold on to this—Elena, Lexi, his family. Reality could wait.

Chapter 20

July fifth broke over Bayshore with a lazy heat, the kind that made the air shimmer above the bluff. Elena woke to Lexi bouncing on her bed and announcing that Papa had made them all pancakes in the shape of Mickey Mouse for breakfast.

Today was Elena's birthday, not that she'd told anyone. And she didn't plan to. Just being here in Bayshore was gift enough.

As with the two previous mornings, Emma and Theo bustled in the kitchen, but this time Will and Gabe were nowhere to be found. After doctoring her coffee with the maple syrup she could no longer live without, Elena went looking for them. It didn't take her long to spot them through the open window in the living room. They were out on the front porch, talking in hushed tones. Whatever it was, it looked too serious to interrupt, so Elena retreated to the kitchen where she helped put on breakfast.

Mid morning, after breakfast had long been cleared away, the doorbell chimed, and Emma perked up. "We've never had so many visitors in one week. What am I going to do when you leave tomorrow? I'll die of boredom."

From behind his paper, Theo chuckled. "You hear that, Elena? The love of my life just called me boring."

"Oh, foo," Emma said with a wave of her hand as she reached for the door handle with the other. "That's not what I said."

Elena smiled at their exchange before returning her attention to her phone. She was back to apartment hunting. Nothing in her price range looked very enticing, so she was going to have to get over the fact that she couldn't count on being inspired by the pictures. She needed to be practical. Her phone rang just as she was about to take down a phone number, and *Tía* Carmen's picture filled her screen. Elena grinned as she answered. She already knew what was coming: a slightly off-key rendition of "*Cumpleaños Feliz*" followed by the English version, "Happy Birthday." It had been a tradition for twenty-six years now. Emma, who came back into the room carrying flowers, stopped—presumably to listen. Elena moved the phone from her ear and turned the volume down with a few presses of the button. "Sorry," she mouthed to Emma who shook her head and smiled that it was no problem.

"*Feliz cumpleaños, mi amor*," her aunt said once she'd finished singing.

"*Gracias, Tía.*"

"I got you flowers, but I don't know when they'll arrive," Carmen said.

Emma must have heard because she held the bouquet up higher.

"They just got here, *Tía*, and they're beautiful. Thank you so much."

"I only wish I could make you your birthday dinner, Elena. I'll make you those *jibaritos* later this weekend when you get back. We'll celebrate with some *tembleque* for dessert, or *tres leches*, maybe, hmm? Whatever you want."

"*Qué rico, Tía*, I was just thinking of *jibaritos* a few days ago." They spoke a few minutes longer, with Emma listening shamelessly all the while, until Elena hung up.

Emma spoke up. "It's your birthday? Theo, It's Elena's birthday. Why didn't you tell us?"

Theo folded the paper and gave her his attention.

"Oh, you know how it is. When you get older, birthdays aren't as important."

"Of course they are!" Emma argued.

"Emma still takes her birthday off from work every single year," Theo offered.

"And don't ask how long I've been doing that. I'm older than I care to admit," Emma said. She handed Elena the vase full of lilies. "These are for you, but you knew that. Happy birthday, Elena." She reached down to hug her.

Theo set down the folded paper and perched on the edge of his chair. "We need to celebrate this, Emma. We can't let Elena's birthday go by without marking the occasion."

Emma clapped her hands together. "We'll throw a party."

Elena chuckled as she stood. "No, no, no. I don't need a party. I've been looking forward to this last night in Bayshore, and all I want to do is spend time with you all tonight. Once Gabe and Lexi get back with Mosie, we can plan something for just us."

"That sounds lovely, dear," Emma said before looking at her thoughtfully. "What's a *jibarito*?"

Elena hid a smile at how Emma had pronounced the word. "Mmm, they're my absolute favorite. It's a type of Puerto Rican sandwich, but instead of bread you use plantains."

Emma looked confused. "Those things that look like miniature bananas?"

"They're similar." Elena laughed at Emma's expression. "They're really good, I swear."

Theo rose from his chair. "Well, let's make these Costa Rican sandwiches."

He'd confused an island in the Caribbean with a country in Central America, but Elena didn't have the heart to correct him. She wouldn't have been able to, anyway, because he and Emma had already gone to the kitchen to make a list of what they'd need to purchase.

By the time Gabe and Lexi got back, Theo was already blowing up balloons and hanging a happy birthday banner in the kitchen. "This banner has survived two decades of use, Elena," he was saying, when Gabe stepped into the kitchen.

Gabe froze as he took in the scene. "Whose birthday is it?"

"Mine," she said, her voice warm with delight.

His eyes widened briefly, and a flush reddened his cheeks. "What? Today?"

She beamed and nodded.

"Elena, I—"

She waved off his stammer. "You didn't know."

"She's a good one for secrets, this one." Emma hugged Elena as she passed by on her way to the closet. "I'll just grab my shoes, and we'll go."

"Go where?" Gabe leaned against the counter.

"We're going to run out for some ingredients." Elena's chest swelled with pride. "I'm going to make *jibaritos* tonight."

Gabe was slow to respond. "I've heard of those," he said cautiously.

"Do you not want them?"

"No, no, they sound amazing." He hesitated, his lips twitching briefly. "Hey, why don't I cook them for us? You shouldn't have to make your own birthday dinner."

Elena stepped closer. "This is my way of saying thank you to you all for having me here in your home. I want to cook for you."

For a second, she thought he looked worried.

As Elena dashed upstairs to grab her sandals, Gabe caught his mother's arm and steered her toward the living room. He kept his voice low. "Listen, Mom, Elena doesn't really cook."

Emma's brow lifted with interest. "Really? But she's so set on making us this dinner. You saw how happy she was."

He spread his hands helplessly. "No, Mom. You don't get it." His voice dropped further. "Elena *can't* cook. She's hopeless in the kitchen. She means well, but—" Visions of scorched plantains flickered in his mind. "I don't want her to be embarrassed."

"You don't think this dinner could turn out?"

He thought back to her early attempts at making them dinner. That rice and bean dish that nearly broke his teeth, the chicken she'd baked that had been raw when he cut into it. He shuddered. "Not a chance."

Emma leaned closer. "Here's a little secret. Maybe it will help. While I kept Elena busy, your dad swiped her phone and called her aunt. She's on her way home from a visit to Grand Rapids, so she'll be passing through on her way to Nicolet. He invited her to stop by and stay for dinner as a surprise." Glancing at her watch, she added, "She and her traveling companions should be here in about an hour. I've never made these ... sandwiches, but this aunt said she makes them for Elena every year. I'm sure she can help."

He exhaled and his shoulders eased slightly. "Yeah, that could work."

Emma smiled. "I haven't seen you like this in a long time, Gabriel." She pulled him in for a kiss. "It sure makes your mother happy."

He smiled. "I suppose you never stop worrying about your kids, do you?"

"No. You don't," she said, smoothing his hair.

Chapter 21

T he doorbell chimed for the second time that day, and Gabe's mom perked up, a playful glint in her eye. "Now, who could that be?" She looked to Elena who was busy trying to peel a plantain that was stubbornly resisting. "I'll be right back, dear." She gave Gabe a pointed look, and he stood from his chair at the table to follow.

He was curious about this *tía* Elena always mentioned so fondly. He'd purchased books from her downtown store, and they'd interacted a few times in that setting, but he wanted to know her better—wanted *her* to know *him*.

Carmen Molina was a striking woman. Despite the silver hair, she looked much younger than he knew her to be. Her skin glowed. She was petite, slightly shorter than his own mother, and very pretty. She smiled graciously as they each made their introductions, and the more he studied her, the more he could see a resemblance to Elena.

Behind her, a tall, wiry man stepped forward. He had salt-and-pepper hair and a timid smile behind his mustache. "John Jarvi," he said, shaking Gabe's hand, his grip firm but his voice soft. "I'm Carmen's ... well, 'special friend,' is what she calls me." He chuckled quietly. "And this is my daughter, Lucy."

Lucy offered a small wave and a big smile. "Hi."

Gabe liked her instantly.

"Nice place you have here," Lucy said, looking around.

Emma thanked her, and Gabe took in the woman's elfin vibe. She was slight and ethereal, like she'd stepped right out of a fairytale and onto their porch.

"You're welcome to come join the chaos," Theo said.

Carmen clapped her hands together. "Chaos is my specialty, which is a good thing because with my *sobrina* in the kitchen, anything can happen." She winked at Gabe.

Preliminary greetings aside, Carmen followed them to the kitchen while Theo took father and daughter out back to look over the bay. Maybe Gabe should have made scarce, too, to give Elena and her aunt privacy, but he didn't want to miss Elena's reaction to the surprise his mother had coordinated for her birthday.

"Look at you glowing like a firefly," Carmen said, addressing Elena from the doorway of the kitchen.

Gabe was glad he'd stuck around. The look on Elena's face was priceless. Her head snapped up, revealing some type of mush clinging to her cheek. "*Tía?* What are you doing here?"

Carmen stretched out her arms and caught Elena in a fierce hug. "*Mija ...*"

The rest of what was said, Gabe would never know since it was spoken in a language he had never mastered. *¿Donde esta el baño?* was all that was left over in his brain from high school. He couldn't help but wish he'd paid more attention. But their radiant smiles and giddy laughter told him all he really needed to know anyway.

Before Gabe could slip away, Elena spun toward him, her eyes alight. She threw her arms around him, the heat of her warming him like the summer sun.

"Gabe, did you know she was coming? This is the best surprise!"

"You can thank Mom and Dad for that one," he said with a grin.

Elena darted back to Carmen, and Gabe caught snatches of their chatter—"*bien*," "*cocina*," "*amor*,"—words he recognized but whose meaning slipped through his grasp. That settled it. He was going to have to learn Spanish. If his six-year-old could do it, so could he.

Gabe had been tasked with grilling the meat for the sandwiches—steak and chicken—and he worked quietly at the table to cut the meat into small strips. Mosie sat like a statue beside him, hopeful for a morsel. Gradually, as he worked, the surrounding conversation became more heightened, and when he looked up, he could see that his mother's tidy kitchen had quickly turned into a battlefield. Carmen took charge again, giving orders like a drill sergeant while Elena wrestled with the plantains.

"They hate me," Elena muttered, tossing a mangled plantain into a bowl.

"Like this, *mija*." Carmen demonstrated how to peel the plantain from the opposite end, completing the task effortlessly before leaving Elena to continue without her as she returned to her *sofrito* sauce.

Platter in hand, Gabe took a detour to the grill, leaning against the counter near Elena instead. Mosie followed him like a shadow. He could tell Elena was aware of him as he watched her struggle, and he smiled when he saw the pink fill her cheeks. He ached to kiss her again, but it would have to wait. "Need a hand?"

She shot him a playful glare and used a plantain to point at him. "You stick to your meat, Gabriel Wright. I've got this."

He pushed off the counter with a chuckle.

Elena didn't have it at all, and she was lucky her *tía* had shown up when she had, or they'd all be going hungry tonight.

Mr. Jarvi's daughter, Lucy, who'd come into the kitchen to be with the women, hovered near the fridge sipping a soda Emma had given her. "I'd help, but I'm useless in the kitchen." Her voice was light but edged with self-deprecation.

Emma smiled warmly. "What do you do, dear?"

She hesitated, almost embarrassed. "Well, I guess I'm a realtor now."

She *guessed*? "That's impressive," Elena said as an encouragement. She pounded a plantain with a mallet and it splattered, dotting her shirt. She cursed under her breath in Spanish.

Lucy smiled faintly. "Thanks. It was Dad's idea. I'm still figuring out what to do with the license. Dad thinks I should start out selling mansions, but I don't think that's how it works."

"Lucy just passed the exam this week in Grand Rapids," Carmen explained. "It's one of the reasons she rode with us."

"My sister is there with my nephew, so we got to visit with them too," Lucy said.

"What does your sister do?" Emma asked, drawing Lucy further into the fold.

"She cleans up garbage."

"Oh." Emma didn't seem to know what more to say to that.

"In outer space."

"Oh!" Emma repeated, clearly impressed this time.

"Carol's the overachiever of the family," Lucy said dryly.

Carmen gave Lucy a brief, one-armed hug. "*Cariña.*"

Emma asked more questions, engaging Lucy further while Carmen ducked out quickly to take a phone call from her bookstore manager.

Elena tried to focus on the conversation between Emma and Lucy, but frying the flattened plantains was going all wrong. She'd followed her *tía's* directions, but they weren't cooking evenly. Some were crisping and others were turning to mush. Maybe they weren't flat enough. She tried flattening the remaining plantains with a plate, then gave up and grabbed the mallet again, hammering away like a woman possessed.

Will popped his head in, grinning. "What's burning?"

Sure enough, a forgotten plantain was smoking on the stove. The cooked ones resting on a plate nearby looked just as inedible. Carmen burst back into the kitchen and intervened, turning off the burner. "Oh, Elena," Carmen breathed, surveying the wreckage in dismay. "How long was I gone?"

Emma jumped from her chair, apologizing profusely for not having monitored Elena more closely. For her part, Elena couldn't speak. She was doubled over from the hilarity of the situation and gasped for breath as she held up a misshapen plantain slice like it was a prize. "Anyone want to try some delicious Puerto Rican cuisine?"

Gabe chose that moment to return with the plate of cooked steak for the sandwiches. He looked around the kitchen his lips twitching before meeting eyes with Elena and declaring, "You're a menace."

That got her and everyone else going all over again, and their boisterous laughter drew the attention of John, Theo, and Lexi who'd heard them from all the way outside. Lexi peeked around Theo's legs, her eyes wide at the mess, before piping up in her small, matter-of-fact voice, "Elena, you're not s'posed to cook bananas!"

Bewildered, Theo looked to his wife who was laughing so hard she was crying. She threw up her hands. "Theo, order some pizzas."

As the laughter dissipated and the cleanup began, Carmen drew Elena aside, her voice a warm murmur. "Your *mami* would've loved this mess," she said. "She'd say it's the trying that counts."

Elena's smile softened and her eyes glistened with unshed tears. "Yeah, she would."

Chapter 22

The Puerto Rican birthday dinner morphed into a pizza picnic on the porch, the failed *jibaritos* now just a funny story Gabe was sure they'd retell for years. He leaned back in his chair, taking in the lively conversations around him, content to watch and listen as everyone else filled the space with talk and laughter.

Lucy opened up a bit, chatting with his brother about his work in the military and sharing her stories from the three months she'd spent working as a loss prevention officer in Chicago. Gabe couldn't imagine a job for which she would be more ill-suited. She seemed too gentle for something like that. He got the sense she was a little lost professionally, and he hoped this latest plan of hers to sell houses would work out.

Carmen and John sat close, their easy banter hinting at a bond deeper than that of just "special friends." Nearby at the patio table, Elena and Lexi giggled, the two of them sneaking pizza crusts to Mosie when they thought no one was looking. Gabe saw it all, of course, and it warmed him to see them bonding over mischief.

By eight o'clock, Carmen and her crew had left, and the house was quiet. Will had gone out to walk Mosie, and Emma was putting Lexi to bed, relishing the last night she'd have with her granddaughter for the next several weeks.

Gabe found Elena in the kitchen, washing plates. She turned to look at him from over her shoulder. It was just them, and the air was thick with unspoken words. "Thank you, Gabe, for today and this whole week. I can't tell you how much I—" she faltered. "It felt like home, and I haven't felt that in a while."

"You make it feel that way," he replied, stepping closer. She turned and stilled, water dripping from her hands. Her dark eyes searched his, vulnerable yet steady.

"Gabriel—" she started, but he didn't let her finish. He closed the gap, one hand cupping her face, the other sliding to her waist. Her breath hitched, and then she leaned in, meeting him halfway. Their lips brushed—tentative at first—then desperate, a hungry edge born of weeks of restraint. She tasted even better than she had last night, like the strawberries they'd had for dessert. Her hands fisted in his shirt, pulling him closer. His heart slammed against his ribs, every nerve lit up.

When they broke apart, breathless, she rested her forehead against his. "Wow," she whispered, a shaky laugh escaping her.

He brushed her hair back. "I'm done pretending I don't feel this, Elena." He stopped short of naming it out loud. He wasn't sure she was ready to hear it.

She pulled him back in for another kiss, her lips a contented smile against his, and he wrapped his arms tightly around her. He never wanted to let her go. They stood there, wrapped in each other's warmth, and for the first time in years, Gabe felt complete.

Chapter 23

The drive back to Nicolet felt shorter than Elena expected, the road humming beneath Gabe's Suburban as Bayshore faded in the rearview mirror. She stole a glance at him—dark blond hair mussed from Lexi's clinging hugs. His hands were steady on the wheel, and a faint smile lingered on his lips from their kiss the night before. Her stomach fluttered just thinking about it—the way his mouth had claimed hers, hungry yet tender. After weeks of dancing around it, they'd finally stopped pretending. But what did it mean now, back in the real world?

She leaned her head back against the headrest, replaying the morning's goodbyes. Lexi had clung first to Gabe, and then to Emma's legs, tears streaking down her cheeks. "I want to stay with Mimi, but I want Daddy too!" she sobbed. Gabe knelt beside her, promising a trip to visit again soon. His voice had been soft but firm when he'd told her it was time to go and lifted her into the car.

Elena spent the first several minutes of the drive turned around to the backseat, holding Lexi's hand. Slowly, her sobs turned to hiccups and then sniffles. Once Lexi had finally let go, Elena turned forward only to have Gabe reach for her. He'd given her hand a squeeze, warm and sure. It felt like a promise.

The Suburban rolled past Nicolet's outskirts, and Elena's mind drifted to the afternoon ahead—unpacking, settling in with Lexi, maybe stealing another moment with Gabe once he was back from a meeting that had come up unexpectedly. He hadn't said much about it, just that it was unplanned, and he needed to be there by two.

Tomorrow, Elena would walk through an apartment, a last-minute lifeline now that Jackson's house had officially sold. The landlord promised to call later today to firm up a time and had promised not to set anything else up until Elena had a chance to see it. She needed this—stability, a place to call hers for a little while. Something that couldn't be stolen away by surprise. It was a year-long lease she'd be signing, and once she did, she'd be able to relax and fully enjoy the rest of the summer.

Elena glanced at Gabe again. The closer they got to Nicolet, the edgier he seemed. His jaw was tight, and his fingers tapped impatiently at the wheel as the pine forests blurred past, their shadows flickering across the dashboard. "You okay?" she asked.

His head bobbed a quick nod. "Yeah. Just thinking about this meeting."

"What's it about?"

His eyes stayed fixed on the road ahead. "A few things, probably. I've been out a few days, so I'm sure I need to be brought up to speed. They had a board meeting last night that I missed. I know for sure we'll talk about the security upgrades and how much we can get done with this second endowment we're getting."

This was the first Elena had heard of a second endowment. She knew where the first one had come from. "Marc?" she asked, testing the name.

He glanced at her then, wary. "I didn't want to say his name, but yeah."

Hearing his name stirred nothing in her at all—a quiet victory. Growth. "It's okay. It'll be good for the schools. What's the money going to be used for?"

"Security updates. Maybe some infrastructure too. The boiler at the middle school is from the early seventies."

"That's ridiculous. The high school bathrooms are ancient, too, and I can't believe we don't have a buzz-in, buzz-out system yet. Nicolet is about a decade behind on all that stuff."

"You're telling me."

"Will Marc be there, then?"

He dipped his chin in confirmation. "Dom Stone, too."

Something, some inner whisper, told her there was something Gabe wasn't saying, and she tried to ignore the nervous flutter in her stomach. She traced a finger along the car's armrest, grounding herself in the memories they'd made together that week.

If something was wrong, Gabe would tell her. When he looked at her again, his smile soft and full of promise, she pushed the doubt aside, choosing instead to trust. Still, the flutter lingered, a quiet warning she couldn't shake.

They pulled into Gabe's driveway just past noon. Lexi bolted out, dragging her backpack, her mood lifted by the promise of playtime. Gabe hauled Elena's bag to her car, and together, they unloaded the rest into the house. It seemed extra quiet after Bayshore's bustle, so Elena could understand why Lexi announced that she already missed it. The truth was, so did she.

Gabe headed up to his loft office to prepare for the meeting, and she and Lexi finished unpacking. Once he left and she'd wished him luck, Elena began a load of laundry and helped get Lexi's clean clothes folded and put back in her drawers. Lexi worked to line her stuffed animals up on the bed in order of shortest to tallest, and when they'd both finished their tasks, she suggested a round of hide-and-seek.

Elena grinned. "Don't you ever run out of energy?"

They were in the middle of their second round when Elena's phone buzzed in the back pocket of her shorts. "Lexi, hold on. I need to take this quick."

Lexi groaned. "But I was in the best spot."

Elena laughed before answering. Lexi had been in her favorite spot, right under the dining room table and in plain sight.

"Elena Torres?" The landlord's voice crackled through.

"Yes?"

"I can nail down a time now. Can you do ten a.m. tomorrow for the tour?"

"Yes, that's perfect. Thank you," she said, jotting it down on a magnetized pad stuck to the fridge. She listened for a few more minutes as the woman reminded her apologetically that, as much as she loved animals herself, the apartment was pet-free. Elena assured the older woman that it wouldn't be a problem before thanking her again and signing off.

Stuffing her phone into her pocket, she walked back into the dining room. "Alright, Lex, I'm ready to—" But Lexi wasn't there. Noticing the sliding door to the patio was open, Elena walked to it and peered outside, calling Lexi's name.

No answer.

A prickle of unease crept up her spine.

Chapter 24

G abe's Suburban rumbled toward the Central Administration Office, his stomach churning as he navigated Nicolet's streets. He hadn't lied to Elena. The meeting at two *was* about the endowment and security upgrades—a win for the district. But something felt off. He'd noticed Joanna's name added to the calendar invite late last night. Why was HR needed? Did it have something to do with her spotting him with Elena at the fireworks? The unease sat heavy, a stone in his gut.

His phone rang as he turned onto Main Street, and Erin Hennings' name flashed on the car's navigation screen. He let it roll to voicemail and silenced his phone while he was thinking of it. He made a mental note to call her later. No doubt she'd found out he'd pushed his candidate for the principal position instead of hers, and he figured she wasn't too happy with him at the moment. His guy was the solid pick, and he didn't regret it.

The conference room was a mess. With Adele still on vacation, no one had been there to tidy up. He flipped on the fluorescent lights and cleaned up the papers on the table, leftover agendas from last night's meeting. Quickly, he glanced over them before pitching them in the trash. Nothing seemed out of the ordinary, so that was good. He dumped the old coffee grounds and brewed a fresh pot of coffee.

Dom's used mug still sat at the head of the table from the night before. Who did the guy think was going to come in and clean up after him? Gabe grabbed it and took it to the break room where he washed it out. It was the mug Dom always used, and it said, "Coffee poured, order restored" and had a graphic of a gavel on it. Pretentious as hell for a school board president, but then Dom did have an overly inflated opinion of himself. Gabe left it to dry in the rack and went to fire up his computer.

Marc arrived first, looking slick in a tailored gray suit, his silver hair catching the light. They shook hands, but a chill hung in the air between them—left over from that night at Rebecca's. Gabe wasn't worried about it. The fact that Marc was here showed he was still willing to do business, personal gripes aside. There'd be no buddy vibes between them, and that was fine. They both knew how to be professional.

They made casual small talk as Gabe poured Marc a cup of black coffee. Marc nodded when he handed it to him. "Thanks. How was your Fourth? I hear you had some time off."

"It was good. Headed back home to Bayshore for a few days. You?"

"I stuck around. Golfed a few rounds with Dom. The guy's not too bad."

Gabe forced a smile. The idea of Marc and Dom palling around bothered him.

Dom and Joanna arrived at the same time. Joanna muttered a greeting, but her eyes skittered away quickly.

Dom ignored him entirely, scowling at the table instead. "Where's my mug?"

"I washed it for you."

Dom stiffened, as if Gabe had committed a felony. "I left it here yesterday because I knew I'd be back. Please go get it."

Before Gabe could suggest that Dom shove that mug and its gavel where the sun didn't shine, Joanna jumped in. "I'll grab it."

She brushed past him, and Gabe mouthed a silent, "Thanks." Her brusque nod said she'd rather be anywhere else at that moment.

Dom launched into the meeting, pausing only briefly to grunt appreciation when Joanna returned with his cup. He outlined the endowment—500,000 dollars for security upgrades—while Marc chimed in with questions and clarifications. The Silver Fox turned to Gabe. "Your proposal mentioned cameras, security systems, and—I believe—included a few infrastructure updates, right?"

"Yes." Gabe ticked off the list. "Thirty new cameras—ten exterior and twenty interior. Reinforced doors with keycard access. Upgraded alarm systems. The bids came in last week—cameras will cost eighty grand, the doors about one-twenty." He ran through priorities and costs, all grounded in the quotes he'd prepped. Solid plans for a safer school.

For the next hour, they hashed out the details—including timelines. Gabe kept half an eye on Joanna, perched silently with a notepad and pen she hadn't touched. Why was she here? Nothing they were discussing had anything to do with Human Resources. As if on cue, she met his gaze and held it this time.

Dom and Marc's chatter hushed, and she took a breath. "You're wondering why I'm here," she said, her voice steady.

Gabe eased back in his chair. "I am, actually."

"We're talking about school improvements, so this is a good segue."

His pulse kicked up. She inhaled again, steeling herself, and he braced for impact.

"Gabe, a good school deserves good staff. Yesterday, alongside approving the endowment and the new high school principal, the board voted on Elena Torres's contract renewal. They decided against it."

"The meeting for staff renewals isn't for another two weeks," he shot back, sharper than he'd intended.

"Given the circumstances," she said, glancing at Marc, "the board thought it would be best to make the decision about Miss Torres in conjunction with the endowment discussion."

Gabe's eyes snapped to Marc. "You knew?"

Marc's hands went up, genuine surprise flickering in his eyes. "This is the first I'm hearing of it."

Dom leaned in, elbows on the table. "Marc didn't know, Gabe, but he's not shocked, I'd wager. Miss Torres's conduct back in January was deplorable, especially for a teacher. That clip is still bouncing around out there in the cyber world, and it's a distraction for this district and our community. Given her willingness to engage in another public confrontation with Marc a few weeks back—"

"Now wait a minute—" Marc tried to cut in.

"—I know, I know." Dom said, pacifying him. "You told me that as a friend, but I had to take it under consideration." He trained his eyes on Gabe. "It's the board's decision to renew or not renew a contract. We've made that decision. Now, I understand, given the circumstances of you living with this woman—"

"Excuse me?" Gabe's voice cut like a blade.

Dom arched his brows, a challenge. "She *is* your nanny." He put air quotes around the word "nanny," and Gabe thought his head might explode.

"She's not a live-in nanny, Dom, contrary to what your sources may tell you." He sent a pointed look at Joanna who had the grace to blush a bright pink.

"But you're involved with her, aren't you?"

Gabe hesitated, their two kisses flashing to mind.

Dom read his silence as an admission and smirked. "Thought so. Your judgment's off, Gabe, but your personal life's yours. Since there can be no conflict of interest now, you're free to carry on with Miss Torres however you see fit."

His insinuation was intentionally sordid, and Gabe wasn't about to let that go unchallenged. "You're twisting it into something it's not."

"This meeting is done. Endowment's a go, and Elena Torres is out." Dom pushed himself away from the table. "I assume you'll be the one to tell her. Joanna will give it a day before sending the letter."

Marc shifted, uncomfortable but silent. Joanna stared at her notepad, her pen still.

Gabe shoved his chair back and stood. "Please lock up behind you."

He stormed his Suburban, his fury reaching a boiling point as he slid into his seat and slammed his hands against the wheel before punching the start button. Immediately, Erin's name appeared on the dash display, signaling her incoming call. He leaned to one side to pull his phone out of his back pocket, sliding the button to unmute it before taking the call through the Suburban's infotainment system.

He didn't want to talk, but he answered anyway, needing a distraction. "Yeah?" he said, his voice tight.

"Gabe, is it true? Is Elena out? Rumors are flying today."

"Is that so? Then how come I'm just finding out now?" he asked bitterly.

Erin was quiet on the other end of the line. "It's true, then."

Gabe let his silence speak confirmation.

"Gabe, this is so wrong."

"I'm heading home now to tell her."

"There's nothing you can do?"

Again, he let the silence speak for him.

She sighed in resignation. "Okay, tell her I'll call her tomorrow. Tonight, I'll give her some space."

"I'll tell her." Gabe hung up, battling the storm in his head the whole way home. The district he worked for was a pit of vipers. Dom's bloated ego, Joanna's spinelessness. How long had she waited before tattling to Dom about what she'd seen in Bayshore? She was a spineless gossip.

He didn't want this job anymore. Not like this. Dom had blindsided him, used Marc as leverage, and twisted the truth into knots. Elena had no house, and now her job was gone. And Lexi—he'd sworn she'd have stability here. Quitting his job would ruin that, so he was trapped, pacing inside a cage of his own making.

Gabe swung into his driveway, and his heart seized as the house came into view. Two cop cars sat parked, lights off, doors open. Elena's name flashed across the display. He answered the call, his voice cracking. "What's happening?"

"Gabe, Lexi's gone!" she sobbed, frantic. "I looked everywhere. She's not here!"

"I'm here, I'm here!" he shouted, bolting from the Suburban, the job news swallowed up by panic. Officers turned to him as he hit the sidewalk.

Two cops—one stocky guy in his mid forties, the other younger and leaner—stood near the porch, radios crackling. Elena flew down the steps and into his arms. She clutched her phone in one hand and gripped his shirt with the other. "She was just playing in the dining room and then the door was open, and she was just ... gone!"

The stocky cop stepped forward, notepad in hand. "Mr. Wright? I'm officer Daniels. We've got her description—dark hair, six years old, pink shirt, right?" He paused, and after a quick nod from Elena, he continued. "We're going to sweep the area. Any places she likes to go?"

Gabe could hardly think, but he heard himself say, "Her tire swing, the creek ..."

Daniels added to his notes. "Another unit's en route. I want you to stay here and—"

"I'm not staying here!" Gabe's eyes, wild with a father's fear, darted to the vast woods at the far end of his property. What if she'd wandered off into the forest? She could be lost for days in there.

Elena's hand tightened on his arm.

The younger cop—Miller, according to his badge—spoke into his radio. "Six-year-old female, straight dark hair, pink shirt, possibly headed to the wooded area behind the residence. Request K-9 if available." He glanced at Elena. "Last seen around ... two o'clock?"

Elena nodded. "That call I took was at ten after."

Gabe shuddered. Lexi had been missing for over an hour.

Elena's hands shook as she gripped Gabe's arm, her voice cracking as she answered the officer. It was her fault—all of it. She'd been on the phone, distracted by an old lady droning on about a no-pets rule that didn't even apply to her. One second, she and Lexi had been laughing and playing, and then that call stole her focus, just for a few minutes. That was all it took. She'd searched everywhere, yelling Lexi's name until her throat burned. Somehow Lexi, the worst hider ever, had vanished in an instant.

The younger cop, Miller, was speaking again. "... neighbors she likes to visit?"

Gabe shook his head. "The nearest one's a quarter mile off."

"Wait!" Elena's eyes snapped to Gabe's, her pulse hammering. "Her sparkle family!"

She spun to the officers. "The woods—on the other side of the creek!"

Daniels straightened. "You think she crossed a creek and went into the woods?"

"Yes! She's very imaginative, and she thinks her sparkle family lives there. She showed me once, but I'm not sure she could find it again."

"The other side of the woods is M-28, and that's at least six miles off," Miller pointed out to his partner.

Daniels nodded. "Okay, you wait here—next unit's five minutes out."

"They said K-9's forty minutes away," Miller added.

"Here's the plan," Daniels said, addressing Elena and Gabe. "Grab something she's worn recently to have ready for the K-9. Then we'll head out. You can show me where she took you."

Elena darted inside, snagging the blue hooded sweatshirt Lexi had worn to the fireworks from a hook near the door, then raced back, thrusting it at Officer Miller. Gabe was already crossing the expansive lawn, shouting Lexi's name. Elena caught up to him and Officer Daniels, her voice joining theirs. They passed the line of dogwoods and the swing before reaching the footbridge a hundred yards later. The woods beyond sprawled dark and endless to the highway. Elena told herself Lexi would never go that far—not on purpose. But what if she'd gotten turned around? People lost themselves in forests all the time.

She shouted louder and picked up her pace.

"Spread out—fifty yards apart!" Daniels ordered as they crossed into the woods. He veered left and Gabe swung right. Elena pushed on straight ahead, brush scraping at her bare legs as her heart slammed in her chest. Ten minutes—fifteen—each footfall beating the drum of increasing despair.

Daniels shouted. "Stop!"

Elena stilled.

"Listen!"

Over her labored breathing, Elena heard it—twigs snapping. It was the sound a deer might make as it bounded across the forest floor. A second later, a flash of pink emerged, and Lexi's voice rang out, bright and oblivious.

"You found me!"

Elena lunged, racing forward, and she could see Gabe doing the same. He beat her there, scooping Lexi up and crushing her to his chest. Elena reached for her, too, and hugged her from the other side. "Lexi," she said, relief choking her.

"I was with my Sparkle Mimi," she said. "We were making mud cookies." She turned to smile at Elena before noticing Officer Daniels. "Who's that?"

Daniels lifted his radio, and through a relieved grin, he said, "Child found safe. Heading back."

Lexi wanted to walk, but Gabe refused to let her down, asking her to let him hold her just a little longer.

Elena trailed closely behind them as they made their way out of the woods. She brushed at Lexi's muddy hair, her guilt easing but not entirely gone.

Gabe spoke. "You can't run off like that, kiddo. Never again. You really scared us."

Lexi answered in a small voice. "I didn't mean it, Daddy. But you get mad about my sparkle family, so I hadda be sneaky."

"I know, baby." He turned to check on Elena, reaching for her with his free hand. They met eyes. She could see the relief in them, but a shadow lingered there, and she wondered if he was as upset with her about losing Lexi as she was with herself.

Chapter 25

Lexi knelt on the living room rug, stacking blocks into a teetering tower. Her freshly washed hair had left a wet spot on her pajamas. "You sure you don't want me to dry your hair before bed?" Elena asked again.

"It's too loud. Daddy only makes me dry it when it's cold outside."

"I could brush it dry," Elena suggested.

"Okay!" Lexi hopped up to grab a brush, blocks forgotten.

As Elena worked the brush through Lexi's hair, her hand slower and more gentle with each repeated stroke, she wondered what was going on with Gabe. Once they'd enjoyed their long, drawn-out reunion with Lexi, he'd become distant. She must have apologized a hundred times, and each time he told her it wasn't her fault. Even though the words were right, she knew something was very wrong.

Then, an hour ago, he'd stepped out on the porch to call Will. Their conversation was still going strong, and she could see him pacing through the window. His words were low and urgent but too muffled to catch. Whatever it was, it was serious, and unease pricked at her. Lexi was safe, she reminded herself. That's all that mattered.

"Can you sing me a song?" Lexi asked.

Grateful for the distraction, Elena agreed. "Which one do you want to hear?"

"How 'bout the one with the *ranas*? The one where they go hop, hop, hopping?"

Elena smiled. She leaned forward, pressing a brief kiss to the top of Lexi's head before she began to sing. Her voice was soft but distant as her mind raced with worry about Gabe and Will's phone call.

Lexi's hair was nearly dry when Elena looked up to see Gabe letting himself back in. "Why don't you finish building your tower before we get you off to bed?" Elena suggested. The young girl needed no further prompting to return to her earlier project. Elena set the brush down on the table and stood to face Gabe, who lingered behind one of the easy chairs, his phone still in hand. "What was that about?" Elena asked, keeping her tone light.

Gabe rubbed the back of his neck before answering. "You have a minute?"

She nodded, dread coursing through her veins. Was he angry with her? Would he fire her? Break up with her?

Was a breakup even possible? They hadn't gotten this relationship off the ground yet, and now it might be over.

He nodded toward the kitchen, then took her hand and led her there. Releasing her, he leaned against the counter near the wall. Elena rested a hip against the island. "What is it?" she asked, fear creeping into her voice.

"There's no easy way to tell you this, Elena, so I'm just going to say it."

She nodded for him to continue, but her shoulders stiffened as she braced herself.

"The board decided not to renew your contract for this year. I found out today."

For a split second, relief flooded her. He wasn't casting her aside. He wasn't angry. His eyes held only compassion—and pity. When his words sank in, panic surged. Her ears rang, forcing her to strain to hear what Gabe said next.

"I took a call from Dom the day we went to Bayshore, and he mentioned his intentions then. I swear, Elena, I didn't think he'd have any luck pressuring the board, but at the meeting I missed, he pushed it through. He golfs with Ghetty and heard about that night at Rebecca's. That clinched it. Tied you and Marc and your situation to the endowment—unofficially, of course. I don't know how he pulled it off, but the board agreed." His shoulders slumped. "I'm so sorry."

She'd swung from anxious to relieved, and then back to anxious in seconds. Anger flickered too. Gabe knew about her job *before* Bayshore? How could he keep that from her? Elena pulled out a counter stool and let her hand linger on its back. "My job," she whispered. One week to leave the bungalow, and now no job.

Gabe stepped closer and took her hand before she could sit. "Elena." He gently tugged her closer, his eyes fierce in the dim kitchen light. "I'm resigning."

Her eyes widened and locked on his. "What?"

"I'd walk away tomorrow just to spite Dom, but it would hurt more than just him if I up and left now. I can't do that to our teachers." He shook his head. "I can't do that to the community. I'll submit the letter next week and stay until they find a good replacement. I owe them that."

Any anger Elena felt vanished. This wasn't Gabe's fault. He'd been her champion all along, and he was still going strong. That he'd even *think* about quitting, and all for her. Taking her side in a situation *she'd* created—

He felt responsible for her, she realized. Maybe even sorry for her. She bit her lip and looked away. "I don't want you to quit for me."

Gabe closed the distance and turned her to face him. "I'm doing it for me. For us. But I need to give them time. I need to make sure I don't rock the boat too much when I leave."

"And then what?" Her question hung fragile in the air, a plea. *Please don't say you're leaving me.*

His lips curved into a broad smile. "And then I'm partnering up with Will. We'd already made a long-term plan anyway, back in Bayshore. I was going to be a silent partner for a few years while he got his bearings, so this just speeds up the timeline. We're taking over Dad's company, and we want to expand out to Brule Harbor. It should double the business."

A searing knot twisted in Elena's stomach. *Bayshore. He's going back to Bayshore.* The words echoed like a slammed door in an empty house. He was leaving Nicolet—and her. Her heart screamed to be happy for him, to celebrate a choice that was so perfect, she didn't even have to think twice about it. Instead, the ground crumbled beneath her. Hot tears blurred her vision. How could she have misread his feelings toward her this badly?

"It makes sense," he went on, oblivious of her pain. "I don't know why I didn't see it sooner. Life's too short, Elena. After that scare with Lexi today—" he shook his head "—I can't waste time on the wrong path."

She nodded, words trapped behind the lump in her throat as she stared at the blurry print on his t-shirt. *Say something. Anything.* She couldn't. She was the wrong path. He wouldn't waste time with her.

"Elena, look at me."

She lifted her eyes to his, and a single tear slipped down her cheek. Her heart ached. He was saying goodbye.

His thumb brushed the tear away. "You and Lexi are my future. I love you. I want us to be a family—to go back to Bayshore and build a life there together. I can't think of anything that would make Lexi happier. That would make *me* happier."

The words broke through her inner storm like rays of sunlight through a dark cloud, and her heart gave a stutter as his meaning sank in. *Together*. He wasn't leaving her—he was choosing her. Choosing *them*. The knot in her stomach unraveled, replaced by a love so fierce, she thought she might burst. He wanted the life she'd scarcely dared to hope for.

"I love you too," she whispered, her voice trembling with the weight of everything she felt. She stepped into his arms. He drew her close, kissing her softly but with the certainty of a man who knew just what he wanted. And he wanted her.

She'd thought this day would never come, that no one could ever love her like this. But this amazing, wonderful man and his amazing, wonderful daughter did. They loved her, and she'd spend every second for the rest of her days proving how much she loved them back.

Lexi's voice broke in from behind them. "Is Daddy your prince?"

They sprang apart, Elena wiping at her mouth sheepishly, and Gabe grinning like he'd just discovered the meaning of life.

Elena laughed. "Yeah, sweetie. He is."

Gabe rounded the counter and ruffled Lexi's hair before scooping her up. "A prince with two princesses." His eyes found Elena's, and she saw everything she needed to see in their warm depths. She trusted it. She trusted him.

Lexi yawned, rubbing her eyes, and Elena glanced at the clock. The late hour settled over her, pulling her back to reality. "I should head back," she said softly, her voice tinged with reluctance.

Gabe nodded, but she could see he was as disappointed to see her go as she was to leave.

"Lexi needs her bedtime stories, and I need to start packing," she said, slinging her bag over one shoulder.

Gabe walked her to the door, Lexi clinging to his leg. "Hey," he said, catching her gaze. "Don't put a destination address on those boxes yet. We've got a lot to talk about."

Elena's heart fluttered at his words, a spark of hope igniting at the thought of unpacking somewhere with him. She shook her head, and a soft laugh escaped as she considered their situation. "We're two people without jobs."

Gabe's smile warmed, and his voice was gentle when he reminded her of the words she'd spoken on the way to the beach just days ago. "Maybe, but we're two people who've finally found home."

Epilogue

Emma and Theo's Bayshore house thrummed with barely controlled chaos. The Thanksgiving turkey roasted in the oven, and the potatoes boiled on the stovetop. Boxes lined the entryway's far wall, and Lexi's toy pony corral sat atop the kitchen table in front of Gabe. He was gluing a horse's leg back on and watching Elena sift through a box of mementos to share a photo of her mother with Will and Emma. The diamond that glinted on her finger filled him with pride and restless desire to make it official.

As Elena passed the framed photo of Marivi to Emma, Gabe's mind flashed to the story Elena had told him a few months back. At eight years old, not much older than Lexi, she'd come home from school to find her father gone, never to return. He'd left no note—hadn't even bothered to divorce her mother. He was just ... gone. Her mother, Marivi, held on for a time before sinking into a deep depression, plagued by ailments she convinced herself were real.

By the time she was twelve, Elena was working odd jobs to cover rent and mothering her own mother as she juggled responsibilities no teenager should have to carry. Just after high school, pancreatic cancer, her one true illness, took Marivi's life. Thank God for Elena's aunt and uncle. They took her in and ensured she finished college and found her way.

A fierce need to shield Elena from all of life's hurts burned inside Gabe. He wanted to be the steady love she'd never had. He wanted to be her rock. She was strong, he knew that, but she deserved someone to lean on, just as he leaned on her.

He caught Elena's gaze across the kitchen and touched the tip of his nose. She mirrored the gesture, her smile soft. It was a communication just for them—a way of saying "I love you" without words. Will asked her a question, breaking the moment, but Gabe knew countless more awaited as they built their life together.

Closing old chapters had cleared the path for that future, like leaving his superintendent role and selling his Nicolet house. Lucy Jarvi had sold it quickly—her first sale. Her quiet efficiency sealed that chapter and forged a fast bond with Elena.

While Elena had embraced the Bayshore move from the beginning, she'd vowed to return to Nicolet every few weeks for a visit. It was important that she kept close ties with family and friends in Nicolet, even though she was happy to call Bayshore home. Talk swirled of her taking over Emma's store in a year or two, though she was in no rush to commit one way or the other. She was content to learn the ropes and help Emma for now.

His parents were saints. He, Elena, Lexi, and Will were all bunked up there, a temporary squeeze until they sorted everything out. Theo and Emma hadn't complained once, and watching his dad play Go Fish with Lexi at the table, Gabe knew their only grumble would come when everyone moved out.

A few things needed to happen first, namely a wedding, but also the full takeover of the construction company. They'd held countless meetings already—with lawyers, the bank, and one another, poring over the books and plans. For the first time in more than a year, Gabe felt a spark of excitement about his professional life. Shaping lives in education was a noble endeavor, no question, but building with his hands offered something visceral—tangible proof of a hard day's work staring back at him.

Gabe imagined the move to their own place would happen sooner than his parents would like and later than he would prefer, not that he didn't enjoy this too. But one big happy family under one roof meant plenty of love and hardly any privacy. His gaze lingered on Elena, longing tugging at him. He wanted her all to himself—and who could blame him?

Lexi glanced up from her cards and peered out the window at the lake. "My sparkle family's out there, Papa," she said, her voice dreamy.

A hush fell over the kitchen. Theo's wide eyes met Gabe's, but Gabe gave his father a faint shake of his head. He wouldn't admonish her. Keeping sparkle family talk out in the open would prevent scares like the one they'd had back in Nicolet.

"But it's okay they left." Lexi went on, studying her cards. "They're on vacation forever across the lake, but I told them I hadda stay here with my Bayshore family.

Gabe swallowed against a mix of emotion. Had Lexi's longing for family, deep inside her little girl's heart, finally been met? He might have cried right then and there, Gorilla Glue in hand, if he hadn't been so overjoyed. She'd sent that cursed sparkle family away, banished to Canada forever. Fine by him.

Lexi looked at each of them in turn, a cherub's smile curving her lips as her gaze settled on Gabe. "We're a real family, Daddy. We'll stick together like your glue, won't we?"

Gabe's heart swelled. He set the glue down and pulled Lexi close.

Elena joined them in a three-way hug. "Glued forever," she whispered.

Lexi giggled. "We're a snuggle family."

Gabe let out a soft laugh, the kind that escapes when a heart is too full to hold everything inside. Maybe they were still living in his parents' house, but Gabe knew—they were already home.

Next in Series

Nicolet Series Book 6

sweet
december

a novel

charlotte everhart

charlotteeverhartbooks.com

In the sixth and final book of the Nicolet series, *Sweet December*, Lucy Jarvi and her young nephew find themselves snowed in at the secluded cabin of Jordan Jamieson, the Minnesota Vikings' celebrated quarterback, just days before

Christmas. As the storm rages outside, the close quarters spark an unexpected connection, blending cozy holiday warmth with heartfelt romance. Will this chance encounter lead to a love that lasts beyond the snowmelt?
Coming 2026.

Books in the Nicolet Series

The Nicolet Series is a celebration of friendship, community, and the power of love. This collection is filled with tender moments that linger long after the last page is turned.

Hope for Tomorrow

Joy of Today

From This Moment

A Time and a Season

When Someday Finally Comes

Sweet December

About the Author

 For Charlotte, few things are more relaxing than an escape into a cozy, little story, and that's what she hopes you'll experience within the pages of her books. An author of contemporary women's fiction, Charlotte writes about small-town women and their families, sprinkling in just the right amount of romance for all the feels. She lives on the Lake Superior shore with her husband and three children, and like most of her characters, she can't imagine ever living anywhere else. Visit her website to learn more, and join her monthly newsletter to receive bonus material and other news.

Website: www.charlotteeverhartbooks.com

Facebook: @CharlotteEverhart.Author

Instagram: @charlotte.everhart.author

www.ingramcontent.com/pod-product-compliance
Lightning Source LLC
Chambersburg PA
CBHW022150240626
47153CB00007B/2587